Death Dons a Mask

Other Books in the Francesca Bibbo Series

Death in the Choir

Death of a Liturgist

Death Dons a Mask

by

Lorraine V. Murray

TUMBLAR HOUSE
' Bona Tempora Volvant'

Arcadia
MMXIII

Printed in the United States of America

ISBN 978-0-9883537-3-2

For my beloved aunt, Rita Pope

CHAPTER 1

The little girl went racing into Latisha's Lovelies, a shop laden with lacy lingerie, which Francesca's grandmother would have dubbed "unmentionables." Francesca's two-year-old niece, Mo-Mo, was enchanted by the window display that featured a pile of plush panda bears nestled among the lingerie.

"Bear!" she screamed as she ran.

Francesca Bibbo followed wearily, wondering if she'd done the right thing by agreeing to watch the child during the day while her younger sister went job-hunting. Much to Francesca's delight, Doris had just moved to town from Tampa with her husband, Dan. Widowed two years ago, Francesca dearly craved the company of family members, but when it came to Mo-Mo—whose real name was Maureen—there were definite challenges.

"It will only be for a few days," Doris had promised, when Francesca agreed to watch the child. "And she won't be any trouble at all."

In just seconds, Mo-Mo grabbed a bear from the display and then snagged a pair of socks and draped them around her ears.

"Socks!" she squealed, doing an impromptu dance in the shop.

"Come on, sweetie, put those back," Francesca said, but just then, the sound of Dixie started blaring through the intercom. She looked around trying to figure out what the celebration was

1

all about. There were only a few people in the shop, including a woman who surely tipped the scales at 250 pounds, surreptitiously examining a flimsy nightgown, and a college-aged girl talking loudly on a cell phone, dishing out dieting advice to a friend: "You can eat all the celery you want!"

A saleslady with a microphone came rushing toward Francesca booming "Congratulations! It's our 25th anniversary—and you're our 25th customer today!"

The beaming salesgirl—"I'm Lu-Lu, honey"—carefully placed a tiara on Francesca's head, while another clerk wheeled in a table displaying a massive cake decorated in hot pink and vivid purple, the shop's signature colors. A small crowd, attracted by the music, began edging into the store.

"We have a wonderful prize for you," Lu-Lu announced breathlessly as Francesca wished she could become invisible on the spot. In the corner of her eye, she spotted Mo-Mo making a beeline for the cake.

Then, as a cluster of curious customers gathered round, the salesgirl presented Francesca with a dauntingly large red-and-purple bra with sturdy, helmet-like cups encrusted with rhinestones. Some teenage boys who had wandered in from the mall expressed their appreciation for the garment by emitting a string of ear-splitting whistles and hoots.

"It's a Va-Va-Va Voom in a double D, honey," Lu-Lu announced proudly, and then in a whispered aside: "We'll get you *your* size later."

"No, uh, this will be fine." The bra was way out of Francesca's league, size-wise, but she figured she could use it as part of a future Halloween outfit.

Thanking the salesgirl profusely, she then turned to get Mo-Mo just in time to see the child—still rakishly sporting the socks on her ears—wolfing down a hefty slice of cake. Her chubby face was smudged with purple and pink frosting and there were colorful sticky streaks in her golden-brown corkscrew curls. She was clutching the bear and grinning. Francesca groaned inwardly as she recalled Doris' warning: "Keep her away from sweets. They make her bounce off the walls."

***

Three miles away, Father Brent Bunt, pastor of St. Rita's church in Decatur, Georgia, stared bleakly at the growing pile of bills on his desk. The weekly collections were continuing to dwindle miserably. He knew it was the economy, but that didn't dilute the fact that he had bills to pay and an archbishop to please.

He ran his fingers through his hair, which had been dark brown when he first became pastor, but was now rapidly turning gray. Was it just his imagination or was St. Rita's causing him to age at a frighteningly rapid pace? I'm only 46, but sometimes I feel like I'm 90, he thought dolefully.

The door eased open, and in came Dopey, his head bent down almost apologetically. The big odoriferous dog collapsed with a sigh at Father Bunt's feet and then put a tentative paw on his knee. Father Bunt wasn't a dog person, but if the rectory had to have one, he'd have preferred a robust German Shepherd, a man's kind of dog. Dopey, a stray, had shown up one day at the rectory, and no one had the heart to turn him out. The dog—named by the children at St. Rita's school because he was not exactly Einstein material—was a yellowish-white mix of poodle and retriever. His crooked paws with their wimpy frills of fur reminded Father Bunt unfortunately of a lady's bedroom slippers.

Despite all his initial misgivings, however, the dog seemed to be growing on him. As Father Bunt scratched the dog's ears, the tail thumped appreciatively against the floor, and Dopey went: "W-w-oof!" There had been some nasty goings-on at St. Rita's, which had left Father Bunt with an arm that still ached whenever it rained, the result of a gunshot wound. The crime eventually had been solved, but Dopey had been so traumatized by the gunman that he'd developed a canine version of a stutter.

After a tentative knock on the door, in stepped Eloise Winkerby, a tall fiftyish woman with a heavily made-up face and poufy blonde hair that reminded Father Bunt of cotton candy. Rumor had it she had shelled out a great deal of money for a facelift, but he tried to ignore gossip. *What does it matter anyway? She could be 35 or 85,* he thought. *It's not like I'm looking for a girlfriend.*

She sank into a nearby chair and clasped her hands together as if she were going to launch into a prayer. "Father, the Ladies'

4

Guild has come up with a wonderful idea for a summer party. We think it will really shake things up here at the parish—and bring in some money as well."

"What do you have in mind?" His voice had a cautious edge to it, as he dreaded rocking the boat too much in a parish that had weathered two shipwrecks in the past two years. First there had been the grisly murder of the choir director, although as Father Bunt reminded himself, that event had not happened on *his* watch—and then the unexpected demise of the liturgist. Both events had put the archbishop on high-alert mode when it came to St. Rita's.

"Well, we thought it would just be lovely to have a masquerade ball and a dance with a big buffet supper," Eloise enthused. "We could have a beach theme—you know, tropical table cloths and drinks with little paper umbrellas, some fake palm trees, and for the buffet we were thinking...."

His mind drifted. This would certainly attract parishioners who like partying, and if there was a good supper and some drinks, he thought, we could charge...well what could we charge? Would ten dollars a person be out of line? Say we got four hundred people, that would be...

"So, Father, what do you think?" Eloise's carefully sculpted eyebrows rose expectantly.

The dollar signs in his head fizzled out as he returned to reality. "Oh, yes, yes indeed, paper umbrellas—and what was the other thing?"

She smiled kindly as if she were dealing with a senile relative. "Well, we can work out all the details later. I just need your go-ahead to start things rolling."

Twirling a pencil in his hand, Father Bunt stood up, walked over to the window and glanced outside. St. Rita's was located on five acres near the town square of Decatur. Despite its proximity to the swarming metropolis of Atlanta, Decatur had a slower pace and boasted an abundance of generously sized oak, pine, and dogwood trees. It wasn't unusual to spy red-tailed hawks swimming through the cloudless blue summer sky, and hummingbirds zooming through the thickets like tiny green jewels with wings attached.

Father Bunt spotted Father William Snortland getting out of his car, a well-worn Honda Civic. Father Bunt was very fond of the pudgy, balding assistant pastor whose round face gave him the look of being much younger than his 30 years. At times the assistant pastor's sermons ruffled the congregational feathers, but William, recently ordained, refused to kowtow, as he put it, to the whims of secular society.

This past Sunday he had come down hard, once again, on people who "threw money away" on animals. "Don't get me wrong," Father William said. "I like dogs as much as the next guy, but Rover doesn't need gourmet chow. And when he dies, there's no reason to spend money on cremation. Dig a hole, for the love of everything that's holy!"

That particular sermon had caused the phones in the rectory to flash like lightning bugs in a summer swamp, but Father Bunt had defended William's position, explaining gently that, yes indeed, the animals at St. Rita's dined strictly on discount food.

Now he watched as the young man opened the trunk and pulled out two large sacks of what looked like wood chips. Must be litter for Ignatius, his hamster, Father Bunt thought. Talk about a low-maintenance pet.

He returned to his chair. "Well, Eloise, what would you charge for this event?

"We were thinking twenty dollars a person, and that includes live music and a delicious buffet. And here's the best part—I think we can get the music *and* the food donated."

Father Bunt began eagerly doodling on the financial report, sketching a little tree with dollar bills as leaves. "But with the economy being what it is, do you think people would spend that much?" He added a question mark to the tree trunk.

She leaned forward as if confiding a secret. "Father, in my experience, even in bad times, folks want to enjoy themselves."

"Well, the collections are down, I have to tell you," he admitted, "and this would be a huge help. So go ahead and start the planning, and keep me posted, alright?"

"Of course, Father," she enthused. "This is going to be so much fun. I already know exactly who I'm going to dress up as." She stood up and looked at him expectantly, as if he could read her mind.

He gave her a questioning look and she burst out: "Scarlett O'Hara! I've always wanted to wear one of those gowns with the hoop skirts!"

Once she'd left, he sat at his desk doodling. A masquerade ball will be just the thing, he thought. And, really, what can go wrong?

***

"Jobs for the jobless, food for the hungry—and a gentle rain to replenish our water supply," Mrs. Reedley called out eagerly. It was time for the prayers of the faithful at the 5:30 p.m. weekday Mass held in the small day chapel at St. Rita's. Francesca sat in the last pew, inhaling the musky scent of the cloying cologne the woman next to her surely had bathed in. She was trying to stem her fast-moving stream of thoughts, which were running to heavily uncharitable at this point.

Why does Mrs. Reedley keep praying for rain when we're now five inches over for the month? she wondered. True, there had been a drought for the past three years in Decatur, but enough was enough. Forgive me, Lord, for complaining about other people's prayers, she thought. After all, Mrs. Reedley headed up the Golden Glories club, the seniors' group, and gave generously of her time to a long list of ministries. Fat chance I'll ever be that unselfish, Francesca thought.

After Mass, Francesca waited for Rebecca Goodman, her friend from the choir. A fifth-grade teacher at St. Rita's school, Rebecca taught pottery during the summer months. She was a self-proclaimed "fortyish discontented singleton" and the same height as Francesca, 5'3", but quite a few pounds heavier. Her honey-blonde hair and creamy complexion led many well-meaning people to assure her she had "such a pretty face," implying the rest of her body needed work.

"Girl, I wish Mrs. Reedley would work on getting me a husband," Rebecca said, giving Francesca a quick hug. "You know—jobs for the jobless and dates for the hopeless."

Rebecca dug around in her purse, extracted a mint, and popped it into her mouth before continuing: "It's probably the only way I'm going to find a guy who isn't married or weird—or both."

"What about that on-line dating service you tried?" Francesca asked.

Rebecca grimaced. "Well, one guy said he was a widower, 42, and tall with dark brown hair. So I agreed to have coffee with him—and I'd say he's pushing 55—and maybe he had brown hair when he was 20, but the few threads remaining are definitely silver. As for tall, he was about five foot six—and he told me that in *his* family, that's considered tall."

"I read in the paper that some guys are getting facials and wearing make-up," Rebecca continued, shaking her head vigorously. "Is someone putting estrogen in our water supply? Do I have to move to Wyoming or something to find a *real* man?"

Francesca was trying to frame a reassuring reply when Rebecca added, "Not that *you* have to worry, what with that gorgeous detective you're dating."

Francesca had a quick mental image of the handsome detective she'd met during a homicide investigation at St. Rita's.

Tony Viscardi was medium-height, like most of the men in her family, with espresso-colored eyes, a strong physique and an endearingly crooked nose, the result of a childhood diving accident. Most amazing of all, he was romantically unattached. He'd left town a few weeks ago, however, to tend to his unmarried sister, who'd been in a car accident and needed someone round the clock to help her.

"Gorgeous, yes, but he's in Miami," Francesca sighed.

"Well, he's not the only show in town. And you know what they say: *carpe diem* before it's too late." Rebecca glanced at her watch, gave Francesca another hug—"Well, I'm off to the kiln"—and headed out the door.

Francesca went to the table where the big book of prayer requests was kept. She looked through the pages, noting the scribbled appeals—"Healing from cancer," "A job for my son," "Healthy pregnancy." As she was jotting down "Tony's safe return," she overheard a woman talking with Father William in the narthex.

"Father, is it a sin if I put Robert in daycare?"

"Well, some children do just fine in daycare," the priest replied.

"Robert's my poodle, Father! He hates being home alone."

Francesca couldn't quite make out the rest of the exchange, but thought she heard Father William mention wasting money. Then, as Francesca was going out the door, she heard the woman exclaim rather heatedly, "But, Father, I put it all on my credit card!"

Driving home, Francesca thought about Rebecca's advice. She knew her friend was right. She shouldn't be dating Tony exclusively if she wasn't ready to settle down with him. But the thought of dating other men made Francesca feel anxious. So did so many things, though, she realized, as she cautiously navigated the streets, ever on the alert for children, bikers, and animals. On Coventry road, a squirrel darted into the street, saw her car, and froze. She slammed on the brakes and hit the horn, which caused the squirrel to skitter backwards and then forwards in an odd, impromptu two-step before scurrying safely to the sidewalk.

Her anxious temperament was surely inherited from her schoolteacher mother, who could string out endless worries even in the most benign circumstances. Francesca was taught never to: get into an elevator containing a solitary man (he might assault her); try on a hat in a store (she might catch lice); or picnic on a deserted beach (there could be a maniac on the prowl). In college, Francesca had spent a year in therapy trying to overcome the fears of childhood, but after marrying Dean, she began accepting herself as she was. When she began spinning out threads of worry (What if we have an accident on the trip? What if a tree crashes on our house?), Dean had quelled her fears with a simple but very convincing, "Everything will be fine."

Unfortunately, his prediction had proven untrue on that fateful day when he'd lost his life in a crash on spaghetti junction, as locals called a tangled series of interstates in Atlanta. After 15 years of marriage, she'd steeled herself to face the future alone, never again loving a man that much. Then she'd met Tony, and she could feel her resolve wavering, which at times worried her.

***

Father William Snortland drove carefully down the street that led to the Eternal Sunrise Nursing Home. He didn't want to be late, but he also didn't want to jostle the small carrying cage in the backseat of the car. He was taking his pet hamster, Ignatius, to the nursing home today.

He had started this practice after reading about dogs that were specially trained to cheer up elderly people. He had considered taking Dopey with him, but the poor animal was so clumsy he might accidentally knock down one of the frail seniors. Ignatius, on the other hand, with his light brown fur and two fuzzy tufts sticking out cheerfully on either side of his rump, was a well-behaved and placid animal.

As Father William parked, he recalled how just yesterday some parishioners had offered to buy him a new car. They had implied the associate pastor needed a more elegant ride than the aging Civic, which his parents had given him. But he'd turned them down gently, explaining that to most people in the world, any car was a luxury.

As Father William entered the nursing home, his nostrils were assailed by an acrid mixture of pine oil, potpourri, and some other odors he preferred not to name. He stopped at the front desk, which was the domain of a stout, cheery black woman named Clarissa. Her close-cropped hair was dyed the color of marigolds, and she had rhinestones attached to her long, blood-red, pointy fingernails, which unfortunately reminded him of an eagle's talons.

"Good morning, Reverend!" Clarissa's blackberry-colored lips parted in a shimmering smile, revealing gold-capped front teeth, while the cross she wore on a chain around her neck rose and fell in time to her breathing. "They's a real nice lady waiting to see you!"

After signing in, he navigated his way through the corridors where some of the patients sat in wheelchairs, staring at the walls. A few smiled when he greeted them, but others gazed at him blankly. Memory loss, he thought sadly, was one of life's biggest crosses. In her room, Mrs. Anastasia Hartwell was sitting in her usual spot, a chair near the window. Her hair was puffed out in a fluffy gray halo around her head, and there were precise circles of rouge on her deeply creased cheeks. Despite her advanced age—she was 96—Mrs. Hartwell reminded him of the dolls his sister had collected when they were both kids in South Georgia.

"Oh, Father William, I'm so glad you're here!" Mrs. Hartwell's voice had the honeyed intonations of someone who had lived all her life in the South.

He placed the hamster carrier in the corner of the room and then pulled up a chair close to hers. After a few moments of small talk about her niece who lived in Unadilla, Georgia, his parents who lived in Valdosta, and the latest goings on at Eternal

Sunrise—"Father, they treat me like a queen here"—they got down to business.

"Would you like Holy Communion today?" he asked gently.

"Oh, yes I would, Father." She bowed her head and clasped her thin hands in prayer.

He opened his black briefcase and extracted the small gold container in which he carried the consecrated Host. He placed a white linen cloth on an end table, which became an impromptu altar, and lit a votive candle. Then he opened his prayer book and read: "I am the Resurrection and the life: he that believes in me, although he be dead, shall live."

After they said prayers together, Father William held up the Host and announced, "The Body of Christ," and she closed her eyes and lifted her face, murmuring "Amen." He placed the Host on her tongue, then sat quietly and let the old lady pray. His eyes swept quickly over the simple room, which could have been a cell in a monastery. Her world consisted of a single bed with a frayed and faded quilt and a few items of humble furniture. On the nightstand were a pair of well-worn Rosary beads and a framed print of a blonde-haired, blue-eyed Jesus. There was also, he noted, a deck of playing cards. No doubt for solitaire, he thought.

In a few minutes, she opened her eyes. "Father, how is Ignatius doing?"

"Quite well." He went over to the carrier and looked inside. The hamster's ears were perked up and whiskers twitching, both signs that Ignatius was alert and ready for action. He carefully scooped the hamster out and placed him in her cupped hands.

"Oh, he's just the cutest thing," she crooned. "I had one when I was a girl. His name was Bob."

There he goes, working his hamster charm on her, Father William thought, as he handed Ignatius a peanut to munch on. After a few moments, he returned Ignatius to the carrier, and then started gathering the cloth and candle as he prepared to leave. He gave her St. Rita's latest bulletin, and she glanced at it quickly.

"Father, I see the church is going to have a masquerade ball! I used to love them when I was a teenager." Now her smile faded. "Those days are over, though."

"Oh, before you go!" She picked up a worn, patent-leather purse and rummaged through it, extracting a crumpled envelope. "It's only ten dollars, for the church. I wish it could be more."

As he pulled out of the parking lot, Father William had an idea. Why couldn't the old lady come to the masquerade ball? He sang one of his favorite hymns aloud—*Tantum Ergo*—on the way home, while in the back seat Ignatius slept soundly.

***

Francesca settled in at her desk at St. Rita's rectory, where she volunteered a few mornings a week answering phones. Although she was 38, in many ways she considered herself retired. Dean had invested wisely, and after his death, she'd discovered that if she lived frugally, there would be no reason for her to work.

This meant more time for things she loved like volunteering at church and taking long walks in the hilly, tree-lined neighborhood of Chelsea Heights, where she often spied mockingbirds, raccoons, and the occasional turtle in a nearby creek. The only downside was that when people found out she didn't have a job, they thought of ways to fill her day. Her sister was one of these people, which meant that today Francesca was again babysitting Mo-Mo.

The little girl was sitting on the floor near Francesca's desk, playing quietly with the bear Francesca had ended up buying for her the other day. The saleslady had patiently explained the bear was not for sale—it was just a prop—but after Mo-Mo collapsed in a shrill, soggy heap screaming "my bear!" the woman had relinquished her position.

Francesca noticed an enticing aroma emanating from the kitchen. The former housekeeper at St. Rita's recently had moved with her family to Chattanooga. Her replacement, Mrs. Trudy Greenstone, had arrived just a few days ago. Father Bunt had told Francesca that the woman, who was "sixtyish," had a long list of references touting her ability to keep things "neat as a pin" and make meals "from scratch." The woman, however, had been somewhat ruffled when he'd explained that he and Father William were not, in fact, interested in exploring the benefits of a vegetarian diet, even though, as she put it, "Your cholesterol will go down, and you can sleep at night without worrying about mad-cow disease."

Father Bunt had told her, ever so gently, that mad-cow disease was not on his list of worries. The woman had relented, agreeing to serve standard fare such as chicken, pork, and beef, although she had looked, according to Father Bunt, somewhat "put off" about it.

As if summoned by Francesca's thoughts, Mrs. Greenstone—who had made it clear she liked being called by her last name—entered the foyer where Francesca's desk was stationed. They had met each other briefly the day before. The woman was barely five feet tall and pencil thin with a face heavily etched in wrinkles, and dramatically arched, darkly drawn eyebrows that gave her a look of perpetual surprise.

"My arthur-it-is is bad today," the cook announced, rubbing her right arm. "My last job, you know, was at St. Jude's, and it was a much smaller place to keep clean. But"—and here she glanced heavenward—"I'll just offer up my suffering for the poor souls in purgatory." She looked somewhat pleased with her self-proclaimed martyrdom.

"My Bertram—that's my husband, God rest his soul—he always said, 'Trudy, you give 200 percent when everyone else gives 50.'"

Now she looked darkly down at the child on the floor. "Do you really want her doing that?"

"Mo-Mo, no!" Francesca leaned down and attempted to wrestle her brand-new lipstick from the child's hands. The bear, she noted dismally, had generous stripes of Peachy Passion painted all over its face.

"Bear wike wipstick," Mo-Mo chortled.

"I raised three children myself, all God-fearing Christians," Mrs. Greenstone offered, "and one thing Bertram and I agreed on is you gotta let them know who's in charge from day one."

Francesca figured that was her cue to discipline Mo-Mo, but setting limits on the child was something she had yet to master. But with Mrs. Greenstone staring at her expectantly, she had to act.

"I'm sure he likes lipstick, but I just bought that, you see," she told Mo-Mo firmly. She tried to gently retrieve the lipstick, but the child's bottom lip trembled and tears pooled in her brown eyes. These were, Francesca knew, early warning signs of a tantrum.

"Well, I'm off to make lunch," Mrs. Greenstone said. "I know His Reverence doesn't like vegetarian, but I'm going to try him on my bean burgers anyway. They taste so good he'll think they're the real item."

A few minutes later, Francesca heard Father Bunt in the kitchen asking about lunch and the cook saying something about burgers. She heard him exclaim, "Oh, I do enjoy a good juicy hamburger!" There was no further comment from the cook.

***

18

That evening Francesca had choir practice. She'd heard there was a new director, but knew very little about the woman, except, as Rebecca had put it, she wasn't known to "suffer fools gladly." After selecting an outfit appropriate to the blazing heat of the Georgia summer—a white skirt, turquoise cotton blouse, and flip flops—Francesca pulled her shoulder-length, molasses-brown hair into a pony tail, and outlined her lips with another of the outrageously titled lipsticks—"Triple Ecstasy Red"—she just couldn't resist buying. She'd always been fiercely critical of her appearance, ever since her school days as a chubby, shy child, but Dean had often praised what he called her "lovely Italian" good looks, even the one feature she most disliked, which was her decidedly Roman-shaped nose.

She peered out the window, noting glumly that the thermometer still read 96 degrees and it was nearly 6 p.m. The brutal heat had wilted the muscadine grape vines Dean had planted years ago, and the fig tree was also drooping. She banged against the window to discourage a squirrel that was shamelessly devouring a fig, but he just gazed at her, unconcerned. Nearby a bedraggled robin sipped from the bird bath. "What a beastly summer," she commented to Tubs, her 10-year-old cat. Pure white except for a tail with raccoon stripes and a black patch on his back shaped like Africa, he sat calmly washing his face in the air-conditioned comfort of the living room.

Arriving a few minutes early, Francesca dipped her hand in the holy-water font and crossed herself before stepping into the church. Some regulars, she noticed, had already arrived—altos Molly Flowers and Rebecca, along with a tenor, Andy Dull, and a few others. This should be interesting, Francesca thought, since someone—probably the well-meaning church secretary—had placed a notice in the bulletin inviting parishioners to join the choir, "even if you've never sung before except in the shower." And there were plenty of new faces, including, much to her surprise, none other than Mrs. Greenstone, chummily leaning against the organ. "My husband, God rest his soul, always said I had a true voice," she was informing the director, whose smile looked a trifle forced.

After everyone had settled in, the director introduced herself—Charlene Gregory—and handed out the music. The fortyish, quite svelte Charlene had ash-blonde hair worn in a tight chignon, and a heart-shaped face. As the folders were passed around, one of the new altos piped up with, "I hope we're not going to sing any of those dreadful songs like 'On Eagle's Wings.' Whenever I hear it, I imagine some big vicious bird swooping down and carrying someone away in his claws."

There were a few appreciative guffaws from the tenors, after which Charlene said calmly, "As you can see, most of the music is from the 19th century, long before anything as egregious as the eagle song was ever written."

"Well, I rather like it," Mrs. Greenstone piped up huffily. "Matter of fact, we had that one played at Bertram's funeral, and it was quite lovely."

At this Charlene looked a trifle discombobulated. "I'm sure it was," she said diplomatically, her face flushing a bit. "OK, folks, let's get down to business."

She hit an opening note on the nearby piano, asking the various voices to sing the scales together. After one go-around it was clear to Francesca that the church bulletin had indeed attracted some people whose voices were best heard in the confines of their own bathrooms.

The director let out a dramatic sigh, and a few wisps escaped from her chignon. "Well, let's try the hymn for next Sunday, why don't we?"

She sat down at the organ and began playing "Lift High the Cross." After the first line, Francesca was uncomfortably aware that poor Mrs. Greenstone, sitting to her left, was hitting at best one out of five notes.

"*Someone,*" Charlene said, glaring at the alto section, "is way off. Now if you're not sure, just turn down the volume."

Francesca didn't sing at all on the next go-around, just in case, but there was no denying that Mrs. Greenstone—and possibly one of the new tenors—was tone deaf. Worse yet, both the offenders continued singing with great gusto.

Charlene repeated her warning. "*Someone,*" she began—and then Mrs. Greenstone raised her hand.

"I don't think it's the altos at all," she remarked. "I'm pretty sure it's one of the sopranos."

There was a titter of giggles emanating from the soprano section, and then Andy Dull chimed in with, "Well, we're all here to praise the Lord, aren't we, and he won't care if we're off a little."

"Maybe the Lord doesn't care, but I'll be darned if we're going to sound like—like cows mooing." Charlene's face was flushed and there were now tendrils of hair poking out every which way from her chignon.

By evening's end it seemed painfully clear to Francesca that they still weren't ready for Sunday, but Charlene tried to put a good face on it. "Well, this has been a fine first start," she enthused. "And we'll go over it again on Sunday, so be sure to arrive a half hour before Mass starts. "

As they were leaving, Francesca saw Mrs. Greenstone standing at the organ talking enthusiastically to Charlene: "Well, I think we did just fine. Didn't sound a bit like cows at all. As for me, I'm real glad I joined—and I hope we do the eagle song sometime too."

After practice, Francesca gathered on the church steps with Rebecca and a few of the other women who were members of the Choir Chicks, a social group Francesca had launched when she first began singing at St. Rita's. The group included Molly Flowers, a nurse in labor and delivery at a nearby hospital, and a new member, Mauve Bundle.

"I've heard there's going to be a masquerade ball at St. Rita's in a few weeks!" Rebecca said excitedly. "It's going to have kind of a tropical theme, but that doesn't mean our costumes have to involve bathing suits, thank the Lord!"

"Why don't we go as characters from our favorite books?" Mauve Bundle smiled shyly. All Francesca knew about the woman, who looked to be in her late thirties, was that she worked as an assistant in a compounding pharmacy. She also was separated from her husband and had a teenage son. Mauve was short and quite pudgy, and tonight had made the unfortunate choice of wearing Bermuda shorts that revealed sunburned calves that brought vividly to mind two Virginia hams.

While the other women made suggestions—Scarlett O'Hara, Bridget Jones, Madame Bovary—Francesca pondered the idea. She dearly loved Southern writer Flannery O'Connor, but had never heard of anyone dressing up as one of her characters, the way people did with, say, Tolkien's hobbits and elves. Her favorite O'Connor character was a girl named Hulga, a self-proclaimed nihilist with a Ph.D. in philosophy, but Hulga had a wooden leg, and that could present problems in the costume department.

"I could do Heidi," Rebecca said, "except I might attract some old weird geezer who likes little girls—you know, she lived with her grandfather and all."

"Little Red Riding Hood could be fun," Molly mused with a wicked grin. "You might run into the big bad wolf."

Mauve's expression was dismal. "I don't know *what* I would go as." She blinked nervously. "I guess there's always Tinker Bell."

Molly suddenly looked at her watch—"Oops, I have to get to work"—and hurried away. Francesca had a strong suspicion that

Molly, who never worked night shift, was actually trying to avoid laughing at the image of the rotund Mauve dressed as a svelte pixie. She felt a pang of pity as Mauve looked at her for reassurance.

"That sounds perfect," Francesca assured her.

CHAPTER 2

The next evening, the streets were flooded with rain when Francesca arrived home after grocery shopping. As she parked in the driveway of her house on Chelsea Drive, she momentarily expected to see Dean peering out the front window. Never again, she thought sadly. He had added so many personal touches to their unpretentious ranch-style house, including a deck overlooking the thickly wooded backyard, which remained Francesca's favorite spot. As she ran down the path, she tried to avoid two things—one was puddles, and the other was the nagging thought that Mrs. Reedley's prayers were to blame for the downpour.

Once inside, Francesca immediately slipped her feet into her hot-pink pig slippers, and then realized she was hungry. She didn't feel like cooking, so she made a peanut-butter sandwich and a cup of tea. A plaintive meow from the kitchen reminded her Tubs had not been fed. She spooned a generous amount of something fancifully entitled "seafood buffet" into his plate, smiling when his loud "brrrow" sounded like a thank you.

Ensconced on the couch, she munched on her sandwich and looked through the newspaper. She usually tried to avoid reading the more grisly stories, but now her eyes were drawn irresistibly to a story about a 90-year-old woman who had blasted a robber with a double-barreled shotgun ("A birthday gift from my grandson.") When the doorbell rang, Francesca put down her sandwich and went to look through the peephole on the door. She saw a man standing there, and although he looked pleasant enough, there was no way she was going to open the door to a stranger. Unlike the grandmother, she didn't have a shotgun, and had read too many grim tales about women living alone who trusted the wrong man.

When she asked who was there, the man replied: "Frank Freeman. I'm Tony's cousin." She could see him smiling through the peephole.

"Tony's cousin?" She repeated the words, stalling for time. How could she tell if he was telling the truth?

"He figured you'd be suspicious, so he told me some stuff to convince you I'm legitimate." There was a pause and then: "Your favorite ice cream is pistachio. You have a cat named Tubs. You majored in philosophy and minored in psychology at the University of Florida. You grew up in Miami. How am I doing?"

Most of this stuff could be on the Internet, she thought.

"And he said you still wouldn't open the door because you'd figure I got all this from the Internet. So here's the deal breaker." He held up a photo in front of the peek hole. "This is me and Tony last year, biking in Stone Mountain."

She slowly opened the door.

***

Father Bunt belched as he sat at the computer. Tonight's meal—some kind of meatloaf—had been quite dry, and had left him feeling gassy and bloated. He hoped he hadn't made a mistake hiring this cook. She was a bit on the dour side and no spring chicken—a favorite expression of Father Bunt's mother— but he would never hold age against someone. And she had impressed him during the interview with her proclamation that she made everything "from scratch." He just hoped she wasn't sneaking too many healthy ingredients into the meals. He was no fan of bran or bean sprouts.

There was a knock at his door, and then someone pushed it open. It was Mrs. Greenstone, and she looked flustered. "Father, there's a dog that keeps trying to get in the kitchen door."

"No worries—that's Dopey, a rather unmovable force." He suddenly had a thought: "Our last cook doted on him. You wouldn't happen to have any experience training dogs, would you?"

"Well, I certainly would try, Father, except"—here she moved her arm and winced—"my arm's pretty bad today."

He remembered her mentioning that she had a touch of arthritis now and again.

"And to tell you the truth, Father, I'm more of a bird person myself. I have a canary, Little Leonora, and that's enough for me."

Now she suddenly let out a yelp of surprise as Dopey bounded into the room. Father Bunt braced himself, but he wasn't quick enough. The dog threw itself joyfully upon him, placing large muddy paws against his freshly pressed shirt.

"Get down!" He kneed the eager beast in the chest, and then grabbed the collar.

"Well, he looks like a fine fellow," she remarked dubiously. The truth was Dopey was in sore need of a bath, and his pungent aroma was hard to miss. "I wonder if he'll get along with Little Leonora," she added.

"Is she...uh...is your bird here in the rectory too?" Father Bunt was rifling through his drawers for a dog biscuit, while Dopey sat patiently nearby, tongue dangling out in anticipation.

"Yes, she is. You see, I can't leave her home alone, ever since my dear Bertram—God rest his soul—died five years ago." She crossed herself as she spoke.

Father Bunt paused for a respectful moment of silence. She had told him all about Bertram during the interview. "Is the bird in the kitchen then?" He deposited a biscuit into the dog's gaping maw.

"Oh, no, the fumes are bad for them." She wrinkled her brow. "Little Leonora's in a quiet corner of the sitting room."

***

Father William was sitting patiently in the confessional. All too often he would only be visited by four or five people in the three-hour time slot set aside for confessions. Last Sunday he had jokingly suggested during his homily that most of the parishioners must be saints, since so few went to confession. To pass the time today, he was re-reading *The Dark Night of the Soul*, one of his favorite books.

Now he heard someone entering the booth, and he put down his book to say the opening prayers. The woman then launched into a recitation of her sins, mostly minor: a few outbursts of temper, some instances of taking the Lord's name in vain. Then came the zinger.

"This is all in confidence, right?" she asked.

When he assured her that it was, she told him she had lied to "someone." This someone, she said, thought she was feeding him a wide range of cuisines, when, in fact, she refused to prepare dishes containing meat. She explained that she had discovered a few years ago that vegetarian cooking was healthier, and she had completely stopped eating meat. Cooking it now, she said, "gives me the willies."

Father William gave her absolution, after she promised— quite reluctantly—to put an end to the deception. Afterwards, he pondered what to do. He was sure the penitent was Mrs. Greenstone, who had tried unsuccessfully to disguise her voice. And he knew Father Bunt should be informed about this matter, but he couldn't break the secrecy of the confessional.

***

Tony's good-looking cousin fit very well in Francesca's living room. He had green eyes and slightly thinning, close-cropped brown hair dusted with gray. He was quite a bit taller than Tony, maybe six feet, and he had broad, solid-looking shoulders.

"Have a seat." She cleared a few books off the couch, and brushed away some of the omnipresent cat fur. "Would you like a glass of iced tea?"

"Yeah, something cold would hit the spot." He sat down and apparently noticed Tubs staring at him with feline interest. The cat's arthritis prevented it from jumping easily onto the couch, so Tubs' usual modus operandi was to sit and stare at whatever piece of furniture he desired to inhabit.

"Great cat," Frank murmured, extending his hand, which the old cat sniffed cautiously before allowing the newcomer to scratch beneath its chin.

Francesca went into the kitchen to get the tea, while her visitor continued talking to her from the living room: "Tony said you might need a hand with things while he's away, you know, like repairs and stuff. I'm pretty good with that sort of thing, so I told him I'd drop by."

That makes sense, she thought, as she got ice from the freezer. Tony was good about doing things for her without her even asking, things that Dean had once done, like cleaning gutters, trimming the ivy on the trees, and changing the oil in her car. As she handed Frank the glass of tea, she noticed he didn't have a wedding band. She wasn't sure why that mattered to her, except that it was one thing about attractive men she always noticed. Must be a reflex, she thought.

"Do you live in the area?" She sat down in the nearby rocker. "And, uh, do you have a family?" That was one way to figure out his marital status.

"I live over in Oakhurst, so just a few miles away," he said, sipping the tea. "But I'm like Tony—footloose and fancy free! My job takes up a lot of my time—I'm in computer security—and it seems all the good women are either married or going with someone."

He drained the glass and placed it on the coffee table. "Well, I just wanted to stop by and say hello. And I have to say, Tony was right about you." He smiled somewhat shyly. "He said you were a real good-looking lady."

She laughed. "Well, that's Tony for you. He's big on compliments." She noticed Tubs staring at her, and leaned down and picked him up. A large cloud of cat hair descended on her lap.

Frank stood up and brushed the front of his shirt. "Look, I'll leave you my number, if that's OK. This way, if you need anything done, you can just give me a call."

"That's really nice of you." After he wrote his number down on a nearby scrap of paper, she walked Frank to the front door. On the porch, he turned around suddenly and said, "I hope I'm not out of line here, but would you like to have a drink sometime? This way, I can give Tony a full report on you!" Then he laughed. "I'm kidding—about the report, that is, not the drink."

She had a sudden impulse, which she decided to go with. "Our church is having a masquerade ball in a few weeks. You know, dancing, food, costumes—the works. Would you like to go?"

"Hey, that sounds like fun," he nodded. "I'll have to figure out something good to wear."

After he left, she picked up Tubs again. "Well, I did it, Tubs. I asked a man out for a date." The old cat began purring, and she took it as a vote of approval.

***

Father Bunt settled down in the sitting room with his newspaper. Finally, a moment's peace, he thought. He sometimes wondered if he should have become a monk rather than a priest. In a monastery he wouldn't have to deal with stray dogs, financial reports, development committees, seniors' groups, and masquerade balls. Surely in a monastery things would be all precise and orderly, the way he really liked them. But for some reason the Big Guy upstairs had called him to be a pastor. It's a mystery, just like the Holy Trinity, he thought wryly.

He thumbed through the paper, noticing the usual grisly assortment of news items. A child had come home to find her parents and the housekeeper dead. A plane had crashed at a county fair, killing a crowd of people gathered to have fun. If anyone doubts that it's a fallen world, he thought, just let them read the newspapers. Then he turned to the entertainment page, where there were ads touting movies about demented killers, escaped zombies, and teenage vampires. He felt a frisson of fear when he spotted a notice in the entertainment calendar, proclaiming in bold print: "Masquerade Madness at St. Rita's." He'd hoped to keep the event small and confined just to parishioners, but it looked like it was too late for that. The proverbial cat was out of the bag.

He fished out his Rosary beads to calm himself. He was well into the third decade when a shattering string of obscenities suddenly burst forth from a corner of the room. He dropped the beads and sat up straight in the chair. What in the name of God is that? he thought as the curses continued. At that precise moment, Mrs. Greenstone entered the room, looking flustered and wiping her hands on her apron.

"Oh, Father, I hope you'll forgive Little Leonora."

He stared at her blankly, since he hadn't the foggiest idea what the woman was talking about.

"It's my bird, Father—she has a bit of a problem inherited from Bertram, may God rest his soul—but I'm sure we can overcome it."

He followed her as she hurried to the corner of the room. There, slightly blocked by a set of bookshelves and a large potted plant was a good-sized cage. He peered inside, noticing Lenora was not little at all; in fact, she looked like a hulking hawk someone had dipped into red-and-green paint.

"I thought she was a canary?" The words flew out before he could edit them; he suspected it wasn't wise to contradict the cook.

"Oh, no, Little Leonora is a *parrot.*" Mrs. Greenstone spoke slowly and precisely as if correcting a small child.

He looked dubiously at the bird, which was now quiet but had fluffed out its feathers rather ominously. He knew Mrs. Greenstone had described it as a canary, but he wasn't going to argue.

"Does it...she...bite?" As the bird crept nearer to him on its perch, Father Bunt backed away.

"Not once she gets to know you, Father. Then she's sweet as sugar." Mrs. Greenstone put her finger right into the cage, and the bird nibbled at it affectionately.

I'd better stay away from the blasted thing, he thought. He'd heard tales about parrots who had nearly sliced off the fingers of unsuspecting people who had been foolhardy enough to get too close.

"***#$%@*&!" The bird chose that moment to unleash another storm of obscenities, which caused Father Bunt to recoil even further.

He had to wonder about Mrs. Greenstone's dearly departed husband. Had the man gone on like this all the time? But he didn't dare bring up the topic. Besides, the woman seemed nonplussed, as if the bird had just sung a particularly stirring rendition of a Gregorian chant.

"As soon as I feed her, Father, she'll be as quiet as a lamb."

More like a vulture, he thought.

"Uh, Mrs. Greenstone, the archbishop, you know, is coming for lunch tomorrow. It might be best to move, uh, the…uh, Little Leonora, just in case, you know."

Her lips twitched ominously. "Little Leonora has become accustomed to the sitting room. I'll cover her cage, and I'm sure she'll be quiet."

***

It was early the next day, and Father Bunt was in his office, saying his morning prayers. He had a long list of things to be grateful for, including the fact that the bird had been angelically quiet after the initial horrifying outbreak. Thank God for small mercies, he thought. All I need is a parrot wreaking havoc in the rectory. After his prayers, he tidied up his desk, hoping the office would give the archbishop an impression of order and dignity. He wasn't sure why MacPherson wanted to meet with him, but he figured it was about the dwindling collections.

It was rare for an archbishop to make house calls, but MacPherson had grown up with Father Bunt's father in a small town in Michigan. The two men had kept up with each other over the years, and when MacPherson had been named archbishop five years earlier, Father Bunt's dad had called his old friend to request that he keep an eye on "my boy."

Father Bunt's train of thoughts now veered in a different direction as he recalled suddenly that a first-year seminarian was due to arrive this evening from St. Michael's, a seminary in North Carolina. The young man had been assigned to St. Rita's for the summer. Father Bunt had overseen other seminarians at other parishes, and it had always gone smoothly, and he trusted this one would also work out well.

He glanced anxiously at the clock and then began making his way down the stairs toward the front door. The archbishop was known to be a man who arrived precisely on the button, and today surely would be no exception. But just as the doorbell chimed, Father Bunt heard a tentative squawk from the sitting room. That blasted bird, he thought. That's all I need now.

He opened the door and there was Archbishop Reginald MacPherson, a short, stocky man with a jaunty crew cut. He looked fit and tanned, as he always did, Father Bunt noticed enviously. It was hard to tell the man was 70. Every time their paths crossed, Father Bunt vowed to start an exercise program, but somehow that didn't seem to happen.

"Brent, how are you? How's the arm?" The archbishop shook his hand vigorously.

"Oh, fine, much better." Father Bunt swung his arm around to show how agile it was, despite the gunshot wound he had received—and then gasped when he felt a sharp pain. He was supposed to be exercising it, he remembered, but he was just too busy.

After a few pleasantries about Father Bunt's parents and the archbishop's plans for a late summer vacation, the two men started toward the dining room. Suddenly the older man dropped his volume and moved closer.

"Oh, listen, Brent, I noticed an announcement in the Atlanta paper about a what-cha-ma-call-it, uh, masquerade ball your parish is hosting."

Father Bunt braced himself. Here it comes, he thought. He's going to tell me I never should have publicized it to the outside community.

"I like that approach, Brent. I think we need to do more to invite the community in." The archbishop gave him an approving tap on the shoulder. "You know, welcome people who don't know much about our beliefs."

"Yes, I...I...think so too." Father Bunt felt the knots in his shoulders easing.

"You just never know when someone will be drawn to the Lord because...:"

But the archbishop never got to complete the sentence because there was a sudden, ear-splitting squawk emanating from the sitting room. Father Bunt was starting to suspect that the parrot was some kind of diabolical entity the cook had somehow conjured up.

"What in the world was *that*?" The archbishop's eyebrows shot up alarmingly.

"The cook, sir, she has a parrot. I thought it would be sleeping, but it seems..." His words trailed off miserably as he prayed fervently that the bird would not give a repeat performance of yesterday's recitation.

A slow grin spread over the older man's face, giving him a momentarily boyish look. "My grandmother had one when I was a boy. Well, let's take a quick look at it, shall we?"

There was no getting out of this one, Father Bunt realized, as he led the way, licking his lips nervously and continuing to pray the bird would be on its best behavior. They walked into the sitting room where the covered cage sat ominously in the corner. The archbishop slowly removed the cover and bent closer to look at the bird. He turned to Father Bunt with a big smile:

"Well, what's this fine fellow's name?"

"Uh, it's a female, sir, named Leonora. The...uh... the cook, Mrs. Greenstone, her late husband, uh, trained it."

"Beautiful." The archbishop drew a little closer, and the bird edged its way over and put its beak against the metal rung of the cage. The archbishop put his finger very close, and Father Bunt drew in his breath sharply: "Be careful, sir, she might nip you."

"I'm good with birds," the older man assured him. "You just have to be gentle with them." He lightly scratched the feathers on the bird's head, and Father Bunt relaxed. It looked like the bird wasn't as dangerous as he had feared.

"She's very much like the one my grandmother had," MacPherson said fondly. "His name was Jeremiah, and he sure could talk up a storm." He turned to Father Bunt now: "Does she do any talking?"

"Uh, just a bit," Father Bunt said. "A few phrases actually."

As the two men headed to the dining room, MacPherson related a story about the time his grandmother's parrot had gotten loose and they had... But he never finished the story because at that precise moment the bird let loose with a string of bright purple phrases.

"Dear Lord, was that the bird?" MacPherson's eyes seemed to double in size.

As if on cue, the bird's volume increased. She went through the entire repertoire, starting with garden-variety curse words someone might utter when stubbing a toe, but then escalating to much more colorful phrases. The two men stood stock still, while Father Bunt prayed to no avail that the bird would shut up. And then, almost miraculously, silence descended on the room. The bird mumbled to itself rather contentedly, and the tirade was over.

The archbishop shook his head. "They do tend to pick up the worst expressions and repeat them."

It was at that moment that the bird launched the final verbal missile, the pièce de résistance that had probably been one of the dearly departed Bertram's favorite expressions. As Father Bunt later reported to Father William—trying to avoid actually repeating the statement—the bird's command would have required listeners to do something to themselves that would have been physically impossible.

The archbishop winced. "Does it always go on like this?"

"I apologize, sir. The cook has promised me she is going to do something about this." That was stretching the truth, Father Bunt knew, but maybe he could make the statement somehow come true in the future.

"Well, she'd better, man." The archbishop frowned. "Think about it, Brent: what if parishioners heard this sort of thing?"

"Yes sir, I agree, of course, but, uh, the cook is very attached to it," Father Bunt said weakly.

"*You're* the one in charge here, Brent." The archbishop's tone of voice was grave. "You figure out somewhere else she can keep this bird."

"Yes, of course, sir, I will." Father Bunt silently prayed Mrs. Greenstone wouldn't decide to pack up her pots and pans and her bird, and find a job elsewhere. He sadly recalled the greasy tubs of take-out chicken that had been daily fare in the rectory while he was trying to fill the cook's position.

As he was ushering the archbishop into the dining room, Father Bunt spotted an unfamiliar person at the table talking with Father William. It was a young man wearing a crisp white shirt and beige slacks. When he caught Father Bunt's eye, the man made his way over to him and the archbishop.

"I'm Augustine Hornsby, Your Grace. We met at the seminarian luncheon at the chancery last week." He made a little bow and extended his hand to the archbishop.

"Yes, indeed, I remember." MacPherson pumped the man's hand enthusiastically. "It's very good to see you again."

Then Augustine turned to Father Bunt. "It's a pleasure to meet you, Father. I'm looking forward to my stay at St. Rita's."

"Yes, indeed, so are we all." Father Bunt was trying to figure out how he could have gotten the young man's arrival time wrong.

Everyone stood while the archbishop said the blessing, during which time Father Bunt took a sideways glance at Hornsby. The man was blonde with hazel eyes and an even tan. He was probably over six feet, and with a good build and even features. Father Bunt wondered if women might find him attractive.

The lunch went reasonably well with the exception of one fiasco. A few days earlier, Mrs. Greenstone had asked if her granddaughter, "a real sweet girl, Beatrice," could help with the lunch. Father Bunt knew the archbishop loved children, and he couldn't see any harm in saying yes, so he had agreed.

And then, as Mrs. Greenstone was serving the salads, a woman sauntered in who looked to be in her early twenties. She was attired in all black and instantly called to Father Bunt's mind someone in the deepest stages of mourning. Then he noticed that the girl was literally covered in tattoos of—and here he nearly did a double take—gruesome-looking snakes. There was even, he noticed with horror, a quite realistic rendition of a viper wrapped around her neck as if preparing to asphyxiate her.

Mrs. Greenstone introduced her as "my little granddaughter, Beatrice," and the girl lisped as she said, "Pleased to meet you." It took a few moments for Father Bunt to realize that the speech impediment came from a particularly strange fashion quirk. He knew that today multiple piercings were as familiar as Tupperware parties had been in his grandmother's day, but he just couldn't fathom why someone would stick an earring in their tongue.

41

As lunch progressed, Beatrice's presence made him increasingly uneasy. Was it Father Bunt's imagination or did she glance at the seminarian in a somewhat provocative way? The archbishop, however, seemed entirely nonplussed with her behavior and didn't say much during the meal except to praise the food.

"These cutlets are delicious—are they veal?" he asked Mrs. Greenstone as she was replenishing the roll basket.

The cook looked flustered. "No, sir, they're, uh, not veal." Then a timer went off in the kitchen, and she rushed away.

***

Augustine looked over the small, bare-bones room in the upstairs section of St. Rita's rectory with a critical eye. He had known when he made the decision to become a priest that he'd be saying goodbye to the many luxuries he'd taken for granted growing up in Avondale Estates.

The small town, a few miles from Decatur, was known for sprawling, meticulously manicured lawns and well-appointed houses. His family's two-story home had been situated on the lake, and his upstairs bedroom had afforded him a splendid view of the geese and turtles that made their homes there.

The family had always had a maid and a gardener, and he'd never had to do chores like other boys. When his friends at St. Pius X High School in Atlanta complained about having to make their beds or mow the lawn, Augustine had kept silent. Then, when they came over to his house for supper and realized that Yvonne, the family maid, took care of nearly everything domestic, they'd started making fun of him. Although there certainly were other well-to-do families at the school, his parents' extremely opulent lifestyle had set him apart, and there were times when he'd longed to be like the other boys.

It was during his junior year in high school that he'd discovered a way to merge with the in-crowd. He'd begun doing impersonations of the various teachers, and it seemed he had a knack for it. Before long he was being called into the principal's office on a regular basis and listening to lectures on showing respect to one's elders. He'd become extremely popular at parties, where his fellow students would implore him to "Do Mr. Monroe" and "Do Father Paul."

The girls thought his stand-up routines were hilarious, and it became much easier to get dates. The only problem was he found it almost impossible to know where to draw the line. Everyone became fodder for his humor, and when the girls he was dating discovered they were the latest source for all the uproarious laughter in the boys' locker room, they were none too pleased.

He couldn't quite remember when the idea of becoming a priest had entered his mind for the very first time. It seemed it was always there on the edge of his consciousness. The priesthood had always been his mother's dream for him, ever since he had first donned his altar server robes in the third grade. His father, an internist, had wanted his only son to become a doctor, but had acquiesced—"If God's calling, you don't say no"—when Augustine revealed his hopes of entering the seminary. His father had made one condition, which Augustine had met: He wanted his son to graduate from college first, and then make a final decision.

Augustine figured he'd be good at writing sermons since he had made straight A's in college English. But it wasn't just that, of course. He wanted to help people, and he knew this was the way to do it. At times he wavered, though, when he thought about going it alone, with no wife and children. His father warned him the priesthood could be a lonely path. But Augustine, now 22, often reminded himself that he'd be known as "father" to the parishioners. It would be a spiritual family, and surely that would make up for the lack of a biological one.

When he'd started seminary, he'd begun keeping a diary, which was blossoming into a satirical novel. Sometimes he envisioned himself as a famous author with *The Secret Diary of a Seminarian* on the bestseller list, while at other times he suspected the whole writing thing was just a pleasant hobby. And in any event, he didn't think being a priest and an author were contradictory pursuits. Writing was a good outlet for his creative energy.

He began unpacking, taking out a few books and a stack of shirts, slacks, and underwear. He carefully placed his laptop computer on the desk. He also unpacked a small framed photo of a smiling girl, her long brown hair cascading upon her shoulders and her dark eyes widening as she laughed. My dear Susannah, he thought.

CHAPTER 3

Mo-Mo was in Francesca's living room, eating cookies and watching cartoons on TV. Despite her sister's warnings about giving the child sweets, Francesca had quickly discovered that a surefire way to prevent tantrums was to acquiesce to Mo-Mo's requests. She knew this was a highly questionable parenting style, but, after all, she was the aunt, and surely there was no harm in a few animal crackers.

Francesca was putting the finishing touches on her outfit for the masquerade ball. Now she stood before the mirror and surveyed the results with a critical eye. Not bad, she thought, for someone who had made a name for herself in a YWCA sewing class by attaching the pockets on the wrong side of a skirt. True, one sleeve was longer than the other, and the pants' legs were somewhat crooked, but all in all, it would do just fine. At that moment Mo-Mo wandered in, clutching her bear.

"Anny Fwan!" she yelled gleefully, wrapping her arms around Francesca's legs.

Francesca returned the child's hug and then looked down with horror, realizing Mo-Mo had left chocolate-covered handprints on the bottom of her costume. The child had evidently discovered the hidden Hershey bar on the bookshelf.

"Oh, Mo-Mo, what am I going to do with you?" She gazed down at the curly-haired child with those irresistibly chubby cheeks.

"Wuv oo," Mo-Mo cooed.

"I love you too." Someday, she'd laugh at this memory, but right now, she had laundry to do.

Just a few miles away, Tony was trying on a costume he'd brought back from Miami. He'd arrived home in Decatur the day before, but hadn't told anyone he'd returned. While in Miami, he'd put together a costume with the help of his cousin, Rachelle, who was a seamstress in her spare time. The outfit consisted of a long black robe, a large pointed hat, and a staff that actually glowed in the dark. She'd also scoured costume shops and found him a shaggy white beard to cover his face and a mask for his eyes. Rachelle had assured him no one would recognize him. "You look really wise," she had joked. He'd heard plenty about the masquerade ball from Francesca, so when his sister had suddenly seemed much better, he'd quickly booked a flight home.

He had reserved a rental car for the evening of the event, so he wouldn't blow his cover when he took Francesca home. Once there, he planned to surprise her by removing the mask and the beard. He wondered if she would go with Rebecca or another friend. He also wondered what Francesca planned to wear.

***

Francesca marveled at the parish hall, which had been transformed from a dumpy auditorium where schoolchildren had lunch into a fairly decent rendition of a tropical paradise. The tables were decked out with festive cloths patterned in island colors with clusters of bright flowers as centerpieces. Someone had added fake palm trees dotted with tiny lights to the room, along with large posters of seabirds, dolphins, and manatees.

The room resounded with the booming sounds of talking and laughter. Francesca saw people dressed as frogs, unicorns, and bears, as well as hobbits, clowns, cowboys, and cats. The buffet table was laden with a tempting array of roast beef, ham, rolls, and a variety of cold salads and desserts. Against one wall there was a well-stocked bar where a man from the Knights of Columbus, dressed as a Smurf, was cheerfully filling glasses.

"I'll get us some wine and join you at the buffet line," Frank said, making a beeline for the bar. He was decked out in a monk's outfit, complete with brown robe and sandals, and a rope tied around his waist.

As she got on the end of a very long line, Francesca saw Mrs. Greenstone dishing out potato salad. Her costume consisted of a baggy white blouse and long skirt painted with large black dots. Next to her was a widower from the Golden Glories, Arnold Turner, dressed as his version of a farmer, complete with a straw hat, suspenders, and overalls. "But don't worry," she heard him jokingly assure Mrs. Greenstone, "the animals on my farm die happily of old age."

"What are you supposed to be?" A tiny boy, thumb in mouth, stood looking up at Mrs. Greenstone.

"I'm a cow, of course," she replied, "and you shouldn't eat them because they're very friendly animals." The child continued staring at her while his mother put a slice of roast beef on his plate.

At the cook's side was a twentyish woman whom Francesca recognized as Beatrice, her granddaughter. She was wearing a shimmering silver gown along with luminescent paper wings and a halo. Somehow, the juxtaposition of the ethereal outfit with the black serpents drawn on Beatrice's limbs was off-putting to Francesca, but she suspected she was somewhat old-fashioned when it came to tattoos.

"I hope you don't meet up with a cat," Beatrice called out to her, snickering.

"Me too," Francesca laughed as she tweaked one of her sleeves. She had decided to go as one of her favorite characters from the comics. She was wearing a bright yellow jumpsuit, with matching feathers pinned to her hair, and fuzzy yellow slippers. On the bodice of her costume she had attached felt letters reading, "I tawt I taw a puddy tat."

"And you...you're an angel, right?" Francesca asked.

"Yeah, the angel of *death*, that's what I am." The girl laughed heartily at her own joke, but her grandmother gave her a sharp look.

The man ahead of Francesca was dressed as a Viking, and when he turned around, she recognized him as Andy Dull, one of the tenors. After a few pleasantries about the choir, he began filling his plate with slices of roast beef.

"I wouldn't eat that to save my soul," Mrs. Greenstone muttered grimly.

"Is there something wrong with the beef?" Andy cast a worried look at the oozing slab on his plate.

"Oh, it's fine, if you don't mind eating a *dead cow*," Mrs. Greenstone said. But Andy just shrugged and uttered a low "moo" under his breath, which only Francesca could hear.

"Hey, Tweety Bird, I hope you like chardonnay." Frank joined her on the line, carrying two large glasses of wine.

After they'd filled their plates and were making their way to a table, Francesca spotted Father William who was wearing ordinary black slacks and a white shirt along with a cowboy hat and boots. He was carrying a cage and accompanying an elderly lady dressed in a white running suit, and with rabbit ears attached to a headband.

"I used to be a parishioner here, about 100 years ago," Mrs. Hartwell joked, after Father William introduced her. "But don't let me get started about that...you know how old ladies just go on and on!" She pointed to the cage: "Father, do tell them about Ignatius."

"Oh, yes, he's captain of the ship tonight," Father William explained. The cage was equipped with makeshift paper sails and bore a sign reading: "Our Lady's Ship, the Lepanto."

"Where's Ignatius?" Francesca could only see a fluffy ball of what looked like chewed-up toilet paper inside.

"Oh, the captain is asleep as usual," Father William replied, and then, after a few more pleasantries, he and Mrs. Hartwell headed to the buffet line.

Just as they'd settled in at their table, Frank turned to Francesca with a somewhat sheepish look. "I know it's a terrible habit, but I need a cigarette, so I'll be outside a few minutes."

A few moments later, a rather attractive, young man sat down next to her. He was wearing everyday clothes, but had red horns attached to a head band.

"Augustine Hornsby," he announced, extending a hand. "Father William told me you volunteer at St. Rita's, and since I'm stationed here for a while, you'll be seeing me around quite a bit. I'm a first-year seminarian." He grinned in a rather endearing way.

As she was introducing herself, she noticed his hazel eyes had shimmering depths that reminded her of the cats-eye marbles she'd collected as child.

"So…did you dream of growing up and becoming Tweety Bird when you were a little girl?" he chuckled.

She was just about to answer when Frank returned and plunked down next to her. "Lucifer, I presume?" he said to the seminarian. His voice had a sharp, somewhat unfriendly edge.

"No, just one of the minor-league demons, actually," Augustine replied evenly.

Francesca quickly made the introductions, but she noticed Frank looked uneasy, as if the seminarian had somehow been homing in on his territory. Surely he doesn't think this guy—

who is probably in his early twenties—is coming on to me, Francesca thought. But when it came to male territorial impulses, she knew reason didn't always rule.

Augustine suddenly stood up and excused himself. He was a few steps away before he turned around and said, "Oh, by the way, Francesca, you never answered my question."

"Oh, that's right; you asked about childhood dreams," she replied. "Well, I confess I actually used to dress up as Tweety Bird for Halloween when I was a kid, "she laughed, "but that's as far as that went. As for dreams, there was a time in high school when I wanted to be a nun, but then it kind of fizzled out." She took a sip of wine and added, "I guess most Catholic kids go through that phase."

As soon as the words flew out of her mouth, she wished she had a net to capture them with. Augustine's smile faded as he murmured something about getting supper, and then he wandered away. She could feel her face flushing beneath the yellow face paint. I bet I insulted him, she thought, since he probably wanted to become a priest in high school and I said it's just a phase.

"What's up with him?" Frank asked as he tucked into the roast beef. "Doesn't he have a date?"

"Uh, he's a seminarian," she said quietly. "Which means he, uh, he's going to become a priest, so I'm guessing he doesn't date."

"Well, you could have fooled me," Frank replied.

"Oh, this pasta salad is perfect," she said, trying to change the topic. It seemed to work, and they ate with few further comments. When he got up to refresh their wine glasses, she realized they'd forgotten to stop by the dessert table.

"I'll get us some dessert," she offered.

"Great—choose something really fattening."

At the dessert table, Francesca spotted Augustine a few feet away talking with Beatrice, who was laughing, although Francesca couldn't catch what the joke was. When she saw Beatrice tweak the young man's horns, Francesca became more curious and managed to move close enough to overhear them.

"So are you a good devil or a bad one?" Beatrice asked playfully.

And then Augustine: "You ever hear of a good devil?"

Someone came up behind Francesca and put their arms around her waist.

"Guess who?"

She turned quickly, and there was Rebecca, decked out in Snow White regalia, including a glossy black wig and a shiny floor-length gown with elaborate puffy sleeves. Francesca admired her friend's outfit, but Rebecca just crinkled up her nose the way she did when she disagreed with someone.

"Thanks, but some good it's doing me. I still haven't run into an eligible man—and with my luck, I'll probably end up with one of the seven dwarves." As the music started up again, she added, "Well, catch you later!"

It was then that Francesca heard someone shouting outside and saw flashing lights through the large glass windows of the hall. I'll get the desserts later, she decided. Her curiosity piqued, she followed a cluster of costumed partygoers to the doorway and peered outside where two police cars were parked. She spotted a troubled-looking Father William hurrying in from the parking lot.

"What happened, Father?" she asked.

"It looks like some motorcycle guys wanted to join the party, but from what I can gather, a fight broke out and someone called the police." His brow furrowed. "I heard some mention of something going on with drugs. I know Father Bunt is going to be very upset."

She walked outside and stood watching as one of the bikers was being escorted to a police car. Suddenly Frank was at her side.

"Hey, what's going on?" he asked her. As she filled him in, she kept her eyes on the scene. Was it her imagination or did the man nod toward Frank?

"Do you know that guy?" she asked.

"Never saw him before." Frank shrugged. "He must have me confused with some other guy."

They stood outside for a few moments after the commotion died down and the crowd went back inside. The sky was velvety black with a generously full moon.

"It looks like a Communion wafer," Francesca murmured.

Frank guffawed. "More like a poker chip!"

She mentally rolled her eyes. She was starting to regret having invited Frank. He was very handsome, and she rather enjoyed the occasional envious glances from other single women there. But there was something about him that grated on her. Maybe she was comparing him with Tony, and maybe that wasn't fair. Still, with each additional glass of wine, he grew louder and more annoying.

"Instead of dessert, let's dance," he suggested. Although she had her heart set on a piece of coconut cake, she agreed. When they returned to the dance floor, he drew her very tightly against him—and the feel of his muscular arms ignited a definite spark. But, still, she was wary of him. After all, she'd been drinking too, and she worried that her usual defenses were down.

"Frank, what church do you go to?" If that question doesn't throw some cold water on the situation, nothing will, she thought.

He grimaced as if she'd mentioned a highly contagious virus. "Oh, jeez, I don't go to *church*. I mean, I used to go when I was a kid, but once my mother stopped nagging me, I gave up on the whole thing."

He evidently sensed that he had blundered. "Hey, don't get me wrong. I'd go to church every day if I had a beautiful lady like *you* on my arm."

This is just beyond the pale, she thought. He's laying it on way too thick. She didn't want him driving her home in his inebriated and amorous condition, but what could she do?

"Uh, listen, Frank, I have to...powder my nose. Be right back." She gave him a big smile and headed toward the ladies room. Once there, she pulled out her cell phone and sent a text message to Tony.

"Met your cousin, Frank Freeman. Miss you."

Moments later, as she was touching up her yellow face paint, she received an answer back: "Don't have cousin Frank. You OK?"

***

Elbowing her way through the crowd a few moments later, Francesca was suddenly face to face with Mauve Bundle, who was decked out as her version of Tinker Bell in a strapless dress with huge, shimmering wings attached. By her side was a sullen teenage boy—"my son, Brad!"—wearing a hat with skull and crossbones on it.

Brad grunted a reluctant hello and then said he was going to get a Coke. Once he was out of earshot, Mauve's face fell. "It was like pulling teeth to get him to come with me, but I don't want him home alone. I don't want him getting into any more trouble. Nothing serious, but he's been cutting classes a lot at high school. It's hard for me to keep up with him, since I have to work."

"Yeah, that must be tough," Francesca said automatically, although she was hoping the conversation wouldn't drag on so she could find Frank and let him know she was on to him. Why in the world did he invent that cousin story? She fumed inwardly.

"Well, I'm going to introduce Brad to the priests," Mauve said in a few moments, "so we'll see you later." The poor boy looked as if he was headed for a root canal without anesthesia, Francesca thought.

She wandered through the crowd looking for Frank, and mentally planning what she would say to him. The music was getting louder by the minute, and the dance floor was filled with gyrating and shaking bunnies, clowns, surfers, and even an occasional vampire—but no Frank.

"A penny for your thoughts, Tweety." Inches away stood a man dressed in full wizard gear, including a staff with a glowing blue crystal at the top.

"Oh, they're not worth that much, really." She didn't want to admit her date had ditched her.

"Would you like to dance?" The wizard's smile beneath the bushy beard was kind.

"Yes, that would be great," she murmured, and he gently took her into his arms. She was relieved that it was a slow number, since she'd never been adept at any version of dancing that required keeping time to a fast beat. Fortunately, she did know how to follow, and he was a smooth leader. She felt herself relaxing in his embrace.

When the music picked up steam again—"Hillbilly Bones" was now thrumming forth—he made a little bow. "Why don't we go outside and get a breath of fresh air? This place is really getting crowded."

She nodded, relieved, because she was feeling a little claustrophobic. Outside they stood a moment silently taking in the black sky in which the fat moon still glittered accented by a sprinkling of rhinestone stars.

"So tell me, Tweety, where do you work?" His brown eyes behind the mask crinkled when he smiled.

She told him a little about volunteering at the church and babysitting Mo-Mo. When she asked him the same question, he seemed evasive. "Oh, I'm, uh, a consultant, you know, programming and such." A heartbeat later, he said: "Do you have a boyfriend, if you don't mind my asking?"

"Not really. I mean, I go out with someone, but it's not..." Her voice trailed off.

Why was she denying her relationship with Tony? Was it because she didn't really know where she stood with him? And at times she even doubted the story about his ailing sister in Miami?

"Not serious?" The wizard supplied the word.

"That's right," she answered quickly. "What about you?"

"Same here—no ties at all." His voice had an odd edge she couldn't quite identify.

"Look, it's getting very late," he said suddenly. "May I offer you a ride home?"

She laughed. "Do wizards have cars?"

"Well, this one does."

"Are you—are you a member of the parish?" She was a little nervous about accepting a ride from a total stranger.

"Yes, I, uh, I just moved here from another state." He smiled reassuringly.

"Where do wizards live, generally?"

He laughed. "Some of us are from Middle-earth, but I hail from Melrose, Florida."

They talked about Florida for a while, covering everything from manatees, boating, and beaches to double rainbows in the sky. She had grown up there, and their small talk put her at ease.

"Well, yes, I would like a ride, if you don't mind," she finally said. "I don't want to walk home in the dark."

They drove the few blocks to her house in companionable silence. She noted with approval how very clean the car was, inside and out. He must be a real perfectionist, she thought.

"Come on, I'll see you safely to your door," he said kindly when they arrived at her house.

He said a quick good night on the porch and then hurried down the steps. Once inside, she realized she had forgotten to ask his name. She wondered if she'd ever see him again. There had been something about him that had rather enchanted her.

***

Tony sat staring glumly at his computer screen at the station. Last night had been a complete disaster. He took a sip of the bitter coffee that was the hallmark of the Decatur police station, and threw the rest of it away.

Some surprise, he thought bleakly. Why in the world had he decided to ask her about her love life? Well, at least now he knew the truth. She had denied even having a boyfriend, probably so she'd seem available to the wizard, a complete stranger. Well, so be it. From now on, he would keep his distance. That always seemed the best plan when it came to women. He had thought Francesca was different, but all it had taken was one evening to discover the truth. It would be strictly business between them from now on.

He decided to do a quick background check on Frank Freeman just out of curiosity. The name sounded familiar. As he read the file, he clenched his jaw. The guy had a record—drug charges. I hope she isn't serious about him, he thought.

***

Father Bunt retrieved the morning newspaper from the driveway and went back inside. There, on page one of the local section, was exactly what he had feared: "Gang members arrested at local church." He also noticed, much to his chagrin, a photograph of himself with the damning cutline, "Pastor denies knowledge of drug sales at dance." I wonder what time the archbishop wakes up, he thought nervously.

There was a staccato sound of toenails clicking on linoleum as Dopey ambled into the kitchen and sat by his food dish, staring at Father Bunt. I'm starting to feel like his slave, he thought, as he dutifully filled the bowl with food and placed it on the floor. He turned around to refill his coffee cup, and when he looked down again, seconds later, the dish had been polished clean, and Dopey seemed to be smiling.

Normally by this time Father Bunt would expect to hear some sounds of life emanating from the upstairs bedrooms, but the rectory seemed eerily silent. Father William, he knew, was out jogging. He decided to go upstairs to check on the seminarian. He walked up the stairs, making shuffling noises with his feet, hoping to awaken him. After all, the man would have to be up very early when he became a priest.

He knocked, but there was no response, so he pushed the door slowly open. To his surprise, he saw the bed was neatly made, and the room was empty. He recalled seeing Augustine the night before, chatting quite amiably with a number of parishioners. He chewed his lower lip as he realized they had been mostly women.

A few moments later, Father Bunt heard the front door opening. He arrived in the foyer just in time to see a somewhat flustered-looking Augustine, dressed in jeans and a neatly pressed dark green shirt, carrying a laptop computer and a grocery bag.

"Oh, good morning, Father! I couldn't sleep last night, so I went to that all-night diner in downtown Decatur." He yawned as he shifted the computer in his hands. "I figured I could do some writing, you know, use the time productively." Now he held aloft the grocery bag. "Then I picked up a few supplies I need."

Father Bunt nodded. What could he say, really? I have no reason to be suspicious, he thought. Then he recalled the carefully made bed. Had the seminarian actually slept in his room? If someone couldn't sleep, would they make the bed before going out? Maybe the guy is obsessively neat, he thought. No harm in that really.

"So, if you don't mind my asking, what are you writing?" Father Bunt asked.

Little streaks of red rushed into the young man's cheeks. "Oh, it's just a hobby of mine, Father. I write fiction in my spare time. I've been doing it since I was a kid."

"Oh, really? What kind?" Father Bunt asked politely.

"Right now, I'm working on a mixture of realism and fantasy. It's called *The Secret Diary of a Seminarian.*" Augustine smiled broadly.

Father Bunt returned the smile in what he hoped was an encouraging way, but deep inside he was starting to feel a twinge of anxiety. All he needed was someone recording the strange goings-on at St. Rita's and publishing a book about them. With my luck it would be a bestseller, he thought.

*　*　*

After Mass that morning, Augustine quietly entered the kitchen. There was no sign of Mrs. Greenstone, but her purse was nearby, so he figured she was upstairs. He hurried to the refrigerator and rifled through the meat bin. In seconds, his suspicions—that Mrs. Greenstone was indeed serving substitute meat products—were confirmed. His mother had gone on a vegetarian binge when he was fifteen, and he'd never forgotten the acrid flavor of the meat substitutes.

Augustine figured he could have a little fun now with the cook. He pulled out a few packages of pre-made soy-burger patties from the refrigerator and tossed them in the trash. He then substituted the ground-beef patties he'd purchased earlier that morning, replacing the cellophane over them. He also removed the soy breakfast links from their package and replaced them with real pork. He was chuckling to himself as he left the kitchen.

***

Father Bunt stood at the back door of the chapel greeting parishioners, most of whom were in a hurry to get to breakfast. His own stomach rumbled as he contemplated a plate of fried eggs accompanied by a cluster of succulent sausages. His doctor was always droning on and on about cholesterol and the like, but the doctor wasn't living a celibate life. Father Bunt figured a man who lived without the comforts of family life deserved the occasional high-fat meal. And that also applied, in his estimation, to the occasional glass of beer at the local pub.

As Father Bunt was heading back to the rectory, his cell phone rang. He dug it out of his pocket, noting that the call was from the archbishop. He crossed himself quickly before answering. "Yes, sir, how are you this morning?"

There were, however, none of the usual pleasantries, which didn't bode well. "Brent, have you seen the morning papers?"

"Yes, I...I...certainly have, sir, but I assure you that the...uh...altercation at the...uh...event last night was handled quickly and appropriately by the authorities who..." Here his voice trailed off, as he realized exactly how feeble his words sounded.

"I know the police took care of things, Brent," the archbishop said quietly. "That's not why I'm calling. We're being swamped by calls at the chancery, calls from all over the metro-Atlanta area, people wanting to know what in the...blazes...is going on at your church."

Father Bunt clutched the cell phone miserably. What could he say, really? This was certainly not the first time St. Rita's had received thoroughly negative publicity in the local media. First there had been that bad business in the choir, followed shortly by the liturgist's death.

"Sir, I..." he began, but his boss cut to the chase: "Brent, I want you to write a letter to the editor explaining what happened last night. There's no guarantee it'll get published, but if it does, it might do some damage control."

"Yes, sir, I'll get right on it." Even as he uttered the words, dread settled upon him like a heavy fog in a South Georgia swamp. He suspected it would not be easy to get a letter published in the local press.

"And, listen, next time you have a big event, Brent, it might be better to announce it just in the church bulletin rather than the newspaper. This way, there's less chance of this kind of thing happening."

"Yes, of course, I completely agree." Father Bunt bobbed his head up and down as if his caller could see him. He didn't dare mention that the archbishop himself had praised him for opening the event to the outside community. Now wasn't the time to point out any inconsistencies in his superior's behavior.

"Oh, one more thing," MacPherson said, "how's that seminarian doing?"

"Just fine, sir. He's a...uh...a really fine young man." Best not to tell the archbishop about the empty room he'd discovered earlier that morning, he assured himself. No reason to raise any red flags until I've done more investigating.

After the telephone call, Father Bunt headed to breakfast, already drafting a letter to the editor in his mind. He took his place at the table and greeted Father William, whose hair looked damp from the shower, and a sleepy-looking Augustine. Mrs. Greenstone carried in a platter of fried eggs and another of crispy sausage and bacon.

"I think I'll pass," Father William said, when the meat was offered to him.

"You're not turning into a vegetarian, are you?" Father Bunt joked.

Mrs. Greenstone shot him an odd look that he couldn't quite interpret.

"I'm just not that hungry this morning," Father William shrugged.

"Well, suit yourself. As for me, I enjoy fried animal products," Father Bunt enthused, noticing that Mrs. Greenstone didn't crack a smile. *Poor woman, maybe her arthritis is kicking in,* he thought.

He tucked eagerly into the sunny-side up eggs and the tender, greasy slivers of bacon, noting they were cooked just right. The bread was homemade, and the figs in the preserves, Mrs. Greenstone announced, had come from a tree that Bertram had grown.

"Delicious breakfast," Father Bunt remarked. "It's even better than usual!"

"Thank you," the cook replied with the faintest ghost of a smile. "My Bertram, God rest his soul, always said no one made better breakfasts than me."

Father Bunt noticed Augustine smiling to himself. *He's probably planning what he's going to add to that diary thing he's writing,* Father Bunt thought.

"I have to agree with Bertram," Augustine stabbed a sausage patty with his fork. "I've always liked these big Southern-style breakfasts—you know, plenty of pork products, nothing too healthy!"

The cook managed another little smile. "Well, I'm glad you're enjoying it."

The dining-room door swung open then and in came Beatrice, once again dressed in all black. Everything she was wearing looked as if it was two sizes too small. For the love of everything that's holy, Father Bunt reflected grimly, can't the people who work in a rectory realize that celibacy demands discipline and self-sacrifice? She reminded him of a slice of double-Dutch chocolate cake waved in front of some starving soul on a Weight Watchers' diet.

"I see you don't have your horns on this morning," she said, smiling at Augustine.

He said nothing, just stared at his plate.

Father Bunt drained his coffee cup and stood up, hoping to derail any further remarks.

"Augustine, once you're done with breakfast, why don't you accompany Father William to the...uh...senior citizens' home?"

"Sure, Father," Augustine said. "Which one are we going to?"

"We'll start with Eternal Sunrise," Father William replied, "over on Scott Boulevard."

"Eternal Sunrise—that's a good one," Augustine chuckled. "Why don't they tell it like it is? I mean, why not call it 'Banana Peel Manor'?"

Father William gave him a questioning look.

"You know, one foot on a banana peel, the other on the grave." Augustine paused and then added: "Or Prune Parlor."

The young man managed to keep a straight face while delivering the punch line, Father Bunt noted, but not Beatrice.

She covered her mouth as she began snorting with glee. It looked like the seminarian had found an appreciative audience.

***

Father Bunt went up to his office after breakfast, hoping to jot down some thoughts for the letter to the editor before they flew out of his mind. But just as he logged on to his computer, he heard a tentative knock at the door and looked up to see Eloise standing in the doorway. She didn't seem her usual upbeat self.

"Anything the matter?" It was a question he always dreaded asking.

She sat down in the chair opposite his desk with a dramatic sigh.

"It's about the money from the dance," she said weakly.

His stomach fell. "What's the problem?"

"Well, Father, when I went back to the kitchen at the end of the evening, we only had checks. All the cash was missing!" Her lips trembled ominously as if she might burst into tears.

"But...but how is that possible?" He braced himself for the answer.

"We think someone stole the cash, Father." She looked down at her hands. "I had counted it earlier, and at that point, it came to about three thousand dollars. "

He heard the train horn hooting on Coventry Road, and then Dopey chiming in with a lonely baying from somewhere downstairs. He walked over to the window and glanced outside to collect his thoughts. He saw Augustine and Beatrice standing by Augustine's car, talking, and then he saw the young man hand her a large brown envelope. I wonder what's up with that, he thought.

Father Bunt turned around to face Eloise and ask the obvious question: "Did you call the police?"

"Yes, Father, we did, as soon as we realized it was missing, but there were so many people in and out of the kitchen where we had stored the money that the detective said right now there's very little to go on." Her voice was weak and whispery. "Cash is very hard to trace, of course."

"Didn't anyone see someone suspicious near the cash box?" His own voice sounded tinny in his ears.

"Well, there were volunteers in charge of taking the money, of course. But no one saw anything out of the ordinary. I mean, whoever did this must have been very quick."

She looked up at him now. "And the police don't think it was a professional thief, Father, because they would have taken the checks as well."

"So this means it's who—one of the volunteers?" Even as he spoke the words, he could imagine what the headlines might read, something along the lines of "local church robbed by parishioners" or something like that.

"The detective said it *could* be a volunteer, Father—or any of the people attending the event."

Father Bunt looked out the window again. This time, he saw Mrs. Greenstone trying to take Dopey on a walk. She was at least making an effort, he thought. The dog, however, was struggling to resist the leash. When she gave up and released him, he sat there with tongue drooping out, his left back paw industriously probing his ear for a flea. Dopey, Father Bunt reflected drily, was the only dog he'd ever encountered that thought a leash was some kind of deadly predator.

His thoughts ricocheted bleakly back to the present moment. He hated to suspect the cook or her granddaughter, but weren't they the ones who'd spent the most time in the kitchen? But to even bring it up with either of them could cause a major explosion of hurt feelings. Besides, as Eloise had just pointed out, in truth there were hundreds of suspects.

"Well, look, Eloise, don't take it too hard," he reassured her. "I'm sure the police will find this person. And…well, you did a really good job with the whole event." He could tell it was the right thing to say because the worry lines on her face softened.

"Thank you, Father. I have to say that…well…I'm really troubled about this."

"It will all be sorted out, I'm sure." He hoped he sounded more confident than he actually felt.

CHAPTER 4

Father William held his breath as he and Augustine walked into the Eternal Sunrise nursing home. On the drive over, Augustine had regaled him with an assortment of jokes related to the elderly, and when he'd run out of those, he'd turned to hamster jokes, since Ignatius was, as usual, accompanying them. Father William had to admit the guy was funny, but he didn't want the young man doing anything that might offend the old people who always looked forward to visitors.

The first place they stopped was at the receptionist's desk, where Clarissa was holding court. Father William noticed miserably that today she was wearing a ruby-red tank top embellished with large rhinestone letters proclaiming "Jesus Loves Me." A hefty gold cross studded with red stones was prominent against the glittering backdrop. She was on the phone when they arrived, but quickly cut the call short.

"Well, do tell! We have *two* preachers visitin' today, plus that little hamster. Aren't we blessed?" She gave them a big, generous smile.

Father William put Ignatius' carrier down on the floor and then made the introductions. "Augustine is actually a seminarian," he explained.

Clarissa smiled again broadly. "Well, his religion don't matter none to me."

"You see, it's just that I'm studying to become a diocesan—or parish—priest," Augustine said. "I haven't taken my final vows yet." He paused. "In fact, for parish priests, they're not really vows. They're *promises* made to the bishop. The other kind of priest—the Jesuits, Franciscans and such—actually take vows, like poverty…"

But she cut him off with a wave of her hand. "I know all about poverty, honey. My first husband, Ronnie, he practically put us in the poor house with his gamblin'!"

"Parish priests don't make any promises about poverty," he said with a smile, "although I'll be expected to live frugally."

Now she handed him the visitors' book to sign. "So what promises will you make?"

"Well, there's praying the Liturgy of the Hours, obedience to the bishop and"—he cleared his throat discreetly—"there's also celibacy."

"Do Jesus! That sound just like Ronnie too," she said, vigorously shaking her head. "All that man did was bet on football and watch TV. He didn't have no time for romance at all."

***

A few moments later, Father William rapped on Mrs. Hartwell's door, and when he heard her soft reply—"Come in!"—pushed it open. Her face brightened when they walked in, and she greeted the seminarian warmly.

"It's such a comfort to know that young men today are still choosing a life with the Lord," she remarked. Augustine seemed to take this as his cue to sit beside her and take her hand.

"You have a lovely Southern accent, Mrs. Hartwell," he said gently. "Do you mind my asking where you grew up?"

"Oh, please, call me Anastasia." She then cheerfully launched into a description of her childhood days in Unadilla, Georgia, while Augustine seemed to hang on to her every word. Father William sat quietly, waiting for a break in the conversation so he could give her Holy Communion.

"Would you like to see the pictures of my family?" Her eyes gleamed with anticipation.

"I'd love to," Augustine replied. "Do we have time, Father?"

"Oh, certainly, plenty of time." Father William had seen the photos at least five times in the past few years, but he didn't want to dilute the old lady's pleasure at having a new audience.

She indicated a nearby bookshelf where the album was stored, and Augustine retrieved it for her. For the next 20 minutes, she showed them the black-and-white photos and identified various relatives. Her eyes filled with tears as she closed the book. "They're mostly all gone now. I sure miss them."

Augustine squeezed her hand. "I know you do."

***

Father Bunt stared at the phone on his desk with an icy feeling of trepidation. He had to tell the archbishop about the theft, before word got out into the newspaper. Plus, he had to tell him the letter to the editor seemed to be on permanent stall mode. Every time he sat down to craft the opening line, he found himself composing, editing, deleting, tweaking, and then, finally, throwing the whole thing out. Now he said a silent prayer and dialed the number, then waited while the secretary put the call through.

"Yes, what is it, Brent?" The archbishop sounded curt and busy, never a good sign.

Father Bunt decided to cut to the chase, telling his boss quickly about the missing money and then assuring him the detectives were investigating. There was a sharp cough on the other end of the line and then:

"Well, you know the media will have a field day with this, Brent. They already think your parish is some sort of...well, what's the word...hot bed of crime."

"I know it doesn't look good," he admitted, flinching at the description, "but maybe it won't hit the papers."

"Well, at least you have that letter to the editor going, Brent. Here's what I would do—come right out and talk about the theft. This way, the public will know you're an up-front, take-charge kind of guy. Better to come clean now than try to do damage control later."

"Yes, sir, I agree," Father Bunt said miserably. How in the world could he ever write a letter defending himself on two fronts—the mix-up with the motorcycle gang as well as the theft? He had this image of himself with a shovel digging a really deep hole.

"Good! Well, I'll be looking forward to your letter," the archbishop concluded. "Why don't you fax it to me first and I'll take a look at it."

After the call, Father Bunt headed to the little day chapel, knelt down, and put his head in his hands. He needed some quiet time with the Lord, a few moments away from his overcrowded in-box and the phone that seemed to constantly interrupt his scattered thoughts before he could string them together into a coherent chain. Lord, help me with that letter, he prayed. I'm running on empty here.

He prayed that the police would find the thief and return the money, although he didn't have much hope of that really happening. Anyone could have walked into the kitchen and dipped their hand into the cash box. There were just too many people in the hall that night, and most were in costume. Still, he knew it could have been even worse. Someone could have taken the checks as well as the cash. I guess I should be grateful for small mercies, he thought.

He also prayed for Augustine. On the plus side, he had heard glowing remarks from Father William about the young man's apparent ability to minister to the elderly. The visit the previous day had gone very well. Obviously if Augustine did indeed go on to become a priest, his compassion with shut-ins would be a huge factor in his favor.

But Father Bunt still had niggling doubts about Augustine. He sometimes could hear the young man talking on his cell phone very late at night. Although Augustine managed to keep his voice muffled, bits of the conversation still drifted down the hall. Sometimes Father Bunt thought he might be overhearing little lovers' spats, but he could never be entirely sure. He wanted to give the young man the benefit of the doubt as much as possible.

He thought back to his own days as a seminarian. There had been, after all, no hard-and-fast rule that prohibited seminarians from dating. A seminarian was a free agent. But dating had been seen as a red flag indicating a lack of readiness to take on the seriousness of the next step. At summer's end, it would be up to Father Bunt to write a report about the young man's stay at St. Rita's before he returned to seminary. That's assuming he returns, he thought. With seminarians one never knows.

***

Francesca settled in at her desk in the rectory. She was carrying a crumpled, grease-stained paper bag containing a cheese-and-egg biscuit she had just bought at a nearby fast-food restaurant. There had been no time for a healthier breakfast at home, since she hadn't slept well during the night and had evidently turned off the alarm clock in her sleep. She hadn't heard from Tony in a week and was beginning to fret. He was usually good about calling her a few times a week and emailing daily, but lately he'd been slacking off. She was starting to wonder what was going on down there in Miami.

As she was taking her first bite of the biscuit, she heard the front door of the rectory opening. She looked up just in time to see Frank standing in front of her desk. He was wearing old jeans and a faded work shirt, and his face was reddened from the sun. It had been over a week since the masquerade ball and there had been no word from him.

"Look, I gotta apologize for running out on you," he said. "See, I had this emergency and I didn't have time to explain." He ran his fingers through his close-cropped hair.

"Oh?" She put the biscuit down. This should be interesting, she thought.

"See, my mother called—she lives over in Snellville. And she had a flat tire on Lawrenceville Highway. She always calls me when something like that goes wrong. And I couldn't just leave her there on the road all alone. You know how it is, right?" He shifted nervously from foot to foot.

She could feel her temper rising. "I understand emergencies. But what I *don't* understand is why you pretended to be Tony's cousin."

He shrugged. "OK, guilty as charged. But how else is a guy like me going to get a date with someone like you? I admit it was wrong. But I saw you one day when I was working a construction job here at the church. I asked around and found out you were single." Now he sat down on a nearby chair.

"Come on, can you blame me? I mean, let's face it: would a high-class lady, all college-educated and everything, go out with a construction worker?" He looked at her with a pleading expression as if he were a trial lawyer delivering instructions to the jury. Still, there was something in his eyes that put her on high alert, although she wasn't sure exactly what the danger was.

"You bet I blame you! You lied to me! You said you were in computers, for one thing, and you..." Then she stopped herself and took a deep breath, willing herself to calm down. "How did you get that photo of you and Tony anyway?"

He looked almost proud. "I got a buddy who's good at Photoshop."

"But for heaven's sake, didn't you know how easily I could find out you weren't really his cousin?"

"Look, I'm sorry. It was just a little joke, that's all." He didn't look contrite though. "And I was gonna come clean with you that night, but I had to leave."

He pulled out a handkerchief and wiped his brow. "I'm working today—doing some painting upstairs for the priests. How about I take you out for a drink later and make it up to you?"

She was trying to frame an excuse when Augustine showed up right behind Frank. He was carrying a paper bag and dragging a very reluctant Dopey on a leash.

"I'm trying to teach old Dopey here how to follow along, but it sure is slow going," Augustine announced, smiling. Then he turned to Frank: "Hey, aren't you Brother Frank?"

Frank didn't look happy to see him. "Yeah, that's me."

Evidently drawn by the scent of the biscuit, Dopey suddenly lunged for the desk, and chaos broke out. Augustine dropped the leash, the bag fell from his arms, and a cardboard container toppled out of the bag onto the floor.

"Hey, Dopey, drop that," Augustine shouted, but it was too late. Dopey had managed to scoop the biscuit off the desk and downed it in one bite.

"Sorry about that," Augustine said to Francesca. Then he reached down to retrieve what had fallen from the bag, and as he did, Francesca recognized the box as containing Frangelico, an Italian liqueur.

"Pretty fancy booze," Frank remarked. "I'm a beer man myself."

"Beer's fine," Augustine said evenly, "but this stuff's a great after-dinner drink." He put the package back into the bag. "Besides, the recipe was invented by the monks, so you'd probably like it."

***

Father Bunt didn't know what to make of Augustine's antics. He was always making jokes and doing impersonations of various visitors to the rectory. The problem was, the man was definitely funny, and certainly a keen sense of humor should serve him well in the priesthood.

But was he too far over the top? This was one of the questions that kept niggling at Father Bunt. It also made him a bit apprehensive seeing the way Beatrice looked at Augustine. She had been following him around quite openly at the masquerade ball, and he knew how easily rumors could spread. They're probably just friends, he thought, but appearances do matter.

He decided to go downstairs to get a glass of iced tea. On his way, he noticed Augustine's door was open. He peered inside. The bed was made, all the clothing was hanging neatly in the closet, and his shoes were lined up precisely on the floor. Some impulse led him to walk into the room and look around. He noticed the young man had gone out without his watch, which was lying on the bedside table. He recognized the brand as expensive and didn't recall seeing the young man wearing the watch before. A little flash of alarm went off in Father Bunt's brain—the stolen money. No, he refused to think that of the seminarian. This could be a recent gift from the family. They were known to be well-off.

Father Bunt was just about to leave when he saw the gleam of a computer screen on the young man's desk. He had left his laptop on. Now Father felt a quick stab of curiosity. What was Augustine writing about? What was he putting in the diary? Would it be wrong to take a peek? As the pastor, didn't he have a right to know what the seminarian was up to? He was, after all, supposed to keep the young man on the right track. Before he could decide on the morality of his actions, Father Bunt moved quickly across the room and peered at the screen. He recoiled in horror at what he saw there.

***

Francesca ran from her car into the house, trying to avoid the downpour. She was hosting a Choir Chicks' meeting that evening and as usual she was running behind. She looked with dismay around the living room. It seemed her house sank into utter disorder every few days. Wasn't there some biological principle along those lines, something about chaos theory or something? She lit some lemon-scented incense in the living room because she'd read somewhere that the aroma of citrus supposedly made people think a place had just been cleaned. She threw the dishes into the dishwasher and then whipped up a quick batch of brownies. She was just about to head to the shower when the phone rang. She had to pick up when she realized it was Tony.

"Tony! Where are you?"

"Just got back in town, uh, a few hours ago," he said. "My sister's doing a lot better."

"That's wonderful! When can we get together?" She was already trying to decide what to wear.

"Well, I have about fifty fires at work to put out, so it'll be a while," he said, "but there's something important I have to tell you."

"Yes?" She hoped her disappointment didn't show in her voice. Here he was, back in town, and still inaccessible.

"I did some checking up on that Freeman guy. You need to be real careful about him, Francesca."

"What do you mean? He told me he saw me at church and just pretended to be your cousin so I'd go out with him."

"Yeah, well it's not that simple. Turns out he's a guy I arrested three years ago on a drug charge. He served some time—and he's out on parole now. I think he could be holding a grudge, if you get my drift, and possibly planning to take it out on you."

"Oh, dear." She inwardly chastised herself for ever opening the door to Frank. Then she told him about Frank leaving the dance because of an emergency with his mother.

"Yeah, right, his mother." Tony chuckled. "I'm betting someone called him about a drug deal."

"So you think he's still using drugs?" She was hitting the replay button in her mind on the masquerade ball, but Frank hadn't acted strange—or had he?

"According to my sources, he's definitely under suspicion, not just for using but selling too."

She then filled Tony in about the missing money from the church coffers, which Father Bunt had told her about, and he whistled under his breath.

"Yeah, I heard something about it," Tony said. "That could have been Freeman, although I don't know why he'd leave the checks. Maybe he didn't want to run the risk of trying to cash them and getting caught."

"But we don't know for *sure* he took the money, Tony. Anyone could have done it." For some reason, she felt compelled to defend Frank—or was she really trying to make up for the fact that she'd been dumb enough to go out with him?

"Yeah, but my money's on Freeman. He's got a track record." There was the sound of someone talking to Tony, probably another officer. "Look, I gotta run," he said. "I'll talk to you soon."

Francesca hung up the phone with a feeling of uneasiness about Tony, who was being unusually standoffish, and a sense of foreboding about Frank.

***

Father Bunt scanned the screen with a sinking sensation. In chapter one there was a character called Father Dunce, plus another named Father Bill Porkland. Father Dunce was described as a bumbling fellow who had a tendency to make a muddle of things at St. Leila's parish. He was being hoodwinked by the cook, who was—Father Bunt groaned inwardly—feeding him meatless dishes disguised to look like the real thing. Is this fact or fiction? Father Bunt wondered anxiously, thinking back on how evasive Mrs. Greenstone was when questioned about ingredients.

He scrolled quickly down the screen. It seemed Father Dunce also occasionally pilfered change from the collection basket, and was also constantly trying, without much success, to impress the archbishop. The writing was good. It wasn't amateurish at all. And even though he had only read a few pages, Father Bunt could imagine the blasted thing finding a publisher. Just my luck, he thought.

"Ah, hem."

Father Bunt wheeled around and saw Augustine standing there with a little smile playing on his lips. Father Bunt was sure his cheeks were scarlet.

"Oh, Augustine, I didn't hear you come in. I noticed you'd left your computer on and with the storm coming, well, I thought I'd switch it off for you..."

Augustine looked at him as if he were a little boy with a hand deeply immersed in a cookie jar. "Thanks, Father, but I had it on battery, so no worries about the weather."

"Oh, yes, of course, well, I didn't think of that." Father Bunt felt like the proverbial cat discovered in the act of devouring the canary.

He hoped the young man wouldn't ask if he'd read any pages from the diary. He had lied more than enough for one day. But all Augustine said was, "Well, Father, thanks for looking out for me."

The words didn't seem to have even the slightest touch of sarcasm to them.

***

Mauve Bundle knocked over her wine glass, and there was a flurry of activity as the other Choir Chicks grabbed paper napkins to help her mop up the spill. The coffee table was laden with their offerings for the evening—a dessert tray, a cheese platter, miniature puff pastries—and, much to Francesca's chagrin, one of Rebecca's infamous nonfat quiches, which no one had the heart to tell her tasted like cardboard.

"I...I...I'm so sorry." Mauve looked as if she might burst into tears.

"Look, no worries. It's just wine. It cleans up easily," Francesca assured her, as she grabbed a nearby dish towel.

"Well, I wish everything else did," Mauve said mysteriously.

"What's wrong?" Rebecca asked.

"It's that seminarian, Augustine. He stopped me after Mass one day and said he'd be coming over about a donation for the church." Mauve paused now to take a bite of brownie.

"That struck me as a little odd, because I didn't know the parish was having any kind of special...what do you call it...fund-raising drive, but I didn't think much more about it."

All eyes were on Mauve as she continued: "He showed up at my house, really late one night. Brad, my son, was downstairs watching TV, and I was alone. I offered Augustine a drink, and he saw a bottle of Frangelico in the liquor cabinet, and said it was his favorite. But he's kinda funny"—she giggled—"he made a point of saying he never has more than one glass, as a kind of an after-dinner drink, you know." She accepted a fresh glass of wine from Francesca and took a long swig.

"Then we sat and talked a while, about nothing really, just small talk. But when he found out my husband and I separated a few years ago, he was really sympathetic. He seemed to really understand how hard it is to raise a boy alone."

"But that's not all." She picked up a cookie and chewed it daintily while the other women sat transfixed, waiting for the punch line.

Finally Molly spoke: "What do you mean, not all?"

"Well, he got kind of friendly before he left." Mauve coyly dabbed at her heavily painted lips with a paper napkin. Her expression seemed, at least to Francesca, slightly triumphant, as if she was announcing some sort of victory.

"Uh, can you define friendly?" Francesca asked.

"I sure can," Mauve giggled. "He put his arms around me and hugged me real tight. And then he….he…kissed me—right on the lips!" She looked at the other women now, as if expecting a round of applause.

But Molly seemed agitated. "Can't he get in trouble for this? I mean, couldn't you tell Father Bunt? After all, the guy said he was coming over looking for a donation, and…"

Mauve cut her off with a frosty look. "I'm not going to snitch on him, for heaven's sake. I'm a big girl. He didn't force himself on me." Now she speared a cheese cube with a toothpick.

"But this is all in confidence," she went on. "See, I don't want Andy, my husband, finding out. I mean, we're separated, you know, but he still keeps tabs on me and Brad. And, well, I don't want to ruin my chances of getting back together with him."

There was a long stretch of silence, as if the other women were mulling over her words, and then Rebecca said, "Well, well, still waters do run deep, don't they? Here I thought seminarians were all holy and stuff, you know, getting ready to be priests."

"Well, maybe he's having second thoughts," Mauve smiled mysteriously.

"Did he say that?" Molly asked.

"No, but, well, it's just a feeling I have, you know."

Francesca noticed that Mauve looked rather pleased with herself. For just a second, Francesca wondered if Mauve had embellished the story. But that's ridiculous, she concluded. Why would she do that?

***

Augustine was at his desk, tapping away on his keyboard as he worked on his book. He smiled to himself as he described the scene: The rectory's resident dog, Mopey, showed up at Mass unannounced and went loping into the choir section. There, he surprised one of the sopranos who was launching into a solo. Instead of the Ave Maria, the congregation heard a loud scream, and... But just then, there came a knock on Augustine's door. He quickly hit the "save" key. It was nearly 2 a.m. and he'd heard the priests getting ready for bed about midnight. Who in the world can it be? he wondered.

He wasn't aware that anyone else was even in the rectory. He'd heard joking rumors when he first arrived about the ghost of a former pastor who roamed the halls. As Father Bunt had put it, "The guy probably came back to get more paperwork done, since it's never ending." Now Augustine opened the door slowly, and then took a step back. Instead of a ghost there was a very real and quite lively looking Beatrice. Her eye make-up looked a little smudged and she was weaving slightly. He could detect the scent of beer combined with her usual flowery cologne.

"Hush!" She whispered, putting a finger over her plump lips. "No one knows I'm here. I got the key from grandma and snuck in."

Now she giggled as she brandished a brown paper bag. "And I got a party with me!"

***

Father Bunt awoke with a start. He thought he'd heard a woman's voice in the hall. Although he had never been a party animal in his younger years, he certainly had done his share of dating before entering the seminary. And he knew that his past sometimes helped him understand people who came to him in Confession. Many were under the impression they had committed truly original sins, especially when it came to sex, but in all his years as a confessor, he'd discovered there was nothing new under the sun. And romantic trysts in the middle of the night definitely fell into that category.

He put on his robe and fished around for his slippers, one of which he noticed Dopey had recently gnawed on. He dreaded confronting whatever was going on down the hall, but what else could he do? He couldn't risk having a woman seen slipping out of the rectory in the early morning hours. He also knew he needed to exert some kind of moral control over the situation. He said a few prayers for courage and then, as he started down the hall, he heard a door slam, and he thought it was downstairs. By the time he got to Augustine's door, he was starting to wonder if he had really heard a voice at all. Was I dreaming? But he decided to knock, nonetheless.

"It's Father Bunt. Is everything alright?" He stood nervously in front of the door, praying there was no funny business going on. Maybe it was just a TV show, he thought.

There was the sound of shuffling, and then Augustine opened the door halfway and peered out. He was wearing his bathrobe and his hair was mussed up.

"Oh, sure, Father, everything's fine."

"Well, I hope I didn't awaken you," Father Bunt said. "I thought I heard something."

"Oh, sorry—I sometimes play music while I'm working on my book. I'll turn down the volume."

Father Bunt said goodnight and returned to his room. He wondered if he was being bamboozled, but what could he do? Barge into the room and look under the bed? This was a grown man, not a teenager. He had to take him at his word. He also had to get a new pair of slippers or somehow teach Dopey to leave them alone.

***

An owl hooted somewhere down the street, awakening Francesca. There was something about the sound that always brought Dean to mind. He had been the first to tell her that the distinctive call of the barred owl sounded like someone asking, "Who cooks for you?" She sat up in bed and looked at the clock. It was 3 a.m. At her side Tubs was snoring lightly, with his fuzzy head resting on the pillow as if he were a human being. Now he opened one eye and gazed at her with interest.

"Who cooks for you?" the owl repeated, and she switched on the bedside lamp. Then there was another sound—was it a car door slamming? She felt her heart rate accelerating as she got quickly out of bed and put on her robe. She went into the dining room and glanced outside. Oh, Lord, she thought, when she saw Frank's car parked behind hers in the driveway.

She moved away from the window so he wouldn't see her. Then she grabbed her purse from the couch and dug out her cell phone. If he tried anything, she would dial 911. She heard footsteps and then the doorbell rang. She wrapped her robe more tightly around her. When she didn't answer, he began knocking on the door.

"Hey, I know you're in there, so answer the door! I just want to talk!" he yelled.

Her heart was pounding and her hands trembling. She knew she should dial the police, but something—a deep curiosity— prevented her. If she called the police and they showed up and started questioning him, she'd never know why he was there in the first place. Besides, what could she tell the 911 operator? That some guy she'd dated wanted to talk with her?

She shouted through the door: "You'd better get away from my house or I'm calling the police." Please, dear Lord, keep me safe, she prayed.

"Fine, call the police," he replied, "but first there's something you need to know. I'll bet Tony has filled your head with all kinds of stuff about me, but it isn't true. OK, yeah, I got in trouble with the law, but I'm different now. All that drug stuff is in the past."

He must have been drinking, she thought, or doing drugs. Why else would he show up at this hour? She stood there silently, clutching the phone as if it were a weapon. In a few moments, she heard the sound of his footsteps as he left the porch, and then his car door slamming. The owl hooted for a third time, and she shivered.

CHAPTER 5

Mrs. Greenstone rummaged around in the refrigerator. She had a strong suspicion that someone was substituting meat for the vegetarian products she always served, but she didn't know who it was. She winced as she recalled the other day when she had been frying breakfast patties, and she'd noticed an unusual and thoroughly disgusting aroma emanating from the frying pan. But she had served breakfast anyway, because it had been too late to throw out the contents of the pan and start over.

Bertram had kicked up quite a fuss when she'd started serving meatless products, she recalled, but he had finally given in. The fact that he'd died of a heart attack anyway still rankled her. But she also suspected that Bertram had a habit of sneaking out for fried chicken now and again.

She pulled out a package of what should have been a meat substitute, sniffed the links, and shuddered. She'd know that smell anywhere—it was definitely pork. She grimaced as she threw the entire package into the trash. Then she lovingly opened a fresh package of 100% vegetarian "soysage," placed the links in the frying pan, and turned the heat on low.

Then she sat down and drummed her fingers on the table. Who was the culprit? Had one of the priests figured out she was serving vegetarian meals and decided to sabotage her? Her thoughts were interrupted by the sound of a squawk from the living room. She wiped her hands on a dish towel and hastened

91

toward Little Leonora's cage. When she removed the cover, the bird sidled up to her on its perch, muttering under its breath. Mrs. Greenstone filled the dish with seeds and then went into the kitchen to get fresh water for the parrot.

As she put in the fresh water, she scratched Little Leonora's head gently and crooned, "How's my sweet girl?"

"Just fine, granny, how are you?"

Mrs. Greenstone wheeled around and gasped. "Beatrice! What are you doing here so early?" And then, taking a look at the girl's smeared make-up and rumpled clothing, she changed her tack.

"Where were you last night, young lady?" Mrs. Greenstone asked darkly. The girl had moved into a room in her house after Bertram had died. "I heard you come home in the wee hours of the morning."

"Don't worry, granny, just partying with friends. I didn't do nothing wrong." Beatrice yawned widely. "But I sure could use some orange juice. I got a hangover."

"Well, if you didn't go out carousing and drinking until all hours of the night, you wouldn't wake up feeling like..." Mrs. Greenstone tried to stem the angry tide.

"Like what?" The girl yawned again.

"Like hell warmed over, that's what!" Mrs. Greenstone said, and there was an enthusiastic squawk from Little Leonora, who had evidently recognized one of her vocabulary words.

"Oh, you're too old-fashioned," Beatrice said, adjusting a bracelet.

"Where'd you get that fancy thing?" Mrs. Greenstone knew she'd never seen it before.

"I saved up some of the money you give me for helping in the kitchen," Beatrice said defensively.

Father Bunt entered the room. "Good morning!" he called out cheerily. "Is breakfast ready?"

"Hell, yes!" the parrot screeched.

"I thought you were going to move the, uh, bird..." Father Bunt said.

"Well, yes, of course I will, Father, but I've just been so busy, you know." Mrs. Greenstone hesitated and then brought up what was really on her mind: "Father, there's something I need to discuss with you about the groceries."

"Is the cupboard bare or something?" he smiled.

"No, but someone's been going through the refrigerator and—and—switching things around."

Beatrice giggled again, and the old woman snapped at her: "You go in the kitchen and check on the soy...the sausage. This is between me and Father Bunt."

As soon as the girl was gone, Father Bunt asked, "So what's wrong exactly?"

Mrs. Greenstone was starting to wonder if she'd backed herself into a corner. After all, if she admitted she'd been secretly serving soy products instead of meat, she might lose her job.

Just then, Augustine walked into the room. "Why, Mrs. Greenstone, what a pleasure to see you! And you too, Father!"

Father Bunt nodded in Augustine's direction, but then turned back to Mrs. Greenstone. "Now, what's this about the food being...did you say switched around?"

Mrs. Greenstone bestowed a withering look on Augustine, who had a little grin on his face.

"On second thought, Father, I'm sure it's just a misunderstanding," she said. "I'll take care of it."

"Hell, yes!" the parrot added.

***

After breakfast, Father Bunt began searching in the sitting room for the newspaper. Mrs. Greenstone had gone out grocery shopping, Father William was visiting one of the nursing homes, and Augustine had announced that he was going for a short walk.

"Where in blazes is that newspaper?" Father Bunt muttered under his breath. "I wonder if someone took it upstairs."

He went upstairs and stopped in front of Augustine's room. He gently tried the doorknob and discovered the door was unlocked. I'll just look inside quickly, he thought. He was relieved to see the computer was not on. I don't need any more temptation. He looked around quickly and didn't spot the newspaper, but noticed the parish directory was lying on the bed, and it was open.

He picked it up and glanced at it. From the looks of it, Augustine was keeping track of his visits to parishioners and had penciled in dates by the photographs. Well, that's good, Father

Bunt thought. He's taking his time here seriously, really getting to know people. But then he rifled through the pages a bit and let out an exasperated sigh. It looked like the only parishioners with dates by their names were, without an exception, females.

He returned the directory to the exact spot where he'd found it, left the room, and closed the door quietly behind him. A few minutes later, he heard the front door opening and saw Augustine climbing the stairs. He figured this was as good an opportunity as any to finally have a word with the fellow.

"Augustine, you got a moment? We need to talk."

"Sure, Father, I need to drop off some stuff in my room, and then I'll join you in your office." The young man was carrying a grocery bag, plus a few books.

Moments later, the seminarian took the seat in front of Father Bunt's desk. "Oh, before I forget, this is for you." He pulled something out of his pocket. "It's from Mrs.—I mean Anastasia—over at the old folks' home."

Father Bunt glanced quickly at the crumpled envelope and put it in his desk drawer for later. Lord, help me say the right thing, he prayed.

"Augustine, it's been a long time since I was in seminary— the Stone Ages to you, I'm sure. But I can remember there were some, uh, tough issues I had to confront." He coughed discreetly and tugged at his collar, which seemed particularly scratchy today.

Augustine raised an eyebrow, and Father Bunt took it as his cue to continue. "Look, we're both grown-ups, so I'll get right to the point." Father Bunt picked up a paper clip from his desk and started bending it. This was going to be more difficult than he'd first envisioned.

"I'm talking about the whole celibacy thing. It sounded straightforward when I was in high school, but became more— what can I say—problematic the older I got. I had this vision of myself as a priest when I was in high school, and it never, uh, dimmed. But when I got to college, it was another whole challenge, you know, what with the, er, the co-eds and all."

"I don't really understand what you're getting at, sir," Augustine said quietly.

"It's just a general sense I have that you're having some trouble—well, how shall I put it—putting the brakes on, you know, when it comes to women." Father Bunt stood up now and began pacing, as he always did when nervous. This was tougher than he had anticipated. He walked over to the window and looked outside, where a squirrel was perched on a limb staring back at him with its paws clasped together as if in prayer.

"Look, I've heard certain rumors…" Father Bunt returned to his desk, noting that the young man was looking very uncomfortable.

But he didn't get to finish the sentence because Augustine interrupted with a great deal of emotion: "Father, I hope you aren't going to believe rumors about me!"

Was it Father Bunt's imagination or were the young man's eyes suddenly beginning to tear up? Dear God, I hope he's not going to break down, he thought.

"Of course not, but there's usually a grain of truth." Father Bunt tossed the broken paper clip into the trash. "And with all the clergy scandals the Church is dealing with today, you have to be absolutely sure that..." Father Bunt stifled a belch.

That was another thing for his to-do list: Have a talk with Mrs. Greenstone. Some of her recipes obviously weren't agreeing with him. And he especially dreaded gastrointestinal disturbances when he was delivering sermons.

"Absolutely sure?" The young man's question broke the thread of Father Bunt's thoughts.

"You have to be *absolutely sure* before you make your final promises that you can *keep* them."

"You're right, Father, of course." Augustine rubbed his eyes. "But I'm not really having any problems." He adjusted the gold watch on his wrist. "Sometimes things aren't what they seem, Father." He picked up a pencil that had fallen to the floor and a little smile played on his lips.

"Father, have you ever been to the Pin-ups Striptease Club on Ponce de Leon?"

"Of course not!" Father Bunt grabbed the pencil and threw it into the trash. "Someone must be playing a practical joke on me." He looked suspiciously at Augustine now, because he knew the seminarian had a penchant for such things.

"We're getting off track here," Father Bunt said, "so I'll come right to the point. I know you're not a priest yet, but a seminarian isn't supposed to be dating. "

"Dating?" Augustine repeated the word as if he'd never heard it before.

"I don't care what you call it, Augustine: dating, visiting women, inviting them to your room at night!" He was losing his temper, something he always regretted. "Man, haven't you heard the expression playing with fire?"

Augustine stared at his fingernails, which, Father Bunt noted, were carefully trimmed and very clean. "Of course, I have sir, but I'm not dating anyone and I certainly haven't let any women in my room, I assure you."

Father Bunt didn't want to turn this into a cross-examination. The whole point of the interchange was just to warn Augustine and get him back on track.

"OK, I'm glad to hear that. But, look, if you visit parishioners, you can't just go to see the *women,* for heaven's sake!" As soon as the words were out of his mouth, Father Bunt regretted them. What if Augustine asked him how he knew this particular fact? He certainly didn't want to admit he'd been snooping around again in the seminarian's room.

"Oh, that," Augustine said casually. "Well, I figured I'd start with visiting the stay-at-home moms during the day and then move on to working parents, and so forth, in the evenings." He looked completely unperturbed.

"Yes, of course." Father Bunt thought that sounded reasonable, but something still kept nagging at him, a little doubt. "Well, alright, I'm glad we got this out in the open. You know you can come to me anytime, don't you, with any problems or…any situations you need help with?"

Augustine smiled broadly. "Thank you, Father. I really appreciate that. Right now, though, everything is smooth sailing."

***

Francesca could tell Tony was peeved by his tone of voice. She was at home, perched in her favorite armchair with Tubs on her lap. It wasn't so much what he said over the phone as what he didn't say. After she told him about Frank ringing her doorbell in the middle of the night, there was a silence, and she could envision the handsome detective clenching his jaw as he tried to control his temper.

"Why didn't you just dial 911 the moment you saw his car?"

"Oh, Tony, I don't know. I guess I wasn't thinking clearly. I mean, he woke me up, you know, and I guess I should have called, but…" She shifted the old cat on her lap and a cloud of fur descended on the chair. "Well, I was curious about what he wanted. And I didn't just want to call the police and say someone's ringing my doorbell. I'd feel like a fool."

"Francesca," he began, and then paused. She could envision him at his desk, trying to calm down. She wondered if he was getting ready to fire off a rubber band, the way he did when something really got to him.

"Look, you're not a child, and I know you hate being treated like one," he continued. "But this guy isn't just anyone. This guy is someone who got into your house on false pretenses, and someone who has a record. So it's not like you'd be calling the cops on the Avon lady."

She could tell he was really steamed now. "I know, Tony, but nothing happened. I'm OK."

"Yeah, but what if he'd decided to kick the door in?" he asked quietly.

"I had it dead-bolted." She felt like she was in court with a high-pressure lawyer firing questions at her.

"Well, OK, you do get points for that," he said. "But you haven't seen the damage a gun can do to a door, and I have."

"I didn't think he had a gun." The very thought of that possibility made her stomach feel queasy.

"Well, think again. I'd put money on it."

She decided to change the topic. "How about coming over for supper tonight, Tony? I can make something Italian, we can kick back and relax and…"

"I'd really like that," he broke in, "but I'm still trying to catch up with all the work I got."

Now she knew something was wrong. Tony wasn't one to turn down a home-cooked meal.

***

Augustine hadn't stopped talking since Mrs. Greenstone had come in with the salads. Father Bunt had never encountered anyone with such a treasure trove of jokes, and he had to admit some were side-splittingly funny. Even William was chuckling, Father Bunt noted with approval. It'll do him some good to lighten up, he thought. William takes life far too seriously.

Mrs. Greenstone was another matter entirely. She had taken a dislike to Augustine for some reason that Father Bunt couldn't quite put his finger on, although he suspected it could have to do with her granddaughter. When she served the dessert, a Key lime pie, Augustine refused a slice.

"Well, it's all from scratch," she sniffed, "and I used all low-fat, so you don't have to worry about cholesterol." She gave the seminarian a withering look, but that didn't seem to faze him in the least.

Instead, as she was cutting the pie, he went into the kitchen and returned with a dark brown bottle and a few small glasses. The bottle was shaped like the figure of a monk, complete with a piece of white rope encircling the waist.

"This is Frangelico, originally made by the monks." Augustine brandished the bottle as if he were in a TV commercial. "It's made with hazelnuts. Anyone want some?"

"Oh, yeah, I've tried that before, but I'm more of a beer man myself," Father Bunt said, scooping a large bite of pie into his mouth, "but you go ahead."

Father William shook his head. "I'm not big on hazelnuts."

"Mrs. G.?" Augustine held the bottle up and gave her a big smile.

"I don't drink, thank you," she replied, her facial expression suggesting she was turning down an offer to participate in a human sacrifice.

Augustine shrugged. "It's delicious—you don't know what you're missing." He poured a small glass. "One glass is a dessert in itself because it's pretty rich stuff."

The cook excused herself shortly afterwards, saying she would see them in the morning. She was hardly out the front door before Augustine put down his glass and stood up. Scrunching up his face to resemble the dour expression Mrs. Greenstone usually wore, he launched into an impromptu soliloquy.

"Why, if everyone on earth ate low-fat foods, there'd be an end to war and famine and poverty. You know, it wasn't an apple that Adam and Eve ate in the Garden of Eden, no sir, it was a donut! *That's* what started all the trouble!"

At the word donut, Father Bunt burst into laughter. The young man was just impossible to resist. Father Bunt tried to cover his laughter by pretending to cough, and then he took a long drink of water.

"Look, Augustine, that's sufficient," he said. "We don't want to make fun of Mrs. Green..."

But he had hardly finished his sentence before he heard the sound of Little Leonora's shrill voice from the sitting room: "Organic! *Squawk!* All-natural! *Squawk!* Low-fat!"

Augustine chuckled. "That bird is a real quick study."

***

The next morning found Father Bunt up early. After a quick cup of coffee and a jelly donut pilfered from the secret stash in his bedroom, he tweaked a few words in his letter to the editor. He had to get something to the archbishop today. Yesterday's paper had contained a small article about the robbery, and he was well aware that a few sentences could easily explode into a major exposé. He had nothing to hide, but he also knew how the press could blow things out of proportion. He placed the sheets in the fax machine, and then input the chancery's number. With any luck the archbishop wouldn't get to the letter for a while and by then it would be too late to send it to the editor.

As he was faxing, his office door edged open and in came Mrs. Greenstone with a decidedly troubled expression. She walked over to a chair and dropped into it quickly.

"Father, you know I'm not one to snoop." She hesitated now, as if summoning up her courage. "But this morning when I was cleaning, I found *this*."

Father Bunt picked up the papers she plunked down on his desk and glanced at them briefly. He could tell they were pages from Augustine's manuscript, but decided not to comment until she'd had her say.

"You see, it's some diary Augustine's keeping, Father." Her eyes were flashing with anger. "And there's a cook in it named Mrs. Judy Mean Bone!"

"Well, I've read some of this already, Mrs. Greenstone," he said calmly, "and I assure you, it's fiction—and nothing to worry about, you see." He hoped his words would quickly smother this particular fire.

But the cook gripped the edge of the desk and rose slightly from the chair. She spoke clearly and precisely as if he were hard of hearing. "Father, the cook has a bird named Big Nora! Does that sound like *fiction*?"

This was going to be tougher than he thought. For one thing, Father Bunt himself was rather nervous about the thin line between fiction and reality that the young man might be crossing. Still, there was no way he was going to censor the seminarian, who clearly had some talent in the writing department. Besides, the thing would probably never get published, so there really was no reason to worry. However, he didn't want to state this opinion, since he didn't want word getting out that he, the pastor, lacked faith in the young man's writing abilities.

"Sometimes, authors use names *based* on people in real life," he said, " but that doesn't mean the writer's actually describing these, uh, real people, you know." He spoke slowly as if he were addressing a child on the verge of throwing a tantrum.

She didn't look convinced. "Well, Father, he describes this Mrs. Mean Bone as complete *health nut*, someone who's feeding the priests vegetarian food without telling them."

He thought about his digestive problems. Was it possible the seminarian was on to something here? Was the cook feeding them bean burgers?

"Well, you're not doing anything like that, right?" He watched her face carefully. "So, you see, it *is* fiction."

"Yes, of course, Father, I guess you're right." She was avoiding his eyes. "Well, thank you for your time," she said suddenly. "I've got to start the vacuuming now." She picked up the sheaf of papers and hurried out the door.

His suspicions aroused, he waited a few minutes and then went down to the kitchen. He figured he could poke around a bit in the cupboards and find out the truth for himself. But when he got downstairs, he heard voices in the kitchen, so he changed his mind. He certainly didn't want to eavesdrop, but the twosome— the cook and Beatrice—were making no effort to subdue their words.

"He's not interested in me, granny," Beatrice said angrily. "He told me he's serious about becoming a priest—and swearing off women." The clanging of a pot drowned out the grandmother's response.

***

Later that morning, Mo-Mo was in the kitchen with Mrs. Greenstone, who was allowing her to play with some excess pie dough. At her desk Francesca could hear the cook instructing the little girl: "That's right—you flatten it out, and then we'll make a nice jam tart."

There was a hard-to-hear reply from Mo-Mo, followed by a carefully enunciated correction from Mrs. Greenstone: "No, dear, that's *jam tart!*"

Doris had dropped Mo-Mo off at Francesca's early that morning. "I have a job interview at Decatur Presbyterian, the pre-K school," she explained breathlessly, "and I promise it won't take too long."

"And if I get the job," she added, "I'll be taking care of the 3-year olds each morning, which means Mo-Mo could come with me!"

Francesca hadn't pointed out that Mo-Mo wouldn't be 3 for another year. She didn't want to dampen her sister's excitement.

Now she heard Father Bunt coming down the stairs, and then heading into the kitchen. "Well, what are you up to, Mo-Mo?" she heard him ask.

And then the reply: "Make damn tart!"

The doorbell rang and Francesca went to answer it. There stood Mauve Bundle in a black tank top, white jeans, and flip flops with tiny purple and green stones on them. Each toenail, Francesca noted, was painted with stripes in matching shades of purple and green.

"I'm just here to help out with next week's bulletins," Mauve announced. "I don't work in the pharmacy on Thursdays, so I thought I'd volunteer a little at the church."

"Great!" Francesca enthused, since putting inserts into the bulletins was her least favorite task. "Come on in and I'll set you up in the other office."

"Oh, and listen, here's an interesting tidbit of news for you." Mauve's eyes were glistening. "My husband, Andy, has been calling lately. He wants us to consider...well going to counseling and maybe getting back together again."

Francesca didn't know the details of their break-up, but she sensed this was good news. "I'm happy for you. Are you going to do it?"

"Oh, yes, I'll do it," she enthused. "You see, my boy, Brad, really wants us back together."

Francesca didn't ask the question that seemed most obvious: "Do you want that too?" She figured that would be prying, so she just smiled. And then, as she was unlocking a small adjacent office for Mauve, she heard someone behind them and turned to see Augustine standing there.

"I didn't know you were working here, Mauve," he smiled.

"Oh, er, not really working, it's more like just, you know, volunteering," Mauve said.

"We can always use help," he said. "And, by the way, Mauve, I really enjoyed our visit the other afternoon."

Mauve glanced quickly at Francesca. "Yes, I did too."

Francesca wondered what was going on. She was sure Mauve had told the Choir Chicks he'd stopped at her house late at night.

***

It was 7:00 a.m. the next morning, and Father William, still in his bathrobe, was already at his computer. After checking email, he went downstairs and retrieved a spinach leaf from the refrigerator to give to Ignatius. He delivered the treat to the hamster and then sat staring at the glowing screen and praying for inspiration for a sermon. He and Father Bunt had gone to the pub last night, and he was regretting his fourth beer. Not only that, but something was troubling him.

Late in the afternoon yesterday, he had taken a short nap, but something had awakened him, the sound of a woman giggling, and he was pretty sure it was Beatrice. It had taken him a few minutes to get downstairs to investigate, but no one was there, so he figured she'd heard him stirring and had left. The incident left him feeling vaguely unsettled because he didn't like the idea of her being in the rectory without the stabilizing influence of Mrs. Greenstone.

He turned his attention back to the matter at hand. He knew many parishioners thought his sermons were too harsh. Many came to church on Sunday and figured they were good to go. They didn't want anyone reminding them about sins. But wasn't that his responsibility as someone they called "father"? And then suddenly, almost like magic, his fingers began moving on the keyboard. His sermon for next Sunday would be about what teenagers called "hooking up."

It was about time he broached the topic. He was hearing far too many confessions these days about sins of the flesh. Even though St. Rita's looked like a run-of-the-mill, middle-class church with people busying themselves making ends meet and raising children, there was plenty going on beneath the surface, and it all came out in the confessional. With all the TV shows heralding premarital and extramarital sex, plus hooking up and shacking up and all the other dismally accurate descriptions of a world in trouble, was it any wonder people were losing their way?

There were just too few role models of married couples who tried to do the right thing. Now *that*, he thought, would be a truly creative TV show, one that showed a husband and wife who truly loved their kids and lived by the Ten Commandments. Well, I guess that was "Father Knows Best," he mused, but today that show would probably be considered politically incorrect.

He heard a door open down the hall and a few moments later, heard someone moving around in the kitchen. He yawned and stretched, envisioning a cup of coffee and maybe a cookie. He saved the document and went downstairs, where he saw Father Bunt sitting at the table, reading his breviary with Dopey stretched out by his feet.

"Good morning, Father, I thought I heard you upstairs, or maybe it was Augustine."

"Must have been me," Father Bunt said. "As for Augustine, I doubt he's up yet."

Father William poured himself a cup of coffee and then rummaged in the cookie jar. He took a tentative nibble of what tasted suspiciously like a low-fat, sugar-free oatmeal cookie, but it would have to do for now. He took five of them, figuring they'd equal one real cookie in pleasure value.

"Oh, before I forget, would you knock on Augustine's door?" Father Bunt asked. "If he's not up yet, he should be. There's a meeting this morning at the chancery for seminarians."

***

An icy nose prodded Father Bunt's ankle, and he dutifully got up and fetched a few dog biscuits for Dopey before returning to his prayers. The dog had already had breakfast, but he liked his own version of a canine dessert. Just as Father Bunt was putting the biscuit box back in the cupboard, he heard an alarmingly loud crashing sound from upstairs and then the sound of William yelling, "Oh, God!"

His stomach dropping in alarm, Father Bunt went running from kitchen just in time to see William clambering down the stairs, his face ashen and the front of his bathrobe stained with coffee.

"Call 911! It's Augustine!"

"What is it, man?" Father Bunt was reaching for his cell phone.

"I can't wake him up. He's just lying there. I think he's in a coma or something." The young priest, ashen-faced, dropped down on a stair step and sat there, trying to catch his breath.

Father Bunt went running up the stairs, his cell phone at his ear. "This is St. Rita's church in Decatur. We need an ambulance immediately," he shouted.

Still talking to the emergency operator, he rushed into Augustine's room. The door was open, but just as he crossed the threshold, Father Bunt stopped. The young man, fully dressed, was lying on his back on the bed. One arm was dangling off the bed, the fingers grazing the carpet. There was a putrid aroma in the room and signs on the bedding that the poor man had been violently ill. Father Bunt felt his stomach churn as he crept toward the bed, willing himself to stay calm.

On the phone, the emergency operator continued barking questions: "What is the emergency? Has there been an accident?"

He couldn't speak though. His heart was pounding ominously, and he was sweating profusely. He stood by the bed and noticed that the young man's eyes were open. It took every ounce of courage for him to bend down and feel for a pulse in Augustine's neck. As his fingers touched the clammy flesh, Father Bunt was overcome by a wave of dizziness and nausea. Even in his shock, though, he'd seen enough TV shows to know what to do. He gently closed the young man's eyes before dropping weakly into a nearby chair, still clutching the phone. The operator continued babbling at him.

"He's dead!" he shouted at her. "He's dead, for God's sake!" The phone fell from his hands, crashing onto the floor.

It took him a few seconds to regain his composure. Then he went over to the bed and made the sign of the cross over the body. "I grant you pardon for all your sins, in the name of the Father, and of the Son, and of the Holy Spirit." He then picked up the breviary from Augustine's bedside, sat down, and began the prayers for the dead.

CHAPTER 6

As she opened the front door of the rectory, Francesca immediately had a feeling that something was wrong. There was no lingering aroma of breakfast, for one thing. But it was something more than that, an unsettling quiet. The only one greeting her was Dopey, who approached in his usual way, head bent down almost apologetically. She scratched behind his ears the way he liked, but that encouraged him to flop down on his back so she could rub his stomach. She did so, smiling to herself because Dopey was impossible to resist.

She cleared away some debris from her desk, noting that yesterday's volunteer had evidently consumed a box of ginger snaps, a banana, a soft drink, and a bag of chips. As she was tidying the desk, she noticed the telephone lines were all busy. That's odd, she thought, for this time of morning. Then she heard someone in the kitchen and went to investigate. She saw Mrs. Greenstone sitting at the table, but there were no signs of breakfast. The woman's face was very pale, and she was staring straight ahead as if lost in thought.

"Are you alright? Is something wrong?" Francesca hurried over and sat beside her.

The cook ran a trembling hand over her face. "I'm afraid I've got some very bad news."

Francesca's stomach lurched. When her husband had been killed in a car wreck, the police officer who'd come to her house to tell her had used nearly the same words.

"Is someone ill? What's happened?" She rattled off the questions nervously, dreading the answers.

"It's Augustine." The old woman clenched her lips together nervously. "I hate to tell you this, but, something has happened, something really bad." She took a drink of water and then continued: "Father Bunt found him this morning—dead!" She crossed herself and added, "God rest his soul."

"Oh, my Lord, I just can't believe..." A storm of tears suddenly overcame Francesca. She put her head in her hands and hunched over. In the background she detected the sounds of someone entering the kitchen, looked up, and saw Father Bunt approaching. His eyes were red, as if he had been crying too.

"Here, now, it's alright," he said gently, handing her a Kleenex from a nearby box. "Now just take it easy."

"Oh, Father, how terrible! What happened?" Francesca dabbed at her eyes with the Kleenex.

Father Bunt sat down wearily. "All we know is he died during the night. The medics said he was probably already dead by the time Father William and I got back home last night at about eleven." There was a muscle twitching in his cheek. "We have to wait for the coroner's official report."

"Father, did he have heart trouble or something?" Francesca continued blotting her eyes, while also aware that Dopey was now situated at her feet, lightly licking her toes.

"Not that I know of—and he seemed just fine yesterday," Father Bunt said, reaching down to pet Dopey.

Mrs. Greenstone walked over to the coffee pot and brought it back to the table with three mugs. She rummaged in the refrigerator and came back with a container of non-fat creamer. She poured them all coffee and then resumed her spot at the table.

"Maybe it wasn't natural causes," Mrs. Greenstone declared grimly.

"What on earth do you mean?" Francesca asked.

The cook poured a generous amount of creamer into her coffee and then added a sweetener that was packaged in a tiny pink envelope reading "all natural." As she stirred her coffee, she said quietly, "Maybe someone did him in."

***

Francesca wasn't sure what to wear for the funeral. She knew on one level it didn't matter, but she wanted to look respectful. Some people wore bright colors to funerals nowadays, but she recalled that she had appreciated the people who attended Dean's funeral dressed in traditional dark garb. Even if Christians believe in life after death, she thought, there's still the sorrow of knowing we won't see the person again here on earth. She settled on a navy-blue dress and low-heeled black shoes. As she drove to the church, her mind felt like a beehive swarming with ideas. What had really happened to Augustine?

Had it been a freakish heart attack—or was the cook right? Was it foul play?

Father Bunt mentioned that he hadn't seen any obvious bruises on the body, but he also admitted he had been in shock when he found Augustine. Although the coroner's report had not come through yet, rumors were traveling fast and furious at St. Rita's. The possibility of another homicide was stirring up disturbing memories of past misdeeds in the parish.

After parking, Francesca walked the short distance to the church, noting that it was another sizzling summer day. Glancing up, she spied a massive cloud formation that reminded her of a castle some giant had built in the aqua sky. When she got to the church, the castle had broken into little pieces and drifted away. Tears stung her eyes as she stepped inside the heavily air-conditioned church. She glanced at the choir section where Charlene was busily poring over music at the organ. Francesca had heard through the email list that instead of enlisting the choir's services, the family had hired professional singers for the funeral.

She found a pew near the back, and knelt down to pray. In a few moments, she looked over and saw Mauve genuflecting by her pew. Mauve was dressed in a hot-pink cotton blouse, beige slacks, and open-toe high heels that revealed her well-manicured toenails. As she settled in next to Francesca, she began sniffling.

"Are you alright?" Francesca whispered, groping in her purse for Kleenex.

"It's just…it's so hard to believe. I mean…" But Mauve was interrupted by the arrival of her son.

"Oh, there you are!" Mauve shifted over to make room, and then whispered in Francesca's ear: "I insisted that he come. Brad has to learn about showing respect for others."

A few moments later, Brad left the pew, and Francesca assumed he'd headed to the men's room. As if she couldn't bear the silence, Mauve said, "I'm at my wits' end. He's been spending more money than I give him for allowance lately, and when I ask him where it's from, he gets angry."

She blotted her eyes and continued: "Sometimes his father sends him money without letting me know, so that could be it." At that moment, Brad reappeared, and Mauve grew quiet as Augustine's family was ushered in.

Watching Augustine's parents slowly move up the aisle was heart-rending. It reminded Francesca of Dean's funeral, when she had been accompanied by her brother-in-law, Dan. She recalled it had been the longest journey of her life. Now she watched as the mother leaned heavily against the father, who looked like he might break down at any moment. There was also a much older couple, who Francesca assumed were the grandparents. She also spotted a young woman who stood out from the rest of the family members. She was strikingly lovely with shoulder-length, brown hair and delicate pale skin. I wonder who she is, Francesca thought.

***

A week later, Father Bunt sat staring at his computer screen, willing himself not to succumb to the temptation of checking email until he had at least jotted down a preliminary outline for his upcoming sermon. Somehow the relentlessly brutal heat of summer had burned away every trace of his creativity. But it wasn't just the weather; it was also the worry about Augustine. He was anxious to learn about the coroner's report. The archbishop had been calling nearly every day to see if there was any news. Plus, the cadre of lawyers at the chancery had been on the phone to him as well. Rumors that the seminarian's death had been the result of foul play were circulating widely at the parish.

The only bright side—and he hated to think of it that way—was that the letter-to-the-editor project was on permanent hold. The archbishop had made it very clear that, as he put it, "There isn't a chance in heck a letter will help at this point."

As for the missing money, it now seemed like a mere niggle to Father Bunt, given the young man's sudden death. Besides, the police hadn't come up with any leads in the theft, so it looked like a total loss. He wondered if there was any connection between the missing money and the death—but until he knew how Augustine had died, all he could do was speculate. He had spoken with the heartbroken parents as they arranged the funeral, and the mother tearfully had insisted that her son had been in perfect health.

Now he rested his head in his hands and said a quick prayer for the repose of Augustine's soul, and just as he got to "amen," the phone rang. It was Francesca.

"Father, there's a Detective Ryan Baker on the line for you."

Father Bunt had hoped Tony Viscardi would be assigned to the case, because he had great respect for the way he had handled the liturgist's death. But for some reason Baker was handling it, so that was that.

"Reverend Bunt?" Baker's slightly high-pitched voice sounded nervous. "I've got some news on the case."

"Yes?" Father Bunt licked his lips nervously.

"Well, according to the coroner's report, Mr., uh, Hornsby was poisoned."

Father Bunt felt a sudden wave of dizziness. "But...but how is that possible? We all had the same thing to eat at supper..."

"According to the report, it looks like someone doctored an after-dinner drink Hornsby had before going to bed—just a second." There was a rustling sound, and Father Bunt imagined Baker going through his notes.

"Uh, let's see, Frangelico, that's right. We found the bottle in the kitchen." More rustling and then: "But here's the thing: whoever did this—they could have been trying to poison everyone in the rectory. I mean, doesn't everyone take a nip now and again?"

"Well, sure, we have a beer or a glass of wine, but Augustine was the only one who liked this particular drink. It was his special bottle."

"OK, let me jot that down. That makes sense. This means whoever did it was definitely targeting Hornsby." There was a second of silence. "Assuming they *knew* he was the only one who drank the stuff, that is."

"What...what kind...of poison was it?" Father Bunt rubbed his eyes wearily.

"Nothing fancy; just your common, garden-variety arsenic, the kind you find in rat poison."

"Oh, Lord, that's terrible." Father Bunt felt his stomach turn over when he remembered Augustine lying on the bed.

"Yeah, pretty nasty stuff," the detective agreed.

"But the taste—I mean, wouldn't he have noticed?" Father Bunt asked.

"Well, here's the thing: The booze has a strong taste of hazelnuts, so it would make a pretty good cover-up for the arsenic. See, arsenic has a kind of almond flavor—not that I've ever tasted it, you know." There was a snorting sound, suggesting the detective found his own wit irresistible.

"And if he drank the booze down quickly," Baker continued, "he might have noticed something slightly off with the taste, but by then it would be too late. So probably someone got into the kitchen earlier that day, someone who knew Hornsby drank this stuff, and doctored the bottle."

"That would mean....wouldn't that mean someone who works here?" Father Bunt could feel his heart rate increasing. He could just imagine the newspapers having a field day with this one, and he knew it would take far more than a letter to the editor to calm down the furor. But far worse was the fact that the killer, whoever it was, was still out there somewhere—and was familiar with the eating and drinking habits of the occupants of St. Rita's rectory.

Father Bunt suddenly recalled how furious the cook had been after discovering what Augustine had written about her in his book. He also remembered how angry Beatrice had sounded about Augustine's apparent lack of romantic interest in her.

"Well, not necessarily someone who works there, although that's possible," Baker conceded. "But it could also be someone else, anyone really who knew he drank this stuff."

"Yes, of course." Father Bunt clenched his jaw nervously, as he realized the list of suspects appeared to be growing by the moment.

"We'll be talking to everyone who works in the rectory, especially in the kitchen," Baker said, "and I already have that list." A short pause and then: "How did the cook and Hornsby get along, by the way?

"Uh, well, they did have their differences at times," Father Bunt said discreetly.

He heard a garbled conversation on the other end of the line and then the words "double cheese," and he realized the detective was ordering lunch. Then Baker came back on the line, loud and clear.

"Differences, huh? OK, we'll definitely be talking to the cook. Can you also tell me if he had any friends, anyone that visited him at the rectory?"

Father Bunt squirmed in his seat. There was no way around this one. "Well, there was one, uh, girl that was, uh, interested in him."

"Interested as in...dating?" The word seemed to hang in the air like a bomb about to detonate.

"I think so," Father Bunt said. "You see, there was one time when I was pretty sure that this, uh, girl, was with him pretty late, although..." He struggled for a way to complete the sentence that would make it somewhat less damning.

"You mean late at night, alone in his room?"

Father Bunt had the impression the man was practically salivating on the other end of the line. *He probably thinks there are all kinds of salacious goings-on here at the church.*

"Yes, but here's the thing: When I asked him about it, he thoroughly denied it. And, well, I took his word for it."

Baker chuckled in a knowing and somewhat annoying way. "But wasn't this guy in training for the priesthood?"

"Yes, he was in the seminary," Father Bunt said patiently, "but he hadn't made a promise of celibacy yet. That doesn't happen until later, you see. And in some cases young men studying for the priesthood discover, over time, that, uh, they really *don't* have a vocation."

There was a low whistle over the phone. "So you think he was planning to drop out?"

"I have no reason to believe that." Father Bunt was growing impatient now with the detective's tendency to draw rather hasty conclusions.

"OK, so there was this woman," Baker said, and there were more rustling sounds. "What's her name and address?"

Father Bunt pulled out his address book and provided the information, explaining she was Mrs. Greenstone's granddaughter.

"One more thing," Father Bunt said. "I, uh, I got the impression that the relationship or friendship or whatever it was, uh, that Augustine had called it quits."

"So maybe this Beatrice had a big axe to grind," Baker said eagerly. "Or maybe she was in cahoots with grandma, who didn't like the way he was treating her."

Father Bunt decided not to comment. Somehow the very idea that there could be two murderers working in the kitchen was too much to deal with.

"OK, anyone else you can think of?" Baker asked.

Father Bunt then mentioned the parish directory he had found in Augustine's room and the check marks by women's names. "It's not that he was doing anything wrong, you see, but I did find it odd that they were all females, so I talked with him— and he explained he was starting with the stay-at-home moms."

Father Bunt could feel perspiration starting to mar his clean shirt. *I'm getting the feeling Augustine is on trial here*, he thought.

"How many women did he visit?" Baker's tone suggested he wasn't buying the stay-at-home mom scenario.

"I can't say for sure," Father Bunt said, swallowing hard, "but when I saw the directory, he was already in the D's." He knew how damning this all sounded, but what else could he do? He had to tell the truth.

There was a long "hmmm" on the other end, and then: "Man, this case is going to be harder to solve than I thought."

***

Poison! Francesca shuddered. She had been thoroughly shocked when she'd heard the news from Father Bunt a few days ago. She knew he was concerned about fueling further rumors at the church, and she had promised not to tell a soul about the detective's report. But somehow the news had spread like the proverbial wildfire, and now it seemed like everyone knew about it.

She had been fielding phone calls all morning from concerned parishioners who wanted more details, especially those with children in the school. "Is it safe for the kids to eat lunch there?" one mother had asked, and Francesca had put the call through to Father Bunt, as he'd directed. She had a feeling there would be lots of kids toting lunch sacks until the case was solved. While answering calls, she was also trying to keep Mo-Mo occupied. Doris had called in desperation early that morning, begging her to take the child since Doris had a second job interview that day at the pre-school. Francesca had agreed, and then Doris had added the zinger.

"Listen, I'm not sending a pacifier along with her."

"Oh?" Francesca personally thought pacifiers were wonderful because they did exactly what their name implied, which was bringing peace to chaos.

"Dan and I are trying to wean her off them," Doris explained. "She's getting too big for them."

"How's it going so far?"

There had been a moment of silence and then: "Horrible, to tell you the truth. She's cried herself to sleep for the last three nights, and it goes on for about two hours. We're totally exhausted."

Francesca hadn't said anything. After all, she wasn't a parent, and surely they knew what they were doing. But Mo-Mo was grumpy this morning and had already had one meltdown, and it was only 10 a.m. Somehow that didn't bode well for the rest of the day.

She gave the child a coloring book. "Here, draw me something pretty," she cooed.

"Dwa pwetty!"

While Mo-Mo busied herself by coloring a pig bright green, Francesca decided to jot down everything she knew about the case. This way she could figure out who might be a likely suspect. She could almost hear Tony warning her to stay out of it, but she excused herself on the grounds that she was naturally curious. Besides, for some reason Tony wasn't on this case and she didn't know who would be handling it. Whoever it was might need her help. Just as she had sharpened a pencil, the doorbell rang. She waited for Mrs. Greenstone to answer it, but heard no sound of footsteps, so she figured the cook had gone out on an errand. When the bell sounded again, Francesca went into the foyer and opened the door.

There stood a decidedly pudgy man, maybe 30 or so, his face flushed from the heat, and his wrinkled, blue-and-white checkered shirt straining across a classic beer belly. He had squinty eyes and a sunburned face, and her first unfortunate impression was that he reminded her of Porky Pig.

"Detective Ryan Baker here." He held out his hand.

She grasped his hand, which was meaty and quite moist, and introduced herself quickly. "Would you like a glass of iced tea?" she asked. The whole front of the poor man's shirt, she noted, was soaked in sweat.

"No, I'm good. I grabbed an early lunch over at Dusty's Barbecue." He belched, then extracted a large handkerchief from his pocket and blotted his face. "You ever eat there?"

"Uh, no, but I've heard it's good." Francesca led him toward her desk and indicated a nearby chair. "Should I call Father Bunt?"

He ran his eyes up and down her body in a way that immediately put her off. "Not just yet. You're Tony's...uh...friend, right?"

There was something about the way he said "friend" that instantly grated on her. She had the distinct impression that he thought she and Tony were lovers, and she wondered suspiciously if it was because of something Tony had said—or if

Baker was just prone to jumping to salacious conclusions when it came to male-female relationships.

"Yes, that's right, we're *friends*. I met him when he was working a homicide case here."

"Yeah, this church sure has a track record." The detective took out a small notebook and pen from his pocket. "You'd think a church would be a more peaceful place, but around here, it seems you never know when someone's going to turn up dead."

He gave her a little smile, as if a string of deaths at St. Rita's was something to laugh about. "As I'm sure you've figured out, I'm here to question you about the Hornsby death. It's routine. We have to talk to anyone who knew him, especially anyone who works here at the church."

She nodded, and he continued: "So we're putting the time of his...uh...death at roughly ten p.m. on August 15." Baker pawed through his notebook and nodded.

"Yeah, that's right. He wasn't found until the next morning, but 10 p.m. is about a half hour after the coroner thinks he actually ingested the...uh...substance. This stuff works fast." Now he raised his eyes from his notes and looked at her.

"We think someone put the poison in his booze earlier that day—or maybe that evening. So we're checking people's whereabouts."

Francesca took out the small calendar she kept in her purse. Just as she did, she felt a slightly damp hand pat her knee. She looked down and saw Mo-Mo who was snuffling loudly. The child's lips were trembling and her eyes were filled to the brim with tears. Francesca had a definite sense of what would come next, and she was right.

"PASSY! PASSY!" the child screamed. She had clearly become bored with the coloring book, which Francesca saw lying on the floor, crumpled and torn.

"Well, who is this?" Baker bent down and extended his big hand to the child.

"My niece, Mo-Mo. I'm babysitting her."

"Well, she's very cute…"

"YOU DOPE!" Mo-Mo screamed at the top of her lungs.

Baker retracted his hand as if he'd been stung by a bee.

"Sorry about that," Francesca said. "You know how kids are—they don't know what they're saying."

"Yeah, sure." The detective looked unconvinced.

"PASSY! PASSY!" Mo-Mo threw herself on the floor, kicking and screaming.

"Excuse me a moment," Francesca said to the detective while she rummaged in her purse, found the emergency pacifier she always carried with her, and handed it to the child. The little girl stood up, popped it into her mouth, and wandered off, making happy sucking noises.

"Now where were we?" Francesca said. "Oh, yes, what I did that day. Well, let's see—I didn't volunteer here. I spent most of the day with my friend Rebecca. We went shopping in the afternoon at Seventeen Steps, that little shop in Decatur, and then to the Purple Elephant bookstore. Then we went to the mall and finally out to supper at about 7:30. We went to the Mediterranean Grill on North Decatur."

Francesca waited a few seconds before continuing, since he was writing in his notebook. "Then we headed over to Bruster's on Lawrenceville highway for ice cream. We came back to my house for coffee, and she finally went home...let me see...I'm pretty sure it was nearly midnight."

"What flavor?" he asked

"Huh?"

"The ice cream—I just wondered what flavor you like."

"Oh, pistachio, definitely."

He jotted something down. "We'll have to talk to her too, this Rebecca person. You got her number?"

She took out her cell phone and found the number. Meanwhile, Mo-Mo had climbed into her lap and was dozing, still making contented gurgling sounds as she gummed the pacifier.

Baker removed the wrapper from a stick of gum, popped it in his mouth, and began chewing vigorously. "What do you know about this Hornsby fellow that might help us?" A strong scent of peppermint wafted toward her.

"Not much really. I mean, we talked now and again." She had a sudden vivid memory of the young man standing by her desk and felt her throat tighten.

"Was it widely known that he drank this Frangelico stuff instead of, say, beer or something?" The detective licked the tip of his pencil and waited for her reply.

"Well, I can't say. I mean, I saw him drinking wine at the masquerade ball, but...well, I knew the bottle in the kitchen was his—and I guess other people did too."

"Who else was he seeing?" Baker asked with an expression that looked suspiciously like a leer.

She felt a quick stab of anger. "Well, I can assure you he wasn't seeing *me*—if you mean dating." She suspected her face was reddening, but couldn't control the reaction.

He smiled in an infuriating way, as if her little outburst of emotion was proof of her deception.

"You got any leads for me?" he asked. "You know, maybe a friend, or someone who was, shall we say, more than a friend?"

She didn't want to give him Mauve's name because the poor woman had enough trouble. Besides, Francesca needed some time to do some investigating on her own. If Mauve's actions proved suspicious, she could always tell Baker then. She considered giving him Beatrice's name, but figured he already had it.

"No, I can't think of anyone else." She avoided his eyes.

"Yeah, well you let me know if something comes to mind." The wary look on his face suggested that he knew she was lying.

A question popped into her head. "Uh, listen, I was wondering: how hard is it to get the poison that was used? I mean, wouldn't that kind of narrow down the killer in some way?"

"You've been reading too many detective novels," he chuckled. "See, this poison isn't that hard to find. You can buy it in any hardware store." He pulled out the pack of gum again, removing another slice. "Most people don't realize how much poisonous stuff is readily available."

"Yes, but whoever did this, wouldn't they have to have some special knowledge or something?" She could feel herself starting to do what Tony called "putting on her detective cap," but it was hard to stop. "I mean, in terms of how much to use—and things like that?"

He jotted down another note. She started wondering if she was incriminating herself in some way with her questions.

"Yeah, well, we're investigating all this, you can rest assured," he said, sucking his teeth as if searching for a last remnant of barbecue. "Ring the pastor for me, would you?"

CHAPTER 7

"Of course, show him up." Father Bunt quickly put down the phone. He had been working on a sermon that was currently going nowhere, and was relieved to have an excuse to abandon it. Dopey was ensconced cozily beneath his desk, snoring lightly, and every now and again Father Bunt would hear a little growling sound, as if the dog was dreaming about hunting squirrels. In reality, whenever Dopey saw a squirrel, he whimpered and ran away.

Father Bunt ran his fingers through his hair and made sure his collar was fastened. The knock came at the door, and he went to answer it.

"Come in, Detective Baker, and have a seat. How can I help you?"

The detective looked much younger than Father Bunt had envisioned him on the phone. I wonder how much experience he actually has, Father Bunt thought. It would be just my luck if this is his first case.

The man lowered himself into the seat slowly, hitching up his trouser legs. "We have to question anyone who worked with Hornsby—and that includes you and the other priest, uh, what's-his-name, Snortland."

"Of course, I'll help in any way I can."

"Yeah, well first we need to know where you and this, uh, Reverend Snortland were the day of the incident. That would be

August 15." There was a sudden snapping sound as the point on Baker's pencil broke.

"Here, use one of mine," Father Bunt said absently.

The man picked up a well-sharpened pencil from the desk and then gave Father Bunt an odd look. "You go to the Pin-Ups club much, Reverend?"

"What? Oh, no, of course not! Someone's planted those here as some kind of joke." Father Bunt didn't add that he suspected the prankster had been Augustine. I thought I'd gotten rid of those blasted things, he thought.

The detective chuckled in an almost conspiratorial way. "Yeah, a joke—I get it."

Father Bunt cleared his throat. "Well, you asked about my whereabouts on August 15."

He studied the scrawling notes on his desk calendar. "Father William—that's Snortland—and I were both here in the afternoon. I was working on my sermon in my office and he was over in the church hearing confessions. Right after supper, we went out and made hospital visits. He went to DeKalb Medical Center and I went to Emory. I guess we left here about 7."

"What time did you get back?"

Father Bunt glanced at the ceiling. "Let's see, we met after the visits and had a few beers at the James Joyce pub over in Avondale Estates. We got home...let's see now..." He pushed back in his chair. "It was eleven—I remember because I went to my room and turned on the TV, and the news was coming on."

"Was Hornsby's car outside?"

"Yes, it was." Father Bunt chewed his lower lip. He was beginning to feel like he was on trial here.

"Did you hear anything unusual? You know, voices, music, anything out of the ordinary?"

"Everything was very quiet. I figured...." Here he was surprised by a catch in his voice. "I figured Augustine was asleep. There was no light coming from his room, and no sounds. Some nights I'd hear him typing on the computer or maybe taking a phone call, but that night...well, there was nothing."

Baker jotted something down. "OK, well, look, we have to verify all this, your alibi I mean."

"You can check the registers at the hospitals where we signed in," Father Bunt said, "and as for the pub, the waitresses there know us pretty well."

"You go there often?" Baker asked, chewing his gum vigorously.

"Well, about once a week." He felt like reminding the man that having a drink now and again was not a sin—but he suspected Baker would see that as defensiveness on his part, so he remained silent.

"OK, so you were both here that afternoon. Obviously you had plenty of opportunity to go into the kitchen..."

"You're not suggesting that one of us did it!" Father Bunt gasped.

There was a loud scuffling sound and Dopey now emerged from beneath the desk, making a low growling noise in his throat. Although the dog was basically afraid of everything, he did at least have a protective instinct when it came to Father Bunt.

Baker recoiled in the chair. "Hey, now, down, boy, easy does it. I didn't know you had a dog under there."

Father Bunt patted Dopey on the head. "Don't worry, he's completely harmless."

As if to demonstrate, Dopey now began wagging his tail eagerly and creating a small puddle of drool on the floor. He also let out a tentative woof, which Father Bunt knew was a request for a biscuit.

Baker moved his chair back a few inches. "I've never heard a bark like that. It almost sounds like he's stuttering or something."

Father Bunt decided now was not the time to explain that the dog did in fact have a speech impediment. No doubt Baker already thought the rectory was a strange enough place without his adding fuel to that particular fire.

"Let's see, where were we?" Baker murmured. "Oh, yeah: any reason you or the other priest didn't like Hornsby?"

An image of the diary flashed in Father Bunt's mind. Did William even know about it? They'd never discussed it, but the cook might have told William about it. Should he bring it up? Why suggest a motive, though, to someone who already seemed suspicious?

"We liked him just fine. No problems with him at all." As he spoke, Father Bunt wondered if he should mention the stolen money. He didn't want to give the impression that he thought a theft was as serious as murder, but maybe the theft could in some way shed light on what had happened.

"Uh, Detective Baker, I don't know if there's any connection between the, uh, murder and another thing that occurred here at the parish not too long ago. You see there, uh, there was some money stolen."

Baker looked through his note pad. "Yeah, I remember, the money that went missing at the masquerade ball. To tell you the truth, I doubt there's any connection." A half smile played on his lips. "Unless you're suggesting that maybe Hornsby took the money, and someone bumped him off for it."

"No, not at all. I mean, Augustine certainly wouldn't have..." Father Bunt's eyebrows shot up in surprise. Where in the world had the detective gotten that idea? But then he suddenly remembered seeing the expensive watch in the seminarian's room.

"As far as the theft goes, we've come up with exactly nothing," Baker said. "I gotta tell you, when it comes to cash— and when there are tons of fingerprints all over the cash box— well, you get my drift."

"Of course, I understand," Father Bunt said miserably. He regretted even mentioning the matter.

Baker stood up as if getting ready to leave, but then added: "Oh, yeah, almost forgot: you mind if I talk to the cook?"

Father Bunt reached for the phone and rang Mrs. Greenstone, who appeared a few moments later, wiping her hands on her apron. As soon as the introductions were made, she sat down in a nearby chair and pursed her lips nervously. Father Bunt began to excuse himself, but Baker motioned for him to stay. "No reason you can't be in on this."

"Ma'am, we're questioning people who knew Mr. Hornsby," Baker explained, "and trying to find out where they were the afternoon when the, uh, poison was added to the bottle."

"Well, you don't suspect *me,* do you?" she sputtered angrily.

"We're just checking everyone's whereabouts that day," Baker sighed.

Mrs. Greenstone looked at Father Bunt as if expecting him to answer for her. When he remained silent, she said, "It was my day off. I went shopping all morning, and that afternoon I was taking my tai chi class at the YWCA."

She once again glanced at Father Bunt as if she thought he would chime in, but he kept his eyes downcast. He'd had no idea she was training in the martial arts. I wonder what else she does in her spare time, he thought.

"Your what class?" Baker looked startled.

"Tai chi: It helps with balance," she said. "My Bertram— that was my late husband, God rest his soul—signed me up for it as a birthday gift a few years ago. He was going to take the class with me, but he never got a chance to."

"And that evening, did you return to the rectory?"

"As I mentioned, it was my day off," she said icily, "so of course I didn't come back. I went over to my friend's house, Mary Lou Barker, for supper at 6, and got home at 10."

"That's pretty late, isn't it?" Baker asked.

"Well, it's not like I'm 90-years old or something." Once again, she shot a glance at Father Bunt, as if hoping he would join the conversation, but he refused to meet her gaze. He was starting to wonder why she was being so confrontational with the detective. Did she have something to hide?

"What was your relationship like with Mr. Hornsby?" Baker asked.

"I cooked the food, and he ate it. I did the cleaning. That's about it."

"Did he like your cooking?"

She looked surprised. "I don't know. I never really asked him. But he always cleaned his plate, I can tell you that—except he wasn't much for dessert. He preferred that, what's the name again, that fancy drink."

"The drink that was poisoned, you mean?"

"Yes." She clasped her hands tightly together.

"Let's see, according to my notes, Mr. Hornsby was rather...uh...friendly with your granddaughter, is that right?" Baker chewed more enthusiastically on his gum.

"Well, you'll have to ask her about that," the cook replied. "She's a big girl and I don't butt into her personal affairs. But she's a good girl and there wasn't anything...anything bad going on. They were just friends," she said emphatically. Then she abruptly glanced at her watch and stood up. "Well, I've got work to do, so I'd better get to it."

After she had left, Baker scratched his head with the eraser on his pencil. "She's a hard nut to crack, isn't she? I get the feeling there's more to the story than we're hearing."

Now he suddenly changed the topic. "Wasn't some guy found dead here last year—a what-cha-ma-call-it—a liturgist? And wasn't there a homicide before that, involving someone in the choir?"

Father Bunt nodded glumly. "That's right. But the, uh, the choir incident, that was with the, uh, previous pastor."

He knew, however, that it really didn't matter under whose watch the crimes were committed. The dismal fact was that St. Rita's parish had earned itself a very questionable reputation with the police.

***

A few days later, Francesca was working on the bulletins when she heard the front door swing open, and then Mrs. Greenstone rushed in.

"You're not going to believe this!" The woman's face was pale and her thin hands were trembling as she stood in front of Francesca's desk.

"What's happened?"

"I'll tell you what's happened! The police are questioning my Beatrice about the murder! And not just once either; they've been by our house now *three* times—as if *she* could hurt anyone!" The cook broke down in sobs, and sank into the nearest chair.

Francesca went into the kitchen, returning with a glass of water. "Here, drink this, and try to calm down."

Mrs. Greenstone drained the glass. "Calm down! I don't think I'll ever be calm again. They're framing her, that's what they're doing. She couldn't hurt a fly!"

"But they haven't arrested her, have they?" Francesca gently tried to interject a note of logic.

The cook placed the glass on the desk. "No, but it seems they're going in that direction. They found a letter from Beatrice to...to Augustine, an angry letter. I didn't realize it, but she had fallen really hard for him. I thought it was just another one of her crushes, but it was more serious, at least in her mind."

Mrs. Greenstone wrung her hands. "The letter makes her look guilty, I'm afraid. You see, my Beatrice, well, she made some threats in it."

"Threats against his life?" Francesca was mentally moving Beatrice to the top of her list of suspects.

"No, not like that, but you know how easy words can be misinterpreted." Mrs. Greenstone gazed at the ceiling as if seeking divine inspiration. "Beatrice said something like 'You'll be sorry if you do this to me.'"

Francesca didn't say anything, and the cook went on: "She was, well, she was running after him, you know. I told her it wasn't ladylike, but she wouldn't listen to me. And it turns out he wasn't interested—and Beatrice isn't one to take rejection lightly."

"But is the letter the only evidence against her?" Francesca was beginning to feel like she was cross-examining a witness.

The cook blinked rapidly, as if trying to decide how to respond to this one. "Well, no, that's not all. You see, it seems Father William said he heard a woman laughing in the living room on the day when the police think the...the bottle was poisoned. And Father William told the police he thought it was Beatrice."

"Did Father William actually see her?"

"I don't know."

Francesca wanted to say something to comfort Mrs. Greenstone, but this last piece of information sounded very incriminating to her.

"There's something else," Mrs. Greenstone continued. "Father Bunt told the police he thought he heard a woman in Augustine's room one night." She sighed heavily. "That could have been Beatrice."

"Did she admit to that?"

"When I asked her about it, she just got angry. She wouldn't tell me what happened."

She grabbed a Kleenex from the box on Francesca's desk and wiped eyes before going on. "Beatrice has no alibi for that entire afternoon and evening. She told me she was home alone, watching TV, and that's what she told the police. But there's no way to back that up, since I wasn't home that day."

The whole situation was sounding bleaker by the moment, Francesca thought. She was starting to wonder why the police hadn't taken the girl into custody, but she didn't want to upset the grandmother even further by bringing this up. As she saw a tear make its way down the woman's thin face, she felt a stab of pity. On an impulse, she reached out and patted the cook's hand.

"What can I do to help?" Francesca asked.

The cook let out a shuddering sigh before responding shakily: "You can help me find the real killer."

Francesca hesitated before replying. Despite the damning evidence, her gut instinct said Beatrice wasn't the murderer. The girl was guilty of terrible taste in clothing and perhaps some questionable approaches to romance—but murder? She didn't seem the type. Still, Francesca had majored in philosophy in college, which had left her with a deeply ingrained tendency to look at both sides of every issue. And she had to admit that if the girl was really angry with Augustine, then she definitely had a motive. And she certainly had easy access to the kitchen.

Francesca knew what Tony would tell her. "Don't do the police's work" and "Leave it to the experts" were his typical pieces of advice. But in this case she surely needed to do some investigating on her own. For one thing, she doubted if the guy assigned to the case was up to the task. Tony had admitted that Baker was new to detective work. "Wet behind the ears" had been his exact words.

"Of course I'll help you," she said. "Where do you want me to start?"

The cook rooted around in her well-worn canvas purse. "Well, there's something I found in Augustine's room the day before...before he died." She pulled out a small framed photo of a young woman.

"This was in his shirt drawer. I found it when I was putting some fresh laundry away. I think it could be his girlfriend." She handed the photo to Francesca.

"What makes you think that?"

"Well, he told Beatrice he wasn't interested in her because he was going to become a priest. But maybe the truth was he already had a girlfriend!"

Francesca turned the photo over in her hands. The woman was quite lovely; there was no doubt about that. And there was something familiar about the face, but she couldn't quite place it. At that moment, her conscience sent out a little warning signal.

"Don't you think we should give this to the detective?" Francesca asked.

"Yes, of course we will," Mrs. Greenstone replied, "in a day or so—but first can you find out who she is? She could be a really important lead in the case. Maybe she was jealous of Beatrice, or maybe she and Augustine had a lover's quarrel. She could be the killer."

Francesca hit the snooze button on the warning alarm in her head. This wouldn't take long to investigate, she assured herself, and then they could give the photo to Baker.

"I'll look into it," she agreed.

***

After leaving the rectory, Francesca drove over to the Publix grocery store in the Emory Commons shopping center to get cat food and a few bottles of white wine. As she was parking her car, she noticed a new beauty shop called the Goddess Salon had opened in the past week. A sign printed in perky pink on a chalkboard outside the salon proclaimed in big letters: "Adore yourself!" I wonder if they expect customers to erect altars to themselves or something, she thought.

Once inside the grocery store, she noticed the usual motley mix of customers, which today included two college-aged girls in black leather shorts with their spiked hair—dyed purple—sprouting horn-like from their heads. There were also a few elderly ladies with blue-tinted hair slowly pushing walkers. As she went through the express line, she wondered what the cashier thought about people like her with an odd assortment of purchases. Does the woman think I enjoy snacking on cat food—or does she suspect that my cat likes Sauvignon Blanc?

Arriving home moments later, Francesca noticed another car pulling up in front of her house. She got out quickly, and, glancing over, she saw that it was Frank's. Oh no, she thought, just like a bad penny, he's back. She rushed toward the house, hoping to avoid him, but when she got to her front porch, she had to put her grocery bags down before unlocking the door, and she lost a few precious seconds. He was right behind her.

"Hey, let me help you with those," he said. She noticed a whiff of something—beer maybe—as he leaned down and picked up a bag.

"No, really, I can get them." She tried to edge her way into the house, but she wasn't quick enough, and he walked in right behind her.

"I see you're stocking up on wine." He chuckled as he glanced into the bag. "You plan on throwing a party or something?"

She refused to smile at his inane humor."What brings you here, Frank?"

"OK, look, I can tell you're still sore with me. I was wrong to give you that story about being Tony's cousin and all, I can see that now. But I was planning to tell you, I really was. I was going to tell you that night, but..."

"But you got called by your mother on an emergency," she finished his sentence. "I know, you told me already."

"And I'm sorry for coming by your house so late that night. I, uh, I'd had a few beers, you know, down at the bar. It was stupid, but I just wanted to talk to you."

She knew what he wanted her to say—"Don't worry about it"—but she couldn't absolve him that easily. She also knew it was wrong to hold a grudge, but if she forgave him too quickly, that could make her look like an easy target for future deception—and right now she didn't want anything more to do with him. She had never been skilled at hiding her emotions, and she suspected her facial expression was conveying her feelings loud and clear.

"Yeah, I know what's coming," he said angrily. "You don't want nothing to do with a guy who has a record, right? Especially an ex-druggie."

What could she say? The truth was she had no desire to have him in her life. "Frank, it's not that. It's just that…well, Tony and I are dating, and …"

"Yeah, well that didn't stop you from asking me out before, now did it? Back when you thought I was, you know, a nice respectable computer guy."

He had her there, so she quickly changed the topic. "Look, I have some things to do this afternoon. I'm afraid I can't invite you in." They were still standing by the open door.

"Oh, I get it," he said bitterly. "You don't want the neighbors to know you have an ex-con in your house, right?"

His tone frightened her. How could she get him out of the house, and fast? Then it dawned on her: She would be the one to leave.

"Oh, gosh, I left the other bag in the car." She hurried out the door, and her plan worked because he followed her. She opened the car door and pulled out the bag of cat food.

"Look, I'm not here to play games," he said. "I heard about what happened to that Augustine guy. That was a real shame. And I'll bet it hit you pretty hard, huh?" The words had a false ring to them.

She felt her stomach churning with some emotion she couldn't quite name. "Yes, it did. The whole parish is grieving over his death."

"Yeah, the whole parish, I'll bet—especially the women," he said sarcastically.

"What do you mean by that?"

"Look, I'm not blind. I'm in and out of the rectory a lot with my job. I got wind of what was going on. He wasn't an angel, if you catch my drift."

"I don't know what you heard, but I don't put much stock in rumors." She shifted the heavy bag in her arms, mentally willing him to leave.

"Yeah, well, that Beatrice was real interested in him." Frank had an odd little half-smile on his face now.

"Well, things aren't always what they seem." She wasn't sure why she was defending Beatrice, but something about Frank's innuendoes was spurring her on.

"I'm just saying people were talking about them," he said evenly. "And you know the old saying, right? Where there's smoke there's fire." He looked like he was enjoying the conversation. "I also noticed you were kind of chummy with him too."

"We were friends—that's all." She could feel perspiration beginning to soak her blouse. "I can't talk any more, Frank. It's broiling hot out here."

"Well, I gotta get back to work anyway." He started walking toward his car, but then turned around suddenly. "I heard about how he was killed—poisoned and all." He grimaced. "Pretty painful way to die, isn't it?" Then he delivered his parting shot. "Someone must have really hated him to do something like that."

She stood there watching him get into his car. Once he'd driven off, she hurried inside the house, bolting the door behind her. She poured a glass of iced tea and took a seat on the couch next to the sleeping Tubs, who immediately began purring when he sensed her presence. As she sipped the tea, she remembered Tony's warnings about Frank.

Did Frank believe that she and Augustine were having a relationship? And could Frank have been crazy enough—and mean enough—to have killed Augustine out of jealousy? Frank was doing work at the rectory, and he could have easily gotten into the kitchen. Then she remembered the day when Frank had seen the Frangelico that had fallen out of the grocery bag. That meant he knew Augustine drank that liqueur. But would Frank have been vicious enough to poison something the priests might also have drunk?

A voice in her head began answering her questions. Tony had mentioned that Frank could still be on drugs. If so, Frank wouldn't be acting completely rationally—and he could be capable of just about anything, including murder. And if he had killed once, he could do it again. The thought made her shiver, despite the heat.

CHAPTER 8

"Well, I just don't think we need those godforsaken cantors perched right up there on the altar." The man on the other end of the line was definitely riled up, and Francesca was doing her best to listen. It was early the next morning, and she was at St. Rita's with Mo-Mo. The little girl was seated on her lap, drawing a blob that she called a dog.

Francesca shared the caller's opinion about cantors, but Father Bunt had been reluctant to send them packing once the liturgist had hired them. Even after the man's death, Father Bunt claimed he didn't want to rock the boat—at least not yet. His plan, as he had explained it to Francesca one day, was to let the cantors go gradually. But it was clear that some parishioners found the cantors' presence extremely annoying.

"They can't even hit the notes," the man continued bitterly. "And have you seen how the guys dress? I mean, blue jeans and T-shirts and sandals! They look like they're performing at a rock concert."

"You dope!" Mo-Mo yelled into the phone.

"What do you mean?" the man asked angrily.

"Oh, sorry, that's my little niece," Francesca explained. Doris had told her that some older kid in the neighborhood had taught the child that unfortunate word.

"Uh, Father Bunt isn't in right now," she added, "but I'll have him call you."

When the phone lines were quiet, Francesca unearthed her notebook from her purse. She wanted some time to string together some of her thoughts about the murder investigation.

"Cookie!" Mo-Mo pleaded, and Francesca sighed.

Doris had dropped the child off that morning on her way to another job interview. The little girl, wearing a pink ruffled dress with a large polka-dotted ribbon affixed to her hair, looked like one of those angelic tykes in a commercial for fabric softener. But Mo-Mo was a force to be reckoned with, as Francesca well knew.

Doris had apparently been up most of the night before trying to wean Mo-Mo from the pacifier. "It's an ongoing battle," she had confessed wearily, "and so far, I think I'm losing."

Of course what Doris didn't know was that Francesca had an emergency pacifier with her, which she didn't plan to toss out until Mo-Mo was truly broken of the addiction. Now the child gazed at her with a longing expression and a slightly trembling lower lip.

Francesca rooted around in her desk for a package of animal crackers and gave them to the little girl, who toddled off happily to a small pile of books on the floor.

Francesca studied her list. She still had Frank on her list of suspects, but something was niggling at her. Mrs. Greenstone had mentioned that the police suspected the killer was a woman because of Father William's report about hearing laughter.

Maybe my suspicions about Frank are completely unfounded, Francesca thought.

At that moment, Beatrice walked in. She wasn't wearing any make-up or her usual elaborate and revealing outfits. Instead, she seemed to be dressed in her version of mourning garb, old jeans and a faded blouse. Francesca felt her heart going out to the girl, whose puffy eyes showed signs of weeping.

"Have you seen granny?" Beatrice asked listlessly.

"Not this morning, no. She might be out grocery shopping." Francesca knew this was her chance to get the girl alone and have a talk.

"Why don't we go out and grab a cup of coffee?" She hoped her voice had just the right upbeat spontaneous ring to it.

Beatrice nodded glumly. "Sure, why not? I'm supposed to help granny, but if she's not here yet, it won't matter."

Francesca quickly put the phones on voice mail and grabbed her purse. "Come on, my car is just outside."

Then, as they were headed toward the front door, she remembered Mo-Mo.

"Uh, just a second," she said.

She went over to the corner where the little girl was tearing pages out of a coloring book.

"Let's go for a ride, Mo-Mo."

The child trundled eagerly toward her, and Francesca scooped her up. A few moments later, the threesome arrived at The Coffee Roasters on North Druid Hills Road, which today was filled with the acrid aroma of freshly ground beans. There was only one other customer, a college-aged girl with a shaven head, who was staring blankly at a laptop computer screen at a back table. The blackboard was covered with the names of various exotic coffees from all over the world.

"What looks good to you?" Francesca asked Beatrice.

"I don't care," the girl shrugged. "It's all the same to me." But then she added: "I'll take some biscotti too."

Francesca paid for two regular coffees and biscotti, plus a cup of milk and a sugar cookie for Mo-Mo. Then they found a table near the front window, where Francesca carefully strapped Mo-Mo into a booster seat.

"How are you doing, Beatrice? I mean, I know you've been through a lot." Francesca took a tentative sip of the steaming coffee.

"Yeah, you can say that again." Beatrice's tone was bitter. "Bad enough that Augustine is gone—but to have the police think I was the one who killed him!" She took a deep breath as if willing herself not to cry, but her lips were trembling. "See, what they don't understand, what no one understands, is that I really loved the guy."

Beatrice broke one of the biscotti into little pieces as she talked. "I knew what people were saying, believe me. You know, he was studying to be a priest, and they looked at me and all they saw were tattoos and mini-skirts. And they jumped to the conclusion that all I wanted to do was seduce the poor guy." She picked up a morsel of biscotti and put it absently into her mouth.

"It must have been really tough," Francesca murmured, while simultaneously helping Mo-Mo to a sip of milk.

"I'll say it was. See, it wasn't like that at all. I wasn't trying to seduce him. I really loved him."

"I see." Francesca hoped her tone was neutral.

"But he wasn't interested," Beatrice explained. "He really wanted to become a priest, you know, go the whole celibate route and all." She took a big gulp of coffee and started coughing. When she could talk again, she added: "I thought he was nuts and I told him so. I mean, why would he give up the chance to, you know, get married and have kids and all?"

As if on cue, Mo-Mo knocked over the cup of milk, sending a white flood across the table directly toward Beatrice. As it hit her lap, Beatrice jumped up.

"Oh, crap!" Giving the child an exasperated look, Beatrice grabbed a cluster of napkins and began mopping up the mess.

"Cwap!" the child repeated, and Francesca cringed as she imagined Doris's reaction to Mo- Mo's newest vocabulary word.

"Did you talk about, you know, the two of you, and marriage and kids and all that?' Francesca asked, once order was restored.

"Not really." She looked uncomfortable. "But I dropped some pretty big hints."

Francesca decided not to pursue the topic. It seemed too painful right now.

"Were you, uh, angry with him?" Francesca asked.

"Yeah, because I thought we were perfect for each other. But he had this thing about some higher purpose or something." She went on: "And here's something else no one knows, not even granny."

"Yes?"

"Well, he gave me some books, you know, on becoming Catholic. See, I was never baptized—and he, well, he wanted me to know about, you know, Christ and all."

"But why not tell your grandmother?"

"I don't want her pushing me into going to church with her. With him, it was different. He just wanted me to know about things. He wasn't like some door-to-door evangelist, all in your face."

Francesca pondered this new piece of information. If his intentions had been to instruct Beatrice in the faith that would certainly explain the attention he was showing her. And if Beatrice had misread his intentions that would account for her disappointment—and her anger—when she realized he wasn't interested in her romantically.

But had Beatrice been angry enough to kill Augustine? Almost as if Beatrice was reading Francesca's thoughts, she said passionately: "OK, I was disappointed that he didn't want me. Especially that night when I went to his room and he—well, he let me in for a few minutes—but he didn't want to drink or party or anything. He called a taxi to take me home because I was, well, I'd had a few, you know, and he cared about me—as a friend. I wanted more than that—but I would never, *ever*, in a million years do something like that to him—or to anyone! I mean, putting poison in his booze." She shuddered.

"It makes me sick to think about it." Beatrice pushed the plate of biscotti away from her as if she couldn't bear to see it. Then she pulled a Kleenex from her purse and held it against her streaming eyes.

"Boo Boo?" Mo-Mo's eyes were growing large with distress.

"It's OK, Mo-Mo," Francesca said gently. Then she touched Beatrice's hand. "I'm sorry. This has to be a really bad time for you. Your grandmother told me about the police and..."

But Beatrice broke in. "Yeah, the police, they decided I'm guilty just because I spent some time with him, and because of all the rumors, you know, how I was trying to seduce him and all."

She looked around as if checking to make sure the girl behind the counter wasn't listening. "And because of that letter they found in his room."

"Oh?" Francesca pretended she'd never heard of the letter before.

"Yeah, I wrote him a pretty angry letter. But how could I know what would happen? How could I know the police would find it? And how could I know it would make me look guilty?"

Beatrice glanced around again and then lowered her volume. "OK, I'll admit I sort of threatened him, but it wasn't serious. I just wanted him to know I was mad, that's all."

"Did he respond to the letter?"

She shook her head mournfully. "No, he never had a chance to." Beatrice now stared out the window as she talked. "He was writing this book, you know, a kind of novel, but he never did let me read it. Then, just a few days before—well, before he died, he told me he planned to destroy it."

"Destroy it, but why?" Francesca released the fidgety Mo-Mo from the booster seat, and the child made a beeline for the display of packaged coffees and cookies.

"Well, he told me he decided writing wasn't his calling," Beatrice said. "He changed his mind. I think at first he thought he could do both—writing and being a priest and all. But then he told me he didn't want anything to distract him from...from being a priest." She uttered the word with a certain degree of sarcasm. "So I guess that meant no women and..."

"NO COOKIES!" Francesca said sharply.

"Huh?"

"Just talking to Mo-Mo." Francesca jumped up and hurried to the display where the child was trying to pry open a box of cookies. She returned order to the jumbled boxes and then gently led the child back to the table.

"Sorry—what were you saying?" Francesca asked.

"No women and no bestsellers," Beatrice replied glumly.

"So did he get rid of the book?" Francesca asked, settling Mo-Mo on her lap.

"I think he was going to, but didn't get a chance to." Beatrice absently rubbed her neck, and Francesca watched in fascination as the serpent tattoo moved. "See, the police mentioned the book, so I think it was still on his computer."

There was something about Beatrice's demeanor that made Francesca feel very strongly that the girl was innocent. Beatrice was obviously upset about Augustine's death and horrified by the whole idea of using poison. Still, Francesca also knew that her gut instincts sometimes failed her miserably.

"Nake!" Mo-Mo was gesturing excitedly at Beatrice's neck.

"What does she want now?" Beatrice's tone was annoyed.

"Uh, I think she's trying to say 'snake.' She must be, uh, admiring your, uh, tattoo."

Beatrice brightened. "Someday, Mo-Mo, *you* can have a snake tattoo also!"

"Nake tattoo?" the child said.

Lord, Doris is going to have a fit, Francesca thought, if the kid goes home talking about tattoos.

"Look, Beatrice, I'd like to help you, but I can't do that unless you can give me some leads. I mean, do you have any idea who the murderer could be?"

Beatrice studied her long fingernails, which today were completely free of polish. "Well, not granny, I know that much. She's a big grouch, but she'd never hurt anyone. But she did tell me something. She thought Father Bunt and maybe Father William had seen the manuscript—and there was some stuff in there that wasn't too complimentary. I mean, it wasn't really about them, but anyone reading it might get the wrong idea."

"You're not suggesting the priests might have…?" Francesca let the sentence trail off because the very thought of completing it gave her a queasy feeling.

"I'm just saying that could be their motive, to stop him from writing more of the book."

"But it was just fiction, and if they weren't doing anything wrong, why would they care about the book?"

Beatrice shrugged. "Well, maybe he touched a nerve."

***

The next day, Francesca decided to drive by Augustine's parents' home in Avondale Estates. Climbing into the car, she noticed a pile of cookie crumbs on the back seat and had a vivid image of Mo-Mo. She had dropped the child off at Doris' yesterday, and as she'd turned to leave, had heard her cry out, "Nake tatoo!" Fortunately, Francesca had slipped away before Doris had requested a translation.

Francesca wasn't quite sure what she was looking for, but thought she might pick up a clue or two. Maybe a gardener would be outside and she could ask a few questions. Or maybe you've seen too many crime shows, that annoying voice in her head replied.

She drove slowly by the house and then parked down the block. She walked down the street and glanced surreptitiously at the house, hoping that if anyone happened to be looking out the windows they wouldn't think she was acting suspiciously.

She knew his father was a doctor, but she was surprised nonetheless by the opulent home. It was a stately two-story white brick house with generous peaks and dormer windows. It rested regally on a lush swath of acreage situated on the lake. The lawn was manicured to perfection with each strand of grass a vivid shade of emerald green and trimmed to a uniform height. The flocks of orange and yellow roses looked almost fluorescent in the sunshine, and glowed with health.

She couldn't help but reflect that her rose bushes recently had been shredded by a hungry horde of green caterpillars. They had persisted despite her attempts to dissuade them, and sometimes, when she was in the yard, she imagined that the diabolical insects were laughing at her. She wondered if caterpillars entirely bypassed the roses of rich people.

Lost in thought, Francesca wandered around the lake, enjoying the sight of ducks and geese, and reveling in the silence. She found a bench where she could pretend to be writing a letter while she glanced now and again at the house. She wasn't sure what she was looking for, but she had learned from Tony that it was smart to follow a hunch and see where it might lead.

She took out her notepad and jotted down some notes by Beatrice's name. A few minutes later, she looked over at the house and saw the door opening. Out stepped a fiftyish, heavy-set woman who might have been the maid judging by the dust mop she was wielding. She seemed to be saying goodbye to a much younger woman, who was wearing a pale-blue sundress. As the younger woman climbed down the stairs and came into better focus, Francesca was so startled that she dropped her notepad. It was the woman from the photo!

***

Father Bunt poured a second cup of coffee, enjoying the morning solitude. Mrs. Greenstone had called in sick with a summer cold, so breakfast would be toast and cold cereal. Still, it was nice to wander around in his bathrobe for awhile and not have to make conversation. As a wisp of light trickled into the kitchen, a Carolina wren began trumpeting its wake-up song in the yard. As Father Bunt picked up his prayer book and began reading morning prayers from the Liturgy of the Hours, Father William wandered into the kitchen.

"Good morning!" Father William said cheerily, heading to the coffee pot. "Oh, sorry, I didn't realize you were praying. But before I forget, I have something for you from Anastasia Hartwell." He fished around in his pocket and extracted a crumpled envelope. "Bless her heart; she seems to think she has to give a donation every time I visit these days." He handed the envelope to Father Bunt. "I told her there's no need, but…"

"There's twenty dollars in here," Father Bunt noted. "That's pretty steep for her, isn't it?"

"Well, she wants it donated for Masses to be said in Augustine's memory." Father William was now rummaging in the cookie jar. "She was pretty upset when I told her about what happened," he added, taking a seat at the table. "She really liked him."

"Yeah, it's terrible," Father Bunt acknowledged.

"Are there any leads?" Father William crunched loudly into an oatmeal cookie.

"Not really. All I know is they're looking at Beatrice."

"I guess that's because I heard her laughing that day downstairs," Father William said. "But what I don't get is this: Who was she laughing with—or at? I mean, she didn't seem like the type to talk to herself."

"Well, she could have been on her cell phone."

"Oh, yeah, that's true. But the fact that she was laughing...I mean if she is the one who"—and here he shuddered—"did the awful deed, well, that makes the whole thing really macabre."

Father Bunt nodded. He had to admit it didn't sound pretty.

"So is that the main reason the police are looking at her? The laughing?" Father William asked.

"That's partly it. But, well, there were also some rumors of romantic entanglements, and you know that can be a pretty strong motive—I mean, if things go sour." Father Bunt glanced at his watch now, mentally calculating how long showering and dressing would take.

"Yes, but if that's the case," Father William replied, getting up to snag another cookie, "why haven't they arrested her?"

"Not enough evidence right now. They've told her not to leave town, though, and are keeping an eye on her."

Father William looked thoughtfully at his coffee cup before phrasing the next question. "You used the plural— entanglements. Were there other women?"

Father Bunt thought about the parish directory. Should he bring it up? He didn't want to cast more doubt on the dead man, who couldn't defend himself. At that precise moment Dopey—who was in the yard—offered a welcome distraction by scratching enthusiastically at the kitchen door and emitting a plaintive howling sound.

"Uh, that's uncertain," Father Bunt murmured diplomatically, as he got up to open the door. Dopey made a beeline for the food dish and looked at him accusingly.

Father William absently snapped a cookie in two. "Maybe romance has nothing to do with this situation at all. I mean, Augustine did have quite a sense of humor and liked to play tricks on people. Maybe he really angered someone with one of his jokes."

"That's possible," Father Bunt agreed as he obediently fetched a can of dog food from the pantry. "But that kind of opens it up to just about anyone he came in contact with, unfortunately. Besides, who would kill someone just because he made a joke about them?"

The two men sighed in unison.

***

It was nearly 10:30 and Francesca was wondering where Mauve was. Today was Thursday, Mauve's usual day to volunteer, but so far there was no sign of her. Francesca knew she could handle the bulletins without Mauve's help, but she was eager to ask her a few questions.

She certainly didn't want Mauve to think she suspected her of involvement with Augustine's death, but she was curious about Mauve's whereabouts on the day he was poisoned. After all, if Francesca was going to "play detective," as Tony often accused her of doing, she wanted to be thorough, and if that meant questioning a Choir Chick, so be it.

She yawned. She knew that at any moment the phones would start ringing, and then it would be impossible to do anything else. She had been relieved when Doris had changed her mind about dropping Mo-Mo off earlier, but now she rather missed the child. There was never a dull moment, Francesca thought, when you had a two-year-old around. As she began collating the bulletin pages, she heard someone stirring in the foyer.

She looked up expecting to see Mauve, but instead it was her son, Brad. He didn't look especially cheery, she noticed, but he seemed to be one of those teenagers who were plagued by perpetual moodiness. Now he stood in front of her desk, chewing his lips.

"Brad, how are you today?" She put an extra dollop of cheeriness into her voice, hoping to dispel the dark cloud hanging over him.

"Great," he said with as much enthusiasm as someone who'd just been diagnosed with swine flu. Then he snuffled loudly before continuing: "Well, my mom, she's got a cold, so she sent me over to, you know, help with the stuff she does over here."

"I'm sorry to hear that, but thanks for coming over. I can sure use an extra set of hands." She stood up and picked up the stack of bulletins. "I'll set you up in another office and show you what to do, OK?"

"Whatever." He shrugged and followed her.

After she handed him the bulletins and the inserts, she turned to leave the room. "Look, before you go," he said, clearing his throat, "there's something I was wondering about. It's about that...you know, that guy, the one that...the one that died."

"Augustine?"

"Yeah, him." He picked up a paper clip and fidgeted nervously with it. "So do they know who did it? The police, I mean."

"From what I've heard, there are some suspects, some leads, but nothing definite yet." She wondered where this conversation was going.

Now he picked up one of the bulletins and creased the corner absent-mindedly. "Yeah, well, I just wanted to know, see, because with my mom working here, I didn't want her to be around any kind of, well, you know, murderers or anything."

It was rather endearing to see how concerned the boy was about his mother, she thought. "Look, Brad, there's no need to worry. It seems that this case, well, it looks like whoever did it had some sort of specific grudge against Augustine. It's not like there's a serial killer on the loose." She gave him an encouraging smile.

His gloomy expression didn't change, however. "Whatever," he shrugged.

Suddenly the door to the little office shot open and in lumbered Dopey.

"W-w-woof!" the dog barked and wagged his tail so hard that his body was nearly bent in two. Brad's expression brightened as he bent down to pet the dog.

"I guess you've met Dopey before." Francesca smiled at the boy's enthusiasm.

"Yeah, my mom introduced us." He kept petting Dopey, evidently oblivious to the tufts of fur the dog was depositing on his jeans.

"So you've been here before?"

"Yeah, what about it?" Brad's smile vanished and he suddenly drew back from the dog.

"Nothing, I was just curious." She hesitated for a second at the door. "Call me if you need anything."

Once back at her desk, she sat quietly for a few moments. Why had he reacted that way? It was almost as if he felt guilty about having been at the rectory before.

CHAPTER 9

Detective Ryan Baker sat at his desk in the Decatur Police Station. The surface was laden with Snickers bar wrappers, empty bags of potato chips, and crumpled plastic cups. He was eating a jelly donut from a grease-stained bag and sipping a cup of bitter black coffee that he had poured from the communal pot. People at the station took turns making the coffee, but it always came out tasting like mud, he thought.

As he ate, he was reading over his notes on the Hornsby case, spilling crumbs onto the pages. After a few moments, he dug through his desk drawer and extracted a thick sheaf of paper. He licked his fingers and thumbed through the pages, leaving a few grease stains here and there, and chuckling every so often.

"*The Secret Diary of a Seminarian*," he muttered to himself. "What a title."

The document was filled with humorous descriptions of characters that Baker figured were dead ringers for the priests and staff over at the church, so he circled sections as he read. Then he picked up the phone and called Father Bunt, making an appointment to see him later that day.

Baker arrived at 1:30, having stopped at the Chicken Barn for lunch. As he stood outside St. Rita's rectory, ringing the bell, he brushed crumbs of fried-chicken breading from his shirt. His doctor had told him to cut down on fatty foods, but in his line of work, that was impossible. He couldn't afford to go to some fancy place in downtown Decatur and shell out ten bucks on a salad. Besides, he was a meat-and-potatoes kind of guy, not to mention chicken and fries.

The door opened and it was that girl, the one Tony was dating. That guy has all the luck; she's really hot, he thought. But he could tell by her expression that she wasn't thrilled to see him.

"Oh, yes, Detective Ryan." She frowned a little. "Come in."

"Yeah, I'm back," he grinned. "Must be your lucky day, huh?"

She smiled weakly at him. "Father Bunt should be down in a second. He's expecting you."

Baker stood in the foyer, rummaging in his pockets for a toothpick. He found one and probed his teeth with it, and then left it dangling from his mouth. As he was checking his phone for messages, Father Bunt came down the stairs.

"Oh, Detective Baker, how are you?"

"Not bad, Father. I found something pretty interesting when I was looking at Hornsby's computer the other day."

"Well, come on up to my office and we'll talk," the priest said, starting up the stairs.

Once they were seated, Baker launched into his report. "Yeah, I found something called, let's see what was it? Oh, yeah, *The Secret Diary of a Seminarian*; that was it. You ever heard of it?"

"Yes, I, uh, I was aware that Augustine was, uh, writing something with that title." The priest looked as if he'd bitten into a sour apple.

Baker threw the toothpick into a nearby trash can, then pulled out a stick of gum, removed the wrapper, and crammed the gum into his mouth. "Did you read it?"

"Ah, yes, I did read a few sections of it, not that much, but just a little." Father Bunt paused. "Uh, why do you ask?"

"Well, it's just that anyone who read this thing might get the wrong impression about what's going on here at St. Rita's." Baker watched the pastor's face closely. He wondered why the man looked so uncomfortable. Did he have something to hide?

"What do you mean?"

"Well, I don't know how far you read, but he's got characters that sound real close to the folks who work here. There's a Mrs. Mean Bone, a Father Dunce, and a Father Porkland. You get my drift?"

"Not exactly," the pastor replied huffily. "I mean, the thing is obviously some kind of satire."

"Well, call it what you will, but here's the thing: Depending on who else read this, we might uncover a motive for the killing. What I mean is, well, it's not exactly a rosy picture of the parish."

Baker added another stick of gum to the wad in his mouth. "So do you know who else read it?"

The pastor picked up a pencil and turned it over in his hands as if it were a foreign object he'd never seen before. "Well, I believe Mrs. Greenstone—I believe she might have read parts of it."

"What about her granddaughter?" Baker licked the tip of his pencil in anticipation of the reply.

"I don't know. It's possible that she did too. But, detective, even if we assume someone killed him because of this...this manuscript, it would still exist—and it could still be published, right? So how would that solve anything?"

"Well, his death made it less likely it would ever get published, see, because he'd never get a chance to finish it," Baker said. "So I'm thinking that whoever killed him wanted him to stop writing the thing. Maybe they even threatened him about it, you know, to get him to stop. You know anything about that?"

"No, he didn't say a word about threats," Father Bunt said quietly.

Baker made a smacking noise with the gum. "Of course, that doesn't mean there weren't some—threats, I mean. He might have kept them to himself."

Baker continued: "He was already on chapter fifteen, and his outline—which I also found on the computer—suggests he was planning on about twenty chapters. So he was getting near the end, and it's possible someone knew that, and was getting nervous about the thing being published."

The detective tossed the gum into a nearby trash can. "If this thing ever got published, it could cause quite a stir, if you catch my drift."

The priest looked like he had indigestion. "Yes, I get it."

"One thing I found real interesting," Baker continued, "is the way the pastor, this Father Dunce, was stealing from the collections. He also was the one who took the money from the cash box at a big church supper." Baker flicked a speck of something off his trousers. "Maybe that's supposed to be the masquerade thing, huh?"

"It was fiction, for heaven's sake," Father Bunt exclaimed angrily.

"Well, I'm certainly no judge of fiction or whatever, but it sounds to me more like a real diary, you know, with real stuff happening, and just the names changed." Baker probed his ear with his pencil eraser as he talked. He was rather enjoying baiting the pastor.

The priest's face reddened. "You're not suggesting that I...that I had anything to do with the theft, are you?"

"I'm just saying this manuscript has quite a few smoking guns in it."

***

After Baker had gone, Father Bunt retreated miserably to the sitting room. He was starting to wonder if Baker suspected him not only of the theft but the murder as well. But surely the detective had checked out his alibi for the murder by now, and knew that he and Father William had been out that night. He put his head in his hands. Yes, they had an alibi for that night, but they'd both been home that afternoon, which meant the detective could still suspect one of them had doctored the bottle.

To make matters even worse, Father Bunt hated the thought that the manuscript could eventually leak out—and people would be sure to confuse fact with fiction when they read it. After all, who looked worse in the book than the incompetent pastor?

Francesca stepped into the room. "Father, I hate to disturb you, but there's a lady—Regina Watson—on the phone and she's pretty upset. It's about her wedding."

What now? What new catastrophe is bubbling up? He wondered. "Of course, put her through. I'll take the call here."

"This is Father Bunt," he said hopefully into the phone. "How are you, Regina?"

"Not so great, Father, to tell you the truth." The voice was shrill. "I'm sure you remember me. I came by about a month ago to talk with you about my wedding, which is going to be in six months. "

"Sure, I remember. What's the problem?" He massaged his left temple as he talked.

"Well, Father, I talked to the wedding coordinator about this, and she thought I needed to talk to you directly. It's about someone I want to be in the wedding."

"Yes—and who would that be?" He hoped it wouldn't be a two-year old flower girl, as the last one had pitched a fit halfway down the aisle and subsequently thrown the flowers at an usher.

"It's my dog, Barney. I want him to be the flower boy."

Oh, God! It's worse than I imagined, he thought.

"Your, uh, your dog, did you say?" He knew he'd heard her correctly, but was stalling for time as he phrased a response.

"Yes, he's very well behaved, you see," she enthused. "He's a dachshund, and I even have this wonderful little tux he can wear."

"A tux?" He echoed incredulously.

"Yes, it's just darling! But the wedding coordinator, Bobbie, she thought a dog was...well, Father, she said it would never do, that animals aren't allowed in weddings." The woman's tone of voice suggested she'd been the victim of a grave injustice.

"Well, I'm afraid that's exactly right," he said, bracing himself for her response.

"But, Father, he's part of the family!"

"Uh, well, you could certainly include him in the, uh, the reception in some way, but I'm afraid the church...well, you see, marriage is a sacrament, and we have to maintain the dignity of..."

She cut him off. "Father, he's very well-behaved. He won't harm the...the dignity of anything!"

"It's not possible," he said quietly. He could feel a headache gaining steam.

"But, but, it's *my* wedding, isn't it?"

She reminded him of a toddler who'd just been denied a toy. "Of course it is, but you see, a wedding is not a social event, like, say the party afterwards. We have to maintain the sanctity of..."

But once again she interrupted him: "Father, I'll bring him by. Once you meet him, I know you'll change your mind."

"No, that really isn't..." But it was too late. She had hung up.

***

Francesca had a plan. She was going to meet the mystery woman one way or another. Since the family belonged to St. Rita's parish, Francesca decided she'd swing by the house on the pretense of conducting a survey. The little voice in her head, which she was fairly sure was her conscience, was whispering that she shouldn't do something that deceitful, and there were surely other, more honest ways of meeting the woman. But Francesca also knew time was of the essence.

Tony had told her more than once that when homicide investigators dawdled too long they often discovered their prime suspects had either left town or assumed a new identity, or both. And even though she could just imagine what Tony would say to her—"Francesca, you're not a member of the police force!"—she decided a few simple questions couldn't hurt anything.

Besides, she would go in broad daylight, and there would be no danger. She heard her mother's voice in her head protesting, "There's *always* danger, day or night," but she ignored it.

Francesca quickly drew up a list of questions on the computer and printed them out. She planned to ask some general questions about how often the family participated in social events at the parish. She hated to interrupt the family, who surely were still in the throes of shock and grief over their son's death, but she knew they wanted to find the killer, and she was just trying to help.

She dressed in tailored beige slacks and a carefully pressed white blouse, plus a new pair of strappy high-heel sandals. She hadn't worn heels in a long time, and as she was leaving the house, she wondered if she'd made the right decision. She was wobbling considerably and felt like she was on stilts. As she backed out of the driveway, she wondered how women in the movies managed to outrun villains, climb fences, and even engage in hand-to-hand combat while wearing heels much higher than hers. As for her, she found it difficult to hit the brake while wearing these particular shoes, so at the end of the block she pulled over, removed the shoes, and drove the rest of the way bare-footed.

It was about 10 a.m. when she arrived at the Hornsby residence. She parked nearby, slipped her feet into the sandals, and wobbled her way to the house, mentally decrying the uneven sidewalks. When she arrived at the front door, she was just about to ring the bell when the door opened. There stood a gray-haired woman with a frosty expression.

"Yes, may I help you?" The woman glanced darkly at the clipboard Francesca was carrying.

"I'm Francesca Bibbo from St. Rita's church. We're conducting a survey of parishioners about various social events at the parish."

"Oh?"

"I just wondered if I might talk with some of the...the Hornsby family." Francesca felt her resolve wavering as she stood there.

"I'm afraid that really isn't possible." The woman started to close the door. "No one is home right now."

But at that precise moment, Francesca heard someone behind the woman saying, "Who is it, Yvonne?" Then the woman turned around and spoke to whoever it was. A few seconds later, the door opened wide.

Yvonne cast Francesca a thoroughly sour look, as if to say, "This isn't something I approve of," but she let Francesca into the foyer. And there, standing right behind the woman, was none other than the mystery lady from the photo.

***

Father William stepped into the sitting room. "Well, I'm off to Eternal Sunrise," he announced to Father Bunt. Then he stopped in his tracks. "Are you alright? You look a little...well distraught I guess is the word."

"Come on in and sit down for a minute, William, and I'll fill you in on the latest about the case."

The young priest looked troubled. "Not more bad news, I hope?"

"It's just that I'm starting to think Detective Baker thinks I'm responsible for some, if not all, of the criminal activity at the parish."

"You! Of all people, Father, you'd be the last person..."

Father Bunt interrupted him. "I appreciate the support, I really do, but until we find out who took the money, Baker is going to have me first on the list of suspects. As for the murder, I wouldn't be surprised if he thought I had a motive for that as well."

"But what motive could you possibly have?"

It was then that Father Bunt told William about the seminarian's manuscript. When he heard the name "William Porkland," the young priest's eyes widened.

"What did he say about this person?"

Father Bunt looked at the floor. "Well, it seems this Porkland character was secretly stealing jewelry from old ladies at the various rest homes he visited."

Father William's face grew ruddy and he stood up suddenly, clenching his fists. "That son of a...that's disgusting! If I'd known about that, I would have..."

"Would have what?" Father Bunt asked evenly.

Father William made an effort to compose himself. "I'm sorry, Father, I can't stand that Augustine would even *think* that about me. I mean, I know it was fiction, but if it had been published..."

"Yes, I know what you mean," Father Bunt nodded. "People would have been quick to think the worst."

"But he seemed sincere about wanting to become a priest. So why would he be writing something like that?"

"Well, writing a book isn't against any regulations, you know. It's something a priest can certainly do in his spare time. You remember St. Augustine and his *Confessions*, right?"

"Yes, of course, but he was confessing his own wrongdoings, not...not casting aspersions on other people!"

"Things have changed, William—to put it mildly! Today a book like St. Augustine's wouldn't raise an eyebrow, but in his day it was quite shocking. So I guess our own Augustine was just keeping up with the times."

***

The woman extended her hand to Francesca and smiled. "I'm Susannah Hornsby. And I understand you're from the parish? Please, come in and sit down."

Francesca was eager to find out how the woman was related to Augustine, but she knew she had to bide her time. After introducing herself, she followed Susannah into a living room appointed with very expensive-looking plush chairs and a few glossy, solid-looking end tables.

There were colorful, plush Oriental rugs positioned here and there on the gleaming hardwood floors, sparkling vases of freshly cut roses, and a huge cluster of greeting cards on the mantel, which Francesca figured could be sympathy cards.

Susannah indicated that Francesca should sit down on the couch and then positioned herself on a chair nearby. Francesca took a seat, trying not to make mental comparisons between her own, quite elderly couch at home, liberally decorated with cat fur, and this rather pristine and posh model, reminiscent of the ones gracing the pages of home-beautiful magazines.

"Would you like tea or coffee, or perhaps a glass of mineral water?" Susannah's glossy lips parted, revealing perfectly aligned, snowy white teeth.

"Tea would be lovely." Francesca returned the smile, hoping there wasn't lipstick on her own teeth.

Her hostess simply glanced at Yvonne who was hovering nearby, and the woman scurried away. Then Susannah turned her attention back to Francesca.

"Well, how can I help you?" As Susannah spoke, she clasped her hands lightly in her lap, and a sunbeam bounced off a pricey-looking gold bracelet.

"Uh, it's just a survey we're doing. We're trying to figure out ways to increase attendance at social events." Francesca could feel her heart rate accelerating ever so slightly as it usually did when she lied.

"Oh, so Father Bunt wants to find out what people like and don't like, is that it?" Susannah straightened up in her chair like a schoolgirl waiting for the first word in a spelling bee.

Francesca felt a definite stab from her conscience. She hoped Susannah wasn't chummy with the pastor. *What if she tells him about my visit? Why didn't I think of that?*

"Yes, that's right." Francesca opened her purse to extract a pen, just as the maid re-entered the room carrying an elaborately carved dark wood tray upon which rested a china teapot

178

embossed with tiny violets, along with matching cups, creamer, and sugar bowl. After placing the tray on the nearby coffee table, the maid handed each woman a thick cloth napkin edged in frothy white lace. Francesca unfurled the napkin and placed it in her lap while eyeing a platter of cookies that the maid had also delivered.

"Please, help yourself to a cookie while the tea steeps," Susannah said. "They were just baked this morning."

Francesca smiled and reached for a cookie, but just as her fingers touched the crunchy surface of what looked like a ginger snap, she felt something cold and wet bump against her ankle. Startled, she jumped and the cookie fell from her hand. Looking down, she saw a West Highland terrier with shoe-button brown eyes and a rapidly wagging tail. The cookie disappeared quickly into its mouth.

"Terribly sorry," Susannah laughed. "That's Benedict, our resident cookie thief. He has a habit of sneaking into rooms very quietly and scaring the daylights out of guests."

Francesca leaned down to pet the dog. "He's very cute."

"He belonged to my brother, but he, uh, left him with me." Susannah's smile faded.

"Your brother?" Francesca asked, her curiosity definitely piqued now.

"Yes, I'm sure you heard about Augustine." Now Susannah picked up her napkin and brought it to her eyes. She sniffed delicately. "He recently...he passed away just a few weeks ago."

"Oh, yes, I knew Augustine," Francesca said. "I'm so *very* sorry for your loss."

Susannah nodded slightly and placed the napkin back on her lap. "Of course, you would know him, since you work over at the church." She heaved a deep sigh. "We just—my parents and I—we don't know how something so terrible could have happened. I mean, everyone just loved him so much."

"Growing up, we were like cats and dogs," she continued as she poured them both a cup of tea. "There was a lot of jealousy, if you know what I mean. But once we were grown, we became good friends." She put cream in her tea and stirred it with a small silver spoon, but instead of drinking it, she picked up the dog and settled him on her lap.

"It's hard to believe my brother's gone." She stroked the dog with pale hands tipped with glossy pink nails that looked expertly manicured.

Francesca didn't know what to say at this point. Somehow the whole idea of the survey seemed ridiculous. But at least she had uncovered one vital piece of information about the woman's identity.

Susannah suddenly stopped petting the dog. "Well, I don't want to waste your time," she said officiously. "What questions does Father Bunt have for us?"

"Well, let's see, the first one is about how often your family has attended social events at the parish in the past year." Francesca looked at Susannah with what she hoped was an expression of intense interest.

"Hmmm, I would say, oh, gosh, I guess if you count the Lenten fish suppers, probably five times."

Francesca retrieved her notebook from her purse and jotted down some notes before taking a long sip of tea. It was delicious, with a slightly smoky flavor, and much better than what she brewed at home.

"Uh, let's see, do you have any suggestions about what we might do in the future to, you know, improve events?" Francesca picked up a second cookie from the tray.

Susannah's expression changed as she suddenly put the dog back on the floor. There was a scuffling sound on the hardwood floor as the animal positioned itself nearby.

"Look, I know you're not here to do a survey." The woman's voice now had a decidedly unfriendly tone.

"What do you mean?" Francesca felt her stomach lurch. I'm such a fool. Why did I think I could pull this off?

CHAPTER 10

Mrs. Greenstone pushed her cart dismally through the Publix grocery store on North Decatur Road. She liked shopping here because the store was relatively small and didn't have ridiculous features that so many other stores had these days.

There was a blessed absence of piped-in sounds of cows mooing in the dairy section, and no recordings of thunderstorms accompanying the moment when a spray of water freshened up the lettuce in the produce section. She also liked the large selection of meat substitutes and health-food items in the big refrigerated case at the front of the store. Now, however, she resolutely steered her cart toward a part of Publix that she rarely set foot in, which was the meat section.

She'd come to a decision a few days ago. It wasn't right to continue deceiving the priests when it came to food. As much as she despised the idea of cooking meat, she would learn to do it. She wasn't going to do anything to jeopardize her job now that Beatrice might need her legal help should she actually be arrested for the crime. As for deception, Mrs. Greenstone was also worried about something else. She'd told the detective she'd been in a tai chi class that day, but that wasn't the truth at all. What if he checked? How would that look?

Mrs. Greenstone had a very small amount of money stashed away for emergencies, and if she had to, she would use every cent to clear her granddaughter's name. But if she were to lose her job, her savings would vanish quickly, and she didn't want that to happen. Now she shuddered as she picked up packages of chicken, pork chops, and a roast. She felt her stomach twinge with nausea as she noticed the blood seeping out of the slabs of meat encased in plastic. Shaking her head, she tossed the packages with great resignation into the cart.

As she did so, she had a sudden image of Augustine, smiling in that smug way on the day when she was sure he had switched out her meat substitutes for the real ticket. She also remembered the terrible things he'd written about her and Beatrice in that book of his. She knew it was wrong to think bad thoughts about the dead, but she couldn't help it. She had never liked the man. He had caused her plenty of trouble, and in some ways, he still was.

***

Father Bunt glanced uneasily at his watch. The archbishop would be coming for lunch in an hour. MacPherson had called the day before to say he wanted to talk with Father Bunt about what he called the "latest goings-on" at the parish. Father Bunt could feel beads of nervous perspiration forming on his forehead. He knew exactly what that meant. The archbishop would want to know all the details of the criminal investigation at this point.

Father Bunt wondered about the menu. It seemed a very trivial matter, on the surface at least, but the fact that the cook had been dishonest about the food she was serving was just one more example of things getting out of his control. He had discovered this piece of information shortly before Augustine's death when he'd found a receipt in the kitchen from a nearby health-food store. The long list of items included tofu, soy hot dogs, soy burgers, and bacon substitutes.

The solution was obvious enough: he would sit down with her and tell her, point blank, that he knew what was going on— and he wanted *real* meat—no more of these wimpy substitutes— served at meals. If she got angry and decided to quit, then so be it. They wouldn't starve. He made a note on his calendar so he wouldn't forget to have a talk with her.

He heard the sound of toenails scraping against the floor and then the door eased open and in came Dopey. He once again needed a bath judging from his pungent aroma, but there was no time for that. The dog ambled over to him, his tongue hanging out, and sat before Father Bunt, eyeing him with what looked like canine interest. Father Bunt knew he wanted biscuits, and he also knew that somehow he always responded to the dog's demands. Even if Dopey couldn't be taught tricks, it was clear the animal had taught his master quite a few.

Now Father Bunt rummaged around in his desk drawer until he found a box of dog biscuits and gave Dopey a handful. As if requesting seconds, Dopey let out a tentative "W-w-woof" and Father Bunt smiled. He had to admit the dog was an instant mood lifter. Maybe someone should figure out a way to market dogs as antidepressants, he thought.

Father Bunt spent a half hour going over financial reports and then heard the rectory doorbell ring. He figured it was the archbishop, although the man rarely showed up early. Somehow, any change in his superior's schedule made Father Bunt apprehensive. He scrambled around his office, making sure things were in order, and then ran to the bathroom to run a comb quickly through his hair. Or what's left of it these days, he thought. Then he hurried downstairs to greet his boss, who was standing in the foyer chatting with Mrs. Greenstone. When she saw Father Bunt, she excused herself, saying she had work in the kitchen.

"Brent, how are you today?" MacPherson's face was somber.

"Just fine, sir, and you?" Father Bunt hoped his voice sounded upbeat and cheery, despite the misgivings in his heart.

"Well, the heat is oppressive these days. Doesn't look like there'll be a break any time soon."

The archbishop brushed an invisible speck off his shirt. "But imagine what it must be like for those poor folks down in South Georgia, near the swamp."

At the word "swamp," Father Bunt felt his stomach twinge uneasily. The word seemed to have an ominous ring to it. Was this just small talk, or was the archbishop hinting that he planned to transfer Father Bunt to a place that he dearly dreaded going? It wasn't just that it would be even more intolerably hot down there, but he didn't want anything to do with swamps. He knew that his father, who lived in Michigan, looked at all of Georgia as a place populated with snakes, alligators, and what he called "hillbillies."

His father was fond of telling Father Bunt jokes about the South when he called him on the phone. ("You know the *tooth*brush was invented in Georgia, because most folks there only have one tooth, ha!") But if his father ever got wind that his son was being sent to South Georgia, the jokes surely would escalate, and the underlying implication would be that Father Bunt was being severely demoted.

"Isn't hell the farthest place south you can go?" was one of his father's favorite questions. His father enjoyed pointing out that, with that logic, living in the Deep South should be avoided at all costs. Father Bunt inhaled deeply now, trying to calm his nerves. He knew his father's opinion shouldn't matter so much—after all, I'm a grown man!—but in fact, it did.

He suddenly realized the archbishop had stopped talking, as if waiting for an answer.

"What was that, sir?"

"Brent, are you with me? I just asked what the news was from the police." The archbishop's tone was exasperated. "Do they think there's a connection between the theft and the murder?"

"Oh, sorry, sir, the police report, of course. No, sir, at this point, they don't think there's a connection. They're continuing to explore leads as to the, uh, the murderer, of course. And there are no leads on the theft at all."

"Well, you have to keep on top of these things, Brent. They have plenty of other cases they're working on, and it's the squeaky wheel syndrome, you know." The archbishop sounded like a second-grade teacher explaining an obvious truth to a recalcitrant child.

"Yes, the wheel, of course," Father Bunt repeated miserably. Was his superior suggesting that he wasn't living up to his responsibilities?

Father Bunt had never been so glad to see Father William, who suddenly appeared in the foyer, greeted the archbishop, and announced that lunch was ready. As they headed into the dining room, Father Bunt felt a growing sense of uneasiness. The archbishop seemed unusually somber today. Of course, what with another criminal investigation in the archdiocese, following on the heels of the one last year, this was to be expected. But Father Bunt didn't like feeling that his superior was suggesting that he, Bunt, was somehow to blame for what was happening.

Was there some way to show the archbishop that he was a take-charge kind of man? Someone who was really on top of everything in the parish? As these thoughts were boiling up in his mind, he took his place at the table and bowed his head as the archbishop said the blessing. He was relieved to see the cook had not enlisted the services of Beatrice, since he was sure the archbishop wouldn't be keen on having a suspect in a murder investigation serving him at the table.

When Mrs. Greenstone entered the room carrying a platter of what looked like slices of roast pork, he hatched his plan. As he helped himself to what he was sure was a meat substitute—no doubt cleverly disguised to look authentic—he knew exactly what he would do.

***

Oh, Lord, she's on to me, Francesca thought nervously as Susannah positioned her teacup carefully in her saucer.

"One of our security guards saw you sitting on the bench the other day, watching the house," Susannah said. "So, tell me, what is it you *really* want?" She managed a polite smile, but Francesca detected a deadly serious glint in her eyes.

Francesca bit into another cookie to stall for time. It was clear she didn't have a promising career as an undercover police agent, so she might as well tell the truth. There was nothing to be gained by further deception.

"OK, you've got me," Francesca admitted. "I'm not really taking a survey at all. I'm here because I'm trying to find out what happened to your brother."

Susannah pursed her lips in annoyance. "Isn't that what the police are doing? You're not an undercover agent or something, are you?"

"No, just a church volunteer, but…" Francesca felt herself losing steam as she realized how idiotic she must sound.

"A church volunteer?" Susannah's voice rang with disbelief. "And how does that make you an expert in a murder investigation?"

"Well, I'll be honest with you: I just don't feel like the police are doing a thorough enough job." Francesca nervously shifted in her seat. "They seem to have their sights set on the cook's granddaughter, but I think they have the wrong person."

"What makes you say that?"

"Call it gut instinct or something. She just doesn't seem capable of murder."

"From what *I've* heard," Susannah said, "and from what my parents have told me about the investigation, Detective Baker is doing everything he can to get to the bottom of this. And frankly, that what's-her-name, Beatrice, she sounds extremely suspicious to me."

Susannah broke off a morsel of cookie and threw it in Benedict's direction. "I mean, she was after him and he wasn't interested. She had a motive, didn't she?"

"Well, if every woman spurned decided to kill the guy, the police wouldn't be able to keep up with the homicides, would they?" Francesca hadn't intended to sound so blunt, but the words were out of her mouth before she could edit them.

"I couldn't say." Susannah was clearly unimpressed by her logic. "All I know is that Beatrice person was after him, big time. She just didn't seem to get the fact that he was in the seminary." Susannah glanced at her watch and began to rise from her seat. "Well, you'll have to excuse me; I have some appointments."

Francesca stood up too, but at that moment, an image of Mauve flashed in her mind. "Before I go, could you answer one question for me?" She figured there was no harm in digging herself in even deeper.

"Yes, what is it?" Susannah's frosty tone suggested teatime was over.

"If Augustine wanted to be a priest, then why was he going after other women in the parish?"

"Other women?" The words had icicles dangling from them.

"Look, the fact is he was rather—well, shall we say interested—in a number of women." Francesca knew she was stretching the truth, but she wanted to see the sister's reaction.

"I don't know what you mean." Susannah's tone was now in the deep freeze. "I'm sure it's all rumors. All I know is he wanted to be a priest, pure and simple."

Francesca's hostess held out her hand. "Well, it was a pleasure to meet you," she said, although her facial expression belied the words. "But if you don't mind some advice, I'd leave the investigation to the police. You must know it could be dangerous looking into an unsolved murder."

After saying a quick goodbye, Francesca hurried to her car. She had the uneasy feeling that she was being watched. The whole house, she realized, might be equipped with surveillance cameras. She also wondered about Susannah's very chilly attitude. Wouldn't a sister be expected to show gratitude to someone trying to find her brother's killer? Still, Susannah had mentioned stormy times between herself and Augustine when they were younger. Was it possible the animosity had followed the twosome into adulthood, despite Susannah's claim that everything had been rosy between them? As much as Francesca hated the thought of a sister killing a brother, gruesome stories of sibling rivalry went all the way back to the Old Testament.

Was it possible Susannah had caught wind of Augustine's book? And was it possible he was brandishing the sword of his caustic wit against his own family members? Or revealing some family secrets?

Francesca unlocked her car door and got inside, but as she turned on the ignition, her stomach started clenching painfully and she felt a wave of nausea overtake her. *Oh, God, I shouldn't have drunk that tea,* she thought. *Did she poison me?*

***

"Really delicious," the archbishop said, taking a sip of mineral water. "Mrs. Greenstone seasoned the pork just right."

Father Bunt cleared his throat. This had to be his cue. "Uh, well, actually, sir, Mrs. Greenstone is a big believer in, uh, vegetarian cooking."

"Vegetarian?" The lonely word seemed to bounce sadly off the dining room walls.

"That's right, sir." Now was Father Bunt's chance to put a good face on things. "She is, you see, very concerned about our health, Father William's and mine. So she has a magical way of making things like, uh, tofu and uh, bean substitutes, taste like pork, beef, and chicken." Now he looked at Father William with what he hoped was an encouraging expression. Surely William realizes what's going on, he thought.

"Isn't that right, William?" Father Bunt asked.

But Father William looked flustered. "I, uh, I guess so, Father."

As if presenting a food demonstration on a TV cooking show, Father Bunt gestured with his fork toward the substance on his plate. "So this has all the appearances of *real* pork, you see, but in fact, it is completely meatless." He cleared his throat and lowered his volume a bit.

"The only problem, sir, and one that I plan to address, as soon as lunch is over, is that she's been—with the best of intentions, I'm sure—serving us these vegetarian dishes without actually telling us. She, uh, led us to believe they were actually meat."

The archbishop said nothing, although he cut another piece of the substance on his plate, put it in his mouth and chewed. Then he took another sip of water.

"I've done my homework, sir, and I assure you I'm about to sort things out." Father Bunt said triumphantly, anticipating the words of praise that would surely be forthcoming from the archbishop's lips.

***

Francesca drove directly home, grateful that it was a short distance. As she was getting out of the car, she felt another wave of nausea. She glanced at the truck parked in front of her house and realized it was Tony's. Oh, she had so longed to see him, but right now all she wanted to do was crawl inside and go to bed. But there he was, larger than life, sitting on her porch swing.

"Oh, Tony, I'm so glad you're here!" She moved unsteadily toward the porch.

Tony jumped up and rushed toward her. "What's wrong? You look really pale."

"I don't know. I feel terrible." She quickly told him about visiting Susannah. A wave of dizziness swept over her, and she grabbed his arm. "I think she put something in the tea."

"Let's not take any chances," he said. "Here, get in the truck. I'm taking you to the hospital."

The hospital was just minutes away, and Tony drove right up to the emergency room door, jumped out, and helped Francesca inside.

"I'm going to park. I'll be right back."

Panicky, she told the nurse on duty that she had been poisoned. Things happened quickly then. Francesca was hurried back to the treatment area, where she was given a dose of a bitter-tasting medicine that caused her to throw up. Once her stomach was completely empty, the nurse helped her into bed, took her temperature, and checked her blood pressure. Francesca quickly fell into a deep sleep, and when she woke up, she glanced at her watch, noting it was an hour later. A young female doctor with wavy red hair stood by her bed looking at the chart.

"Was I...did someone try to poison me?" Francesca asked.

193

"Well, judging by your other symptoms, I don't think so," the doctor said with a little smile. "Generally chills and fever don't accompany poisoning." She made a note on the chart. "What made you think you'd been poisoned?

"Uh, well, I was doing an investigation...into a murder... and it involved poisoning...and I thought..." Francesca's voice trailed off. The whole thing sounded preposterous when she spelled it out like this.

"Are you with the police?" The doctor hiked up a carefully groomed eyebrow in curiosity.

"No, not exactly." Francesca knew she was digging herself in deeper with her deception, but seemed unable to quit. "I'm just sort of helping out with the investigation."

"Well, I think you have a stomach bug, a virus, pure and simple. It's going around right now. We've had a big rush of cases just today. The best thing is rest and a liquid diet—and you'll be good as new in a day or so. Let the nurse know if you need help getting out of bed."

"Thanks, I will." Francesca felt an odd sense of being let down. Not that she had wanted it to be poison, but if it had been, she would have known for sure that Susannah was the culprit in Augustine's murder. But she still wasn't quite ready to remove the woman from her list of suspects.

The doctor left the room, and Tony walked in a few moments later. He took a seat by the bed.

"Are you OK?" He looked genuinely concerned.

"The good news is it's just a virus—not poison." She shifted in the bed. "Oh, Tony, I can't thank you enough for all you've done."

"Hey, all I did was drive you here. I'm really glad I was there." But his expression told her that he was holding back.

"Francesca..."

"Yes?"

There was a long sigh. "Why in the name of everything that's holy did you go snooping around at the Hornsby place? Didn't you know you could be putting yourself in harm's way?"

"Well, as it turned out, I wasn't poisoned, so...." She knew this was an extremely feeble excuse, and braced herself for what would surely come next.

"No, but you could have been, or something worse! Francesca..." He seemed to be groping for the right words.

"Yes, Tony?"

"There's a reason police officers carry guns, you know."

"Do you think I should get one?"

"That's not my point at all! You know what I'm getting at! This obsession you have with investigating—it has to stop. Leave it to the professionals." His face was red with anger.

She waited a moment. "Yeah, I know I should, I really do, but this Baker guy, Tony, he's hardly, well, he's not exactly professional."

"Well, he's the guy assigned to the case, so let him do his job, OK?" His words had a ring of finality to them.

She mumbled her agreement, but kept her fingers crossed. She knew she was on to something with this case, and she suspected Tony was overreacting.

He wasn't going to let the matter drop. "Look, you could have really gotten into trouble going over there. What if she had poisoned you, and what if you hadn't gotten home in time? What if you'd just passed out in the car or something?"

"I know you're angry with me, Tony, but I was just trying to help."

He paused, as if counting to ten. He reached over and pushed a lock of hair off her forehead. "Yeah, I know that. But, look, there's someone out there who killed Augustine. I just don't want you running into that person."

She decided to change the topic. "What brought you to my house?"

"I just stopped by to say hello." He hesitated. "Well, actually I stopped by to say more than that. I'm sorry I've been kind of distant. The fact is, Francesca, I…"

But at that precise moment her cell phone rang, quite loudly. It was sitting on the nearby table and he picked it up. He looked at the screen and handed it to her with an odd expression.

"It's Freeman."

***

The archbishop's reply to Father Bunt was cut short by the entry of a rather flustered-looking Mrs. Greenstone, who, Father

Bunt later concluded, must have been eavesdropping in the kitchen.

"Is there anything else you need, Your Grace?" As she spoke to the archbishop, she managed to bestow a rather withering glance at Father Bunt.

"Everything is fine, thank you." The archbishop dabbed his lips with the napkin. "Father Bunt has just been praising your ability to make tofu taste remarkably like pork loin."

Mrs. Greenstone let out a dramatic sigh. "Sir, with all due respect, this is 100% garden-variety pork loin that we're having. I got it in Publix."

Now she turned to face Father Bunt. "If you want to see the wrappers, they're in the kitchen."

"It's delicious, Mrs. Greenstone." The archbishop smiled fondly at her. "You certainly have a way with seasonings."

As soon as she had left the room, the archbishop put down his fork and gave his full attention to Father Bunt. His tone of voice suggested he was talking to a confused child.

"Brent, it's pretty easy to tell the difference between tofu and pork, believe me."

Father Bunt tried to smile, but his lips felt tense. The archbishop went on: "My Aunt Lillian, may she rest in peace, tried converting the entire family to tofu one Thanksgiving. She served something called "tofurky," and thought we'd all just love it." He buttered a roll as he was speaking.

"Well, some of the younger cousins actually snuck out later and brought back some take-out fried chicken. They tried to hide it from her, but she found out—and all hell broke loose at that particular family gathering." He smiled at the memory while he cut another piece of meat and raised it to his mouth.

Father Bunt toyed miserably with his buttered roll. He knew he must seem like a total idiot in the eyes of the archbishop. He could hear the underlying message in the story, which was that even children could tell the difference between meat and tofu. He could just hear his father's reaction on the phone when he told him he'd been transferred to a parish in the Okefenokee Swamp.

The lunch seemed to drag on forever. As she served dessert, lemon pudding with whipped cream, Mrs. Greenstone announced pointedly: "And this is made from *real* cream from *real* cows." The archbishop chuckled as if he and the cook shared a secret joke.

Just as he'd dipped his spoon into the pudding, Father Bunt's cell phone rang, and when he checked the screen he saw it was Detective Baker.

"Excuse me, sir; this is from the police station, so I'd better take it."

Father Bunt left the room with the phone pressed nervously to his ear.

"I've been checking alibis," Baker said. "And something doesn't add up."

"What's that?"

"Well, it seems your cook isn't signed up for tai chi, so she must have been lying."

Father Bunt felt his stomach turn over with tension. "What will you do now?"

"We'll have to question her again. Meanwhile, if I were you, I'd keep an eye on her."

After hanging up, Father Bunt returned rather morosely to the dining room. Now wasn't the time to mention to the archbishop that they'd just eaten a lunch prepared by someone who might be adept at poisoning people.

"Everything OK?" MacPherson asked.

"Oh, yes, uh, just a question he needed an answer to."

"Well, Brent, shall we go to your office for a few minutes?" The archbishop drained his coffee cup and stood up.

"Of course." As Father Bunt stood up, there was the sound of the front door opening and a commotion in the foyer.

"I wonder what that's..." Father Bunt began, and then Mrs. Greenstone rushed into the dining room followed by a young woman whose face was quite flushed. She was accompanied by a small dog tethered to a leash.

Mrs. Greenstone looked flustered: "Father, this is Regina Watson. I tried to explain that you're busy, but..."

"I'm just going to take a second," the woman said with a big smile for Father Bunt. "Oh, Archbishop MacPherson, it's just wonderful that you're here too! It's an honor to meet you."

After a quick handshake, she picked up the dog and cradled it in her arms. "And this is my Barney. Father Bunt, you remember I told you about him on the phone, don't you?"

With a sinking heart, Father Bunt realized that the dog was wearing a mini-tuxedo.

CHAPTER 11

After lunch, Father Bunt headed to the sitting room to read the newspaper. Thank God the woman had only stayed a few moments. The archbishop patiently had explained that having a dog in the wedding wouldn't do, but perhaps she could include him at the reception. Her face had fallen then.

"But, your Grace, the country club doesn't allow dogs."

The archbishop started to reply when Mrs. Greenstone blurted out, "And if the country club won't allow them, why in the world do you think the church would?"

The woman appeared quite flustered, but she left when Mrs. Greenstone ushered her out, assuring her that Father Bunt would call her in the morning. Afterwards, the archbishop looked at Father Bunt with a raised eyebrow, as if to say, "What next?" and then they went upstairs to discuss the murder case.

That discussion lasted only ten minutes, since Father Bunt didn't want to alarm his boss at that moment with the report about Mrs. Greenstone's having lied to the police. The archbishop reminded him that the rumor mills were churning out theories daily, and the longer it took to find the culprit, the more the stories would spread.

"And these can cause lasting damage to your parish," he added. Then he left, but not before making some pointed joke about tofu, which Father Bunt acknowledged with a hearty, thoroughly forced laugh.

Now Father Bunt stared at the newspaper, although he was too worried to read it. "Lasting damage" wasn't exactly something he wanted to add to his resume, but what could he do? The police had their own time table, and he just had to be patient. He heard the doorbell ringing. Isn't someone going to answer the blasted thing? It rang again, and he put down the paper and rose from his chair. Mrs. Greenstone had evidently gone out after lunch. He noticed that Dopey was snoring contentedly on the couch.

"Some watchdog," he muttered as he made his way to the door.

He looked outside and saw one of the volunteers—Mauve somebody—standing there. Her hair was damp as if she'd recently showered, he noted absently. He opened the door, suppressing a yawn.

"Father, I'm sorry to disturb you. I'm here to help Francesca, but she didn't answer the door." The woman clutched her purse nervously and looked quite apologetic.

"Oh, right, come on in." He stood aside to allow her entry. "Francesca didn't come in today for some reason."

"Well, I can do the bulletins anyway, and keep an eye on the phones too."

"That would be great, thanks." He turned away, planning to return to his newspaper, but she stopped him.

"Father, I was wondering…" She stared down at the floor, as if she were gathering up her courage.

"Yes, what is it?" He hoped this wouldn't take too long, whatever it was.

"Is there any news on...on the murder investigation?" She looked at him with an odd, almost pleading expression.

"Uh, well, the last I heard, the police were still collecting information, but, no, there isn't really anything new." He wasn't comfortable discussing the case right now, since he knew that anything he said could be misinterpreted.

"Now, if you'll..." he started to excuse himself, but the look on her face suggested the conversation wasn't over.

"Well, it's just that..." Mauve toyed with the clasp on her purse, and then, much to his dismay, she suddenly broke down sobbing. She took refuge in a nearby chair, fishing for a handkerchief from her purse.

He waited patiently until she found her voice again.

"Oh, Father, I just can't keep it inside any longer." She held the handkerchief against her streaming eyes. "The guilt is just about to kill me."

"Guilt? What do you mean?"

"I'm the one—I poisoned him!"

***

Francesca was exhausted by the time they got to her house. Tony had driven largely in silence, and she had mentally chastised herself for ever giving Frank her number. He was becoming a total pest. He had called at the exact moment when

Tony had seemed ready to say something really important. Just my luck, she thought ruefully. Even though she'd kept the phone conversation very short, Tony had left the room. A few moments later, after she was dressed and ready to leave the hospital, he'd returned and helped her out to the truck—but he looked glum.

Once she was in the house, she collapsed wearily onto the couch. He brought her a big glass of water, and put a blanket on her.

She wished that he would stay, but she was sure that if she asked him, he'd say he was too busy.

So she took the opposite approach. "Tony, you should go. I don't want you to get whatever this is."

He nodded, but he looked sad. I wonder if he wanted me to ask him to stay, she thought. It's all too complicated, just like this murder case. After he left, she began having chills, and when she took her temperature, it registered 102 degrees. She undressed, put on her pajamas, and went straight to bed.

***

Father Bunt was sure all the blood had drained out of his face. Mauve was clearly in great distress—and even if she were a murderer, he had to comfort her. He felt like he was moving in slow motion as he sat down next to her.

"Here, now, take it easy," he said gently. "Now, can you tell me what happened?" He had to lean forward to hear her because she was almost whispering.

"Father, I know how stupid this sounds, but I was falling for Augustine...you know, in love with him," she said, sniffing loudly. "I know it sounds crazy, believe me. He was much younger, but when I was with him, I just didn't notice the age difference."

He didn't say anything, just waited for the rest.

"I'm not beautiful, Father, I know that. And I should have known better; I mean, why would someone like him be interested in me? But for just a while there, for just a while, I could pretend I was someone else, pretend that in his eyes I really was beautiful and young again."

She began to cry again, crumpling forward like a child's abandoned rag doll.

"What happened, exactly?" Father Bunt asked quietly.

"He came over one afternoon. I invited him, you see, because I needed help with my son. I needed advice about how to handle him. Augustine was a good listener. He prayed with me. But, when he came over a second time, on another afternoon, I guess I misinterpreted his intentions."

"Meaning?" He held his breath, waiting for the reply.

"Oh, I'm such a fool!" she said passionately. "I thought he found me attractive, and I, well, I thought he... I thought he had, you know, feelings for me."

"Did anything happen?" He prayed silently that the answer would be in the negative.

"Well, we had a drink together, just socially, you know," she replied. "And when he was leaving that day, I kind of...I threw myself on him, and I...I tried to kiss him. But he backed off. He told me I'd misunderstood him. He apologized, said he was sorry if he'd done anything to make me think..."

"Yes?"

"Well, to make me think he was interested in me romantically." She wrapped the handkerchief around her hand. "I felt like such a jerk. And then I made matters worse by bragging to the girls in the choir group, as if he were really coming on to me."

"Is that why you killed him, because he wasn't interested in you that way?" Father Bunt asked incredulously. He'd heard the old saying about a woman scorned, but this seemed too far-fetched.

"There's more to it than that," she murmured.

"Now, you do understand this is not the sacrament of Confession," he said quietly, "which means I'm not bound to keep your confidence. So anything you tell me, well, I'm going to have to tell the police. If you want to, you can come upstairs to my office and we'll call them."

She didn't say anything for a moment. Then she looked at him with a mournful expression. "I think you should call them."

"And do you also want to go to Confession?"

She shook her head emphatically. "No."

***

Tony got the call from Father Bunt a few minutes after he walked into the station. He had been assigned to the murder investigation just an hour before. All his boss had said was, "I want you to take over. Baker is dragging his heels."

Father Bunt sounded agitated: "Someone has confessed."

Tony drove right over to the rectory, parked quickly, and jumped out. He knew how important time was, because if the perpetrator suddenly decided to clam up, that could seriously impair the investigation. He rang the bell and was quickly greeted by an ashen-faced Father Bunt, who led him up into his office. There, a rather overweight middle-aged woman with swollen eyes was hunched over in a chair. After quick introductions, Tony sat down near her and took out his note pad and pen.

"Ms. Bundle, did you poison Augustine Hornsby?" Tony decided to cut to the chase.

"Yes—yes I did!" She seemed relieved to get it out in the open.

She went on to tell him about her romantic feelings for Augustine, which had not been returned.

"He was just doing his job, you see, helping out a parishioner, and I took it all wrong," she said. "I made a total ass of myself."

"And was that why you did it—because he wasn't interested in you?" Tony asked.

"Well, no, it wasn't just because of that, you see," she replied. "I knew he was writing a book—a diary thing—and he read me some parts of it. It was pretty funny, all those scenes with Mrs. Mean Bone and all. But I found out, later, that there was also a character called Myra Trundle." She fidgeted nervously in the chair.

"Well, I'm not an idiot. It was obvious Trundle was modeled on me. The character was an older woman with a teenage boy. And this Myra person, she had fallen for a younger man."

"Well, I just couldn't have that, could I?" The color rose in her neck. "I mean, my son and I—we'd be the laughingstock of the whole town."

Tony took down a few notes before asking, "How did you know about that particular character?"

"Once, when I was in the rectory, I had to go upstairs to deliver a message to Father Bunt. Augustine's door was open and I looked in. I saw papers on his desk, and I got curious and read them."

"What made you decide to use poison?" Tony asked.

"I ...I don't know. It seemed easy somehow. I mean, I could never shoot anyone, you know?" A tear made its way down her cheek, leaving a sooty mascara smudge.

"OK, you were mad at him. He didn't want a relationship. And you didn't want him putting you in his book. But here's what I don't get: Why didn't you key his car or let the air out of his tires or something? Rat poison is pretty serious stuff."

"I wasn't thinking straight. I was really angry." She ran a trembling hand over her face, brushing away another errant tear. "It was a crime of passion."

There was something about the way she said that, as if she'd rehearsed it, or had heard it on a recent TV show. He wasn't about to point out to Mauve that people committing crimes of passion generally didn't go out and buy rat poison and then carefully add it to a bottle of booze. That had all been pre-meditated.

He was surprised to find himself feeling just the tiniest spark of sympathy for her as she sat there looking like a caged animal, but he had to do his job.

"How did you manage to put poison in the bottle without getting caught?"

She shrugged. "It wasn't hard. You see, I volunteer here, so I just rang the doorbell and the cook let me in. I told her I had left my cell phone in the office where I was working, and I was there to pick it up."

"And then?"

"Well, Francesca wasn't here yet, so I waited until the cook went shopping, and the priests were in their offices. Augustine was out. I went into the kitchen, found the bottle—and put the poison in."

"Were you wearing gloves?" Tony was watching her face carefully.

"Huh?" She seemed surprised by the question.

"You know, to avoid leaving prints on the bottle." He noticed she was blinking rapidly now, as if trying to come up with a plausible reply.

"Oh, I, uh, used a paper towel when I touched the bottle, so there wouldn't be prints." She gave him the ghost of a smile, reminding him suddenly of a little girl who had delivered the right answer to her teacher.

He shot off the next question quickly: "What did you do with the poison?"

"Huh?" She looked baffled as if she'd never expected such a detailed inquiry.

"The bottle of poison: did you take it home with you?"

"I…uh…I threw it away. I put it in the dumpster in back of the church, right before I drove home."

"And you bought it where and when?"

She appeared quite flustered now. "I got it, uh, it was earlier that same day—at Ace hardware—the one on Scott Boulevard."

"Cash, check, charge?"

She looked at him blankly.

"How'd you buy it?" He was starting to lose patience with her.

"Oh, I always charge everything."

He took a few more notes. "And why did you confess, Ms. Bundle, if you don't mind my asking?"

She glanced at Father Bunt, who was sitting at his desk, staring at a prayer book, before replying: "I couldn't stand the guilt anymore."

***

Francesca woke up to the sound of her phone ringing in the living room. She was going to let the machine pick up the message, but then she heard Father Bunt's voice, so she got out of bed and hurried into the living room and picked up the receiver.

"Francesca? Are you alright? I heard you were at the emergency room."

"Yes, Father, I'm fine. It's a stomach virus." Francesca sank into the cozy chair near the bookshelves, gently moving Tubs.

"Well, you take care of yourself. Get some rest." Father Bunt coughed. "There's something that might interest you—something about the case."

"Yes?" Her heart beat a little faster in anticipation of what he might say.

There was a short silence, as if he were trying to decide how to phrase his words. "Well, for one thing, Detective Viscardi is now handling things. The other one, that Baker fellow, has been taken off the case. But more importantly, someone has confessed."

"Who is it, Father?" she asked breathlessly.

"Unfortunately, I'm not at liberty to divulge anything more," he replied. "But I just wanted to assure you that the rectory is safe. The person has been taken into custody. And that's about all we'll be saying to anyone who calls, you know, parishioners seeking information and all that."

"Of course, Father, I understand," she murmured obediently, although her mind was racing ahead, trying to figure out who the culprit might be.

After hanging up, Francesca immediately dialed Tony's number. Surely he'll fill me in, she thought. But his phone was on voice mail, so she went glumly back to bed, drifting into a feverish sleep.

***

Tony pulled up to Francesca's house and parked his truck behind her car. He noticed her tires were looking rather low; she probably hadn't checked them since he'd left town. The lawn was overgrown, and there were persistent trails of ivy creeping up the oak trees. He cast an appraising eye at the gutters, noting they were crammed with leaves. I'll have to get up there and clean them out for her, he thought.

One thing that really appealed to him about Francesca was the way she thought she had it all together, when in fact her life had plenty of loose ends. He liked the fact that she needed him. He'd dated too many women who acted as if a man was an accessory rather than a necessity. She had once told Tony that her husband had really enjoyed taking care of the practical matters around the house—as she put it, the computers, the car, the roof, the lawn—and after his death, she had felt totally at sea. Tony recalled chuckling then and saying, "Well, you've got a life jacket now."

He approached the front door hesitantly. He hoped that she wasn't angry with him for being so blunt when she was sick. On the front porch two stone angels were perched with their legs hanging off the edge. One had lost its wings, but Francesca had told him that she didn't have the heart to toss it out. There were also a few bottles of plant food and a pair of flip flops. He chuckled when he noticed a huge bag of sunflower seeds that she had evidently bought for the bird feeders. The side of the bag had been chewed open, no doubt by one of the many squirrels that lived in her yard.

He didn't know if this thing with Frank was anything serious. She said it wasn't, but how could he be sure? He felt somewhat guilty for having warned her off Frank so strongly. The fact was that Frank *did* have a record, but Tony had stretched the truth a bit by saying Frank was still doing illegal stuff. He really had no evidence of that. He just hadn't liked the guy showing up at her house at 3 a.m. I just wanted to protect her, he reassured himself.

He still felt like a total ass for dressing up as a wizard. He hoped that she never found about that particular error in his judgment. She'd see it as deception, although he'd only meant it as a joke. But at least he'd found out what her real feelings for him were. Still, he couldn't deny his own feelings for her. They had hit him right in the face when he was driving her to the hospital. He'd realized that he could have lost her.

He rang the doorbell and waited. In about a minute, he saw her peering through the blinds in her dining room window, then the door shot open and there she was. She was wearing her fuzzy pink pig slippers, the ones he always kidded her about, plus a silky floral housecoat.

"Oh, Tony, it's so good to see you, but I wish you'd given me some warning." She began pulling her hair back from her face and tightening the sash on her robe.

"What would you have done—killed the fatted calf?" he joked as he walked inside.

She grinned. "Nothing so serious—but maybe put on some lipstick."

"How are you feeling? Any better?" He noticed how pale she still looked.

"I'm feeling a little better, but I could still be contagious." She backed away from him.

He was suddenly very much aware that she didn't seem to be wearing very much under her robe. He looked away quickly, ashamed of the scandalous images that were prancing through his head.

As if she'd read his mind, she said, "Tony, let me, uh, put some clothes on. I'll be right back. There's some beer in the fridge if you want some."

"Nothing for me." He took a seat on the couch and picked up a nearby women's magazine. They always perplexed him because the covers touted the latest fad diets along with recipes for rich casseroles and chocolate desserts.

After a few moments, she returned to the living room in jeans and a pink blouse.

"It's so good to see you again," she enthused. "I didn't get a chance to tell you the other day—when all that happened at the hospital—that you have a great tan."

"Yeah, well you know how Miami is, just walking to the car you get burned," he replied, replacing the magazine on the coffee table. He bent down, picked up the nearby Tubs, and put the old cat on his lap.

"Look, not to change the subject, Francesca, but I meant to ask you this the other day. What made you go over to the Hornsby house anyway?"

"Well, I was going to tell you, really." She walked across the room and picked up her purse, extracted something from it, and handed it to him. "This was given to me by Mrs. Greenstone. She wanted me to find out who the lady in the photograph was."

He looked at the framed photo. "Where'd Mrs. G. get it?"

"It was in Augustine's room," Francesca pressed her lips together nervously.

"And you both didn't give it to Baker?" Tony was trying to control his temper, but he could tell he was quickly losing the battle.

"I was going to, but she kind of made me promise to find out who the woman was. She—Mrs. Greenstone—thought the woman could be the killer."

Tony willed himself to remain calm because he knew from experience that Francesca would clam up if he came on too strong. "You know you should have given this directly to Baker, right? He was assigned to the case."

"Yes, and I know what you're thinking, mainly that *I* wasn't assigned to it." She was starting to get upset, he noted, and was now anxiously twisting a lock of her hair.

"Well, isn't that the truth?" he asked in what he hoped was a calm tone of voice.

"Yes, but that Baker...he's just a buffoon!" she replied heatedly.

"Look, I agree with you, believe me, but that didn't give you a green light for butting in!" Tony knew he had lost it now. There was no way he could conceal his irritation with her.

"Well, I was just trying to help Mrs. Greenstone," Francesca said in a wounded tone of voice. "She was really worried about Beatrice being blamed for the murder."

"Francesca, how do you know Beatrice *didn't* commit the murder?" He was starting to feel like he was cross examining her, but he couldn't seem to stop.

"Well, I don't, not really, but she just doesn't seem the type."

The room was silent except for the rather loud rumbling purrs emanating from Tubs.

"Unfortunately, Francesca, when it comes to homicide, *everyone* is the type." Tony realized that he was practically shouting now, and by the look on Francesca's face, he knew it was a big mistake.

***

A few hours later, Tony was at his desk again going over the reports on the Hornsby case. He was having trouble concentrating because Francesca was very much on his mind. She had obviously been miffed by his chiding her, and had made an excuse about needing some rest, so he had left. They seemed somehow fated to bump heads whenever she got involved in police work, and he hated the arguments—but he also hated the idea of her inadvertently putting herself in danger.

Now he picked up a rubber band and stretched it absent-mindedly until it snapped. Something doesn't add up here, he thought, his mind returning to the murder investigation. He had a confession from Mauve, and that should be the end of things, but there were just too many loose ends. First, according to the report, Father William said he heard a woman laughing downstairs on the day Hornsby was poisoned—and he was fairly sure it was Beatrice.

Tony circled the word "fairly" because he knew people could make mistakes. But even if Beatrice had been there that day that did not necessarily mean she was the culprit—although the priest's testimony certainly could count against her in court. Clearly that could have been her golden opportunity to go into the kitchen and poison the booze.

Tony pushed back in his chair and stared at the ceiling, noticing a chunk of the plaster was coming loose. Talk about opportunity: Wouldn't the cook, that Mrs. Greenstone, have had a clear shot at the bottle of booze any time she felt like it? He scanned through the notes, and saw that the old lady had said she'd been at a class at the YWCA. Tai chi, he thought with a mental shake of the head. In my grandmother's day, it was quilting. But then he read further and saw that Baker had noted, "No tai chi class at time she said. To do: Question cook again." Had Baker actually done that? Tony continued leafing through the report. He couldn't find any notes suggesting Baker had spoken with the cook again.

And he still couldn't figure out why Baker hadn't taken Beatrice into custody. Was he falling prey to something that many detectives did, which was the belief that the most obvious suspect couldn't possibly be guilty? Unfortunately, when it came to TV shows, viewers would feel cheated if the person who looked the guiltiest ended up being the criminal. TV detective-show writers seemed committed to an unspoken belief that there had to be as many red herrings as possible. But in real life, as Tony well knew, it was often the most obvious person who had committed the crime, someone with a clear motive and easy access to the victim.

Tony picked up another rubber band, stretched it, and this time shot it across the room, where it knocked over a plastic cup, fortunately an empty one, on his office mate's desk. Buddy Mills was running an errand in downtown Decatur, so Tony could shoot rubber bands to his heart's content. Somehow the habit helped focus him. Some people meditate; I shoot rubber bands, he thought.

The next band made a direct hit on an African violet plant, one that had died a few weeks ago without ever getting a proper burial. Just then, Tony saw two faces in his mind's eye: Father Bunt and Father William. What about them? He looked through the notes, and saw that Baker had checked out their alibis, at least for the evening. But they'd been there in the afternoon, and there was no way to know for sure when the bottle of booze had been doctored.

But what about motive? Did they have some vendetta against Hornsby, something they were keeping hidden? He knew they were mentioned in Hornsby's book, but would that be enough for one of them to do something that hideous? He knew the two priests from a previous case at St. Rita's, and they definitely didn't fit the profile of cold-blooded killers. But he still wasn't going to strike them from the list of possible suspects.

Tony fished in his shirt pocket for a pack of cigarettes and sighed. At times like these, he forgot that he had quit smoking years ago. The craving never went away. He opened his desk drawer and found a package of mints. They would have to do. He popped a mint into his mouth. For both Beatrice and Mauve, the motive was a common one, namely unrequited love.

Now he picked up another sheaf of papers, the manuscript found on Hornsby's computer. This complicated matters even further, since it was filled to the brim with incriminating, albeit supposedly fictional, anecdotes about people Hornsby had known. Why can't things be simpler? Tony wondered.

He had been just about to arrest Beatrice when Mauve had thrown a major monkey wrench into his plans. He should be relieved that Mauve had confessed, but something wasn't adding up. The problem was Mauve was quite a few years older than Hornsby, and she had a teenage kid. Would she really have been so naïve as to think Hornsby would get involved with her? Tony crushed the mint into smithereens in his mouth and reached for another one. When it came to women and romance, it seemed all the rules were being broken in the 21st century. Today it wasn't so unusual for younger men to date older women.

Still, there was something about Mauve's confession that was bugging him. He scanned the notes he'd taken when she confessed, then he picked up the phone and called forensics to find out if a bottle of poison had been found in the dumpster behind the rectory. Next he called Ace Hardware. When he was through, he selected another rubber band and shot it at the ceiling. It dislodged a loose piece of drywall, which fell with a little thud to the floor, creating a small pile of white dust. Something doesn't add up here, he concluded.

CHAPTER 12

Father William was alone in the rectory. Father Bunt was out visiting parishioners at Emory Hospital, and Mrs. Greenstone had gone out to Publix. Francesca had called to say she was running late, and wouldn't be in for another hour. He put the phones on voice mail and decided to do something he hadn't done in a while.

He went into his room and rummaged around in the closet until he found the large plastic ball that Ignatius liked to run around the house in. He carefully removed the plastic top, then went over to the aquarium and woke up Ignatius by holding a pecan close to the mound of shredded tissue beneath which the hamster slept. A nose poked out, and finally the entire body of the hamster.

Father William scooped up Ignatius and put him inside the plastic ball. He then took the ball downstairs and made sure Dopey was outside before placing it on the sitting-room floor. Now Ignatius had free rein of the entire downstairs. In seconds, the ball was zooming around the rectory, knocking into the chair legs before the hamster righted his course and then continued in a different direction.

Father William went into the kitchen and dug out a few cookies from the jar, then poured himself a cup of coffee and put it in the microwave to heat up. He was thoroughly enjoying being alone for even an hour, not having to chit chat with Mrs.

Greenstone, answer questions for volunteers, or talk with Father Bunt about upcoming events. Somehow it was incredibly relaxing to have a few moments to just eat a cookie and drink some coffee. He let Ignatius roam for about fifteen minutes and then returned him to his cage.

Then Father William started rummaging around in his office to find a book to read. As he did so, he suddenly heard the rather eerie sound of someone laughing in the downstairs sitting room. He was sure it was Beatrice, and she sounded just as loud as she had on the day Augustine had been poisoned. But he was alone, wasn't he? How in the world had she managed to get into the rectory without him noticing her? Or was there some kind of demonic spirit on the loose? He felt an uneasy chill creep up his spine.

***

After going over the report Baker had sent him, Tony called the man into his office. Baker arrived about five minutes later. Tony couldn't help but notice that he was wearing a wrinkled and dingy off-white shirt that barely buttoned across his expansive belly. He was carrying a super-sized bag of peanut M&Ms, which he was noisily tearing open as he walked into the room. Tony had to restrain himself from suggesting that the man put down the bag and give him his full attention. Try as he might, he just didn't think Baker was the right man for the job of detective. It wasn't just the man's inexperience but also his demeanor, which certainly did not inspire confidence.

Tony didn't expect policemen to look like they'd stepped out of the pages of a fancy men's magazine, and he would have forgiven Baker his sloppy appearance, but Baker also was gaining a reputation at the station as someone who apparently thought taking a shower once a week was sufficient.

"Well, I see we have our killer," Baker mumbled through a mouthful of candy.

"Technically, yes," Tony noted.

"What do you mean, technically?" Baker seemed perplexed as he dipped his large paw back into the bag, and then offered it to Tony. "Want some?"

"Well, she confessed, but I don't think she did it." Tony waved away the offer, and then picked up an extra large rubber band, resisting a strong impulse to shoot it at the bag.

"Come on, man, we've solved the case!" Baker plopped down into the chair, his expression suggesting he was clearly riled by this new wrinkle. "Now you're going to say she's innocent?"

Tony mentally rolled his eyes at the word "we." From what he had heard through the grapevine, Baker had dropped the ball numerous times on this case. Mauve's confession was certainly not the result of any keen detective work on Baker's part, but had instead been handed to them on the proverbial platter.

"I did some digging around. Her story just doesn't hold water." Tony flicked an ant off his desk.

"What's wrong with it?" Baker continued crunching loudly on the M&Ms.

"Well, for one thing, according to forensics, they searched the dumpster thoroughly the day Hornsby's body was discovered, looking for anything suspicious. And they didn't find a bottle of rat poison, although Mauve claims she threw it there. Second, I checked with Ace Hardware and they have no record of selling anyone poison on the day she claims she bought it."

"So?" Baker's word hung in the air like a mosquito that Tony was eager to swat, but he restrained himself from making a bitingly sarcastic reply.

Didn't the man know how to draw an obvious conclusion? Tony thought angrily. And didn't he realize his lips and tongue were stained bluish-green from the candy? He looks like a corpse for God's sake!

"If she's lying about where and when she bought the stuff and also lying about where she threw the bottle, she can't be trusted with the rest of her statement either." Tony spoke slowly as if explaining something to a dimwitted child.

"Yeah, OK, but why would she lie?" Baker extracted another handful of candies and shoved them into his mouth.

"People who confess to murder—or any crime really—when they're actually innocent usually have one of two motives." Tony felt like he was a lecturer in a basic class on police investigations.

"Some do it to get attention," he went on. "Especially today, when newspapers often turn killers into overnight celebrities, some of them just want their fifteen minutes of fame."

Baker was now staring at Tony as if he were divulging a major secret of the universe.

"But others are just covering for someone else," Tony added quietly.

Baker threw the crumpled-up bag into the trash and wiped his mouth with his hand. "So you think maybe this Mauve person knows who the killer is—and she's covering for him?"

"Well, as I said, that's one possibility. We won't know until we do some more digging." He leaned forward in his chair and frowned slightly. "You questioned Beatrice, right?"

"Yeah, three times." Baker stared out the window across the room as if something out there had suddenly caught his interest.

"*Three* times?" Tony looked through the folder. "I only have your notes from two interviews."

"I think I lost some notes." Baker was now gazing at the floor.

Tony could feel his temper rising to the boiling point, but willed himself to stay calm. If the man had lost notes on the case, he was compromising the outcome. When the case went to court, the whole thing could be dropped because of this fool's incompetence.

"You put them in the computer, didn't you?" Tony held his breath as he awaited the reply.

"Uh, well, no." There were large beads of perspiration on Baker's forehead even though the station's air conditioning was set at what Tony thought of as three degrees below freezing.

"See, I was about to, but I lost the handwritten notes before I could do that."

Tony was just about to reply when Baker added, "But I don't think she's the one anyway." He drew in a breath of air and made an odd puffing sound as he expelled it.

"You don't think she's the one?" Tony saw another ant crawling across his desk and smashed his hand down on it. He did not feel inclined to show any more mercy.

"No, I don't," Baker said smugly, as if he were an expert lawyer delivering the closing argument in a winning case.

"Based on what?" Tony clenched his fist beneath the desk. I'd like to smack that stupid smile off his face, he thought angrily.

"Instinct, I guess." Baker shot Tony a blue-lipped, supercilious smile.

That was it. Tony couldn't control himself a minute longer. He stood up and slammed his fist on the desk, and a few errant ants went flying. He knew he was shouting, but he didn't care.

"For God's sake, man, let me remind you that *instinct* doesn't hold up in a court of law!"

Baker's beefy face reddened. "Sure, I know that—but that Beatrice girl, she also had an alibi."

"Alibi? Where's that in the report?" Tony was leafing through the pages.

Baker picked up the report and thumbed through it, leaving chocolate stains on the pages. "This isn't the whole report," he said in a mystified tone of voice.

"This is what you sent me," Tony said. "Where's the rest of it?"

"I must have printed out the wrong version. I got a revised one in the computer, and I'll get it to you, just give me a minute." Baker stood up and started heading out the door.

"Wait, before you go: There's another thing," Tony said. "The cook was lying, according to your notes, about that class she was taking at the Y. So did you follow up on that?"

"Uh, not yet, but I was going to..." Baker was now edging backwards toward the door.

"Meanwhile, she's still in the kitchen at the rectory, man," Tony thundered, "and she could end up poisoning everyone over there!"

As soon as Baker was gone, Tony fired off three rubber bands in rapid succession, knocking the dead plant off Buddy's desk and landing it squarely on the floor.

***

Francesca let herself into the rectory with her master key and went directly to her desk. She was still feeling weak from the virus, but she was tired of staying home. She had heard rumors that someone had been arrested for Augustine's death, and she was eager to find out the details. Even if Father Bunt had been sworn to secrecy, she figured Mrs. Greenstone might have some news to divulge. She went into the kitchen where she saw Mrs. Greenstone standing at the table, rolling out pie dough. The old woman looked startled.

"Oh, I heard you were down with a virus. Feeling better now?"

"Yes, much better." Francesca pulled out a chair and sat down. "I've heard there's been some news on the murder investigation."

Mrs. Greenstone put down the rolling pin. She went to the sink, washed and dried her hands, then sat down opposite Francesca.

"You can say that again." The cook looked around as if checking for spies. "It seems that Mauve, you know that volunteer that was helping you with the bulletins…well, it seems she confessed."

"Mauve? Are you sure?" Francesca couldn't believe her ears.

"Yes, I was here when she…uh…kind of came clean to Father Bunt," Mrs. Greenstone whispered. "You know I'm not one to eavesdrop"—here the cook dropped her eyes discreetly—"but I just happened to overhear them from the kitchen. I just heard bits and pieces, but enough to know what's what."

"But why in the world would she do something like that?" Francesca asked.

"As I said, I only caught a few words—but I think she threw herself on him—and he wasn't interested."

Francesca remembered the night of the Choir Chicks' meeting when Mauve had told the group about Augustine coming on to her. Had Mauve made it all up?

The cook picked up the rolling pin, knocked off a bit of dough that was clinging to it, and then stood up. "That's all I know," she said with a note of finality. "But I'm very relieved my Beatrice is in the clear. And I'm grateful for whatever you did to clear her name."

"Oh, you're welcome, of course," Francesca said, "but I didn't do much at all." She was kicking herself mentally because she'd been on the wrong track all along.

Francesca went back to her desk and dialed Tony's number. He didn't answer, so she left a quick message: "I heard about the confession, and I have some questions."

He called back a few minutes later: "Are you back on the case again?" he asked drily.

"I might be able to help you," she said. "I mean, Mauve talked about Augustine at the Choir Chicks' meeting, you see, but..."

"Who mentioned Mauve? Was it Father Bunt?" Tony sounded irritated.

"Uh, no, it wasn't Father. I probably shouldn't say."

"You know this is all confidential, right? And I can't divulge anything to you about the case while it's in progress," he reminded her.

"Of course, I know all that! But aren't you interested in what I might know about...about Mauve and Augustine?"

"OK, shoot. What is it?"

"I don't think I should tell you over the phone. The walls here have ears." She had a mental image of Mrs. Greenstone in the kitchen hovering by the door.

"OK, Detective Bibbo, where do you want to meet?"

"How about the Dairy Queen on East Trinity?" She was relieved that he was back to kidding her again. His officiousness had been getting to her.

"You got it. How's two o'clock?"

"Perfect. I'll see you there."

***

After lunch, Tony headed over to the rectory. He wanted to see the look on the cook's face when he announced that her alibi had crumbled. He knew people faked alibis, generally, for one of two reasons: One, they had committed the crime and were running scared, and hoping the police would be too stupid to figure out the deception. Or two, they had been doing something else at the time they didn't want to admit to—something embarrassing or perhaps illegal.

Over the years, he'd checked out false alibis from men who had, in reality, been cheating on their wives. There also had been shaky alibis from women who were trying to keep their real whereabouts hidden from their husbands for a variety of reasons. One woman didn't want her husband to know she was at a plastic surgeon's office getting an estimate for a facelift. So she lied to the cops—and to her husband—about where she was the afternoon a murder had been committed.

Of course, the truth nearly always came out, Tony reflected. What was that old quote—something about how lying is like weaving a tangled web? He'd have to check with Francesca on the exact wording. He parked in front of the rectory and walked up to the front door. He knew Francesca's shift was over, so he wasn't sure who would answer when he rang the doorbell. He was relieved when it was the cook, since he didn't want to waste time making small talk with anyone else. When he introduced himself as a detective working on the Hornsby case, she seemed flustered.

"Come in. I'll get Father Bunt for you."

"No, that won't be necessary, ma'am. I'm here to see you."

"Me?" Streaks of red flooded her wrinkled cheeks. "But I thought the case was solved!"

"Is there somewhere we can talk privately?" He now knew where Francesca had gotten her information on Mauve.

"Of course, come in," she murmured and led him into the kitchen where a table was covered with open containers of herbs and various spices.

"You making a pie?" he inquired just to warm her up a bit.

"Yes, for dessert tonight."

He took a seat at the table, and she sat across from him. "Look, I'll get right to the point here," he said. "We checked out your alibi, and there was no tai chi class at the time you said there was. So why did you mislead us?"

She picked up a nearby dish towel and began folding it as if she were stalling for time.

"I was afraid to tell the truth," she finally admitted.

***

The Dairy Queen was one of the few places in downtown Decatur that had withstood the test of time. It seemed that restaurants were constantly opening for business with a grand flourish and then closing a year or so later. Many were quite trendy, some serving buffalo burgers, and others touting locally grown, organic vegetables. The Dairy Queen had survived the economic downturn, in Francesca's opinion, because the menu featured politically incorrect, deep-fried chicken, fattening sundaes, and other comfort foods that people craved during hard times.

Francesca was early for her meeting with Tony, but figured she'd grab a table and read the paper while she waited for him. As she was sitting at a table reading a newspaper, she saw another car, a rather heavily dented Ford Focus, pull up next to hers. She watched as the car door swung open, and out climbed none other than Brad, Mauve's son. He entered the restaurant and ordered a Blizzard.

She was just about to go over and ask how his mother was doing, when he suddenly looked in her direction, turned around quickly, and stormed out. The waitress called out behind him,

"Hey, what about the Blizzard?" but Francesca saw him get into his car and drive off. She was stunned.

Why had he done that? Was the poor kid so embarrassed about what had happened to his mother that he was trying to avoid people from church? As she was scrambling to make sense of his behavior, her phone rang. It was Tony.

"Francesca, look, I'm sorry, but I can't meet you. Something's come up and I can't get out of it."

"That's alright, Tony, I understand," she said trying to hide her disappointment.

"How about dinner tonight at Benedetti's?" he asked. "I can come by for you at seven."

"Yes, I'd love that."

She ordered an ice-cream cone and found a shady spot outside. She had to eat quickly, since it was a blistering day, and a tempting treat could quickly turn into a huge mess. As she took the last bite, she had an idea. She'd go over to Mauve's house and visit Brad. The poor kid is probably really upset about his mother, she thought. I'll see if he needs anything. She made a quick call to the rectory and got Mauve's address from the afternoon phone volunteer.

As she was driving over, Francesca recalled how excited Mauve had been about the possibility of reconciling with her husband, Andy. I wonder what ever happened with that, she thought. I wonder if he knows she's confessed to a murder.

The house on Bluebird Lane was one of those 1940s-era brick cottages that seemed to have "charming" written all over it.

Most houses on the street resembled English cottages, and many had roses out front, plus tendrils of ivy trailing up the sides. One of the yards, she noted, sported a life-size statue of a penguin. What's up with that, I wonder?

She noticed Brad's car was in the driveway. She parked behind him, and then rang the doorbell. It took a few minutes, but finally the door opened, and there he was, looking none too pleased to see her.

"Brad, I just stopped by to see how you're doing—and if you need anything." Francesca decided not to bring up his strange behavior at the Dairy Queen.

"Oh, I'm fine," he said dully.

"Could I come in for a few moments?" She hated to be pushy, but it was really hot on the porch.

He hesitated for a moment, then waved her in. "Whatever."

The shades were drawn in the room, and there was an unpleasant, lingering aroma of something that could have been last night's take-out chicken, plus piles of clothing and old newspapers strewn about. She imagined Mauve would have a fit if she could see her house now. Francesca pushed aside a stack of what she hoped was clean laundry and sat down on the couch.

"Look, Brad, I just wanted to say how sorry I am about what's happened with your mother. I know how worried you must be."

He crouched on the edge of the hearth across from her. "Yeah, sorry is the word alright. If you want the truth, I think the whole damn thing is one big sorry mess!" Now he stood up and started pacing the room. He looked as if he might break down and start crying at any moment.

"There's no way my mother could *ever,* not in a *million* years, do something like that! She just isn't that kind of person!" He stood there before her with his fists clenched and his eyes brimming with unshed tears.

"But you know she confessed to it, right?" Francesca hoped to inject a note of reason.

"Sure, I know all about that," he muttered, dragging his sleeve against his eyes. "But...but she was lying."

"Lying? Why would she lie?" Francesca's curiosity was definitely piqued now.

"She thought she was doing the right thing." Now he sat back down on the hearth and put his head in his hands. His shoulders were shaking, and she knew he was crying. She sat there quietly until he had composed himself.

When he could speak again, his words shocked her to the core: "She was trying to protect me."

***

Mrs. Greenstone looked stricken.

"Why didn't you tell Baker the truth?" Tony asked. "Was it because you were the one who poisoned the bottle?"

"Me! No, my Lord, I would never do that!" Her thin lips trembled ominously.

"Augustine wasn't your favorite guy in the whole world, though, was he? I mean, your granddaughter was pursuing him and he wasn't interested, for one thing," Tony said evenly.

"Yes, it's true. We had our run-ins. But I'm not a...a murderer."

"Then where were you that day?" Tony asked.

"I had a date," she replied with a look that almost dared him to challenge her.

"A date?"

"Yes, a date, as with a man! Is that so hard to believe?" she asked huffily.

Tony didn't say anything. He was remembering the woman who had lied because she'd been at the plastic surgeon's office. Compared to that, Mrs. Greenstone's date was minor league in the strange category.

"Fine, you had a date," he said. "But why did you lie about it?"

"Well, one of the men in the Golden Glories club—that's our senior citizens' group here at the church—Arnold Turner—invited me out for the day." Perhaps noticing Tony's bemused expression, she added, "I may be old, Detective, but I'm not dead!"

"I get that, ma'am, but why didn't you tell us?"

"Because I knew my granddaughter would make fun of me, that's why," she snapped. "Plus, I didn't want the priests thinking, oh I don't know, that I was some kind of loose woman."

Tony pressed his lips together to avoid smiling. He couldn't imagine anyone on earth having that particular thought about the cook.

"I'll need this Turner's phone number so I can double check your whereabouts."

"OK, but can you keep this quiet?" She looked at him pleadingly.

"Well, if it all checks out, there's no reason for me to share it with anyone. It goes in the official report, but that's all."

"Thank you." She rummaged through her purse for the phone number. "We weren't doing anything...anything to be ashamed of," she added. "We had lunch, took a walk, and went to a movie in the evening."

"Oh, yeah, what did you see?"

"It was a thriller, something Arnold really wanted to see, but not my cup of tea."

"What was it?"

She winced at the memory. "Zombie Romance."

***

Francesca thought the room was getting warmer by the minute. Brad probably hadn't adjusted the air conditioning since his mother had left. But this didn't matter. She had to find out if he was telling the truth.

"Brad, did *you* kill Augustine?" There, she had put into words a thoroughly preposterous idea.

"No, but my mother thinks I did." He seemed more subdued now that it was out in the open.

"Why in the world would she think that?"

"I was real upset when he came over—you know, to see her. She thought I was downstairs watching TV and didn't know what was going on. But I could hear them laughing and talking. And then I heard her telling a friend on the phone about how he was coming on to her, and how they had a drink together and all. I told her I didn't like it one bit, but she just laughed." He picked up a nearby wash cloth from a pile of laundry and blew his nose.

"See, my dad was trying to make up with her," he continued. "They were going to—going to see some counselor. And I want them back together. I want us to be like everyone else, you know, a family again." He uttered the word "family" in a hushed tone as if referring to something sacred, and she felt a pang of pity for him.

"So you told her you were upset about Augustine's visits?"

"Yeah, but she wouldn't listen to me. Said I'm just a kid and what did I know." He hesitated. "I told my dad about the two of them too, but he just shrugged it off. And then, one day, when she was in the rectory, I stopped by after school. She was doing the bulletins. The cook was out. My mom told me to go into the kitchen and get a Mountain Dew. While I was in there, I saw the bottle on the counter, you know, that fancy booze, and I picked it up—and I was looking at it when my mother came in. She asked me what I was doing, and I told her I was just curious, that's all. I wanted to read the label."

"And then?" Francesca asked, dreading the answer.

"Then we went home, that's all," he said. "But, see, the next morning, Augustine was found, you know, dead. And when word got out about how it was done and all, she decided I was the one who had done it!"

"But surely she asked you about it?"

"Yes, but when I told her I would never poison anyone, she didn't believe me. She got all hysterical and stuff and then she ran to the police and confessed." He tossed the wash cloth on the floor. "She made me swear that I would never, under any circumstances, tell them I'd been in the kitchen near the bottle that day," he added bitterly.

"But it doesn't make sense. I mean, how would you have even known that he drank Frangelico?" Francesca asked.

"Oh, I knew," he said dully. "See, she mentioned it one time."

"So she lied to the police to protect you?" Francesca was wishing she had a tape recorder.

"Yeah, and there was no reason to. Like I said, I didn't do anything wrong. I would never poison anyone."

"But someone did." Francesca spoke the obvious truth rather slowly.

"Yeah, someone did," he repeated.

"We have to tell the police about this," Francesca said softly. "They'll find the real killer and let your mother go."

"No, we can't!" He was agitated again. "She said not to tell them. She said it was all too incriminating and they'd never

239

believe I didn't do it." He looked around almost furtively now. "See, I have sort of a record."

"For what?"

"Shoplifting and smoking weed at school."

"Well, that's a far cry from murder."

"Yeah, but she doesn't see it that way. She was afraid the police would try to frame me or something."

He stood up, clearly angry now, clenching his fists in a way that made Francesca quite wary. "I shouldn't have told you," he shouted. "I promised her not to tell anyone about all this." Sweat and tears ran profusely down his face. "You can't tell anyone!"

"But you want your mother out of jail, don't you?" She stood up too, and noticed for the first time how tall he was.

"Yes, but she has a good lawyer. She said he'd figure out a way to get her out."

Francesca decided not to push him on his logic, since he seemed on the verge of breaking down again. She picked up her purse and started edging her way toward the front door.

"OK, Brad, I won't tell anyone." He didn't have to know she was crossing her fingers as she spoke. "Now I've got to go."

She got to the door just as the doorbell rang. When she opened the door, she saw an unfamiliar man, somewhat taller than Brad, and quite muscular with gray stubble on his face and straggly brown hair pulled back into a pony tail.

"Dad!" Brad called out behind her.

As he stepped across the threshold, the man gave Francesca a decidedly unfriendly look.

"I'm Francesca from St. Rita's." She held out her hand. "I was just checking to see if Brad was OK."

He ignored her hand. "We don't want anyone butting in here," he growled. "Brad's fine. This is a family matter, and we're handling it."

"Of course, I was just leaving." She couldn't wait to get out of the house.

CHAPTER 13

Driving home, Francesca started to wonder if Brad had told her the truth. Maybe he really *was* the one who had killed Augustine—and his mother was indeed covering for the true criminal. After all, the boy certainly had a motive, given how much he wanted his parents to reconcile. It sounded like he had seen Augustine as an obstacle to that ever happening. And surely Mauve had a very compelling reason to believe her son truly was guilty, else why would she have done something as extreme as confessing to a crime she apparently hadn't committed? Maybe the kid had told his mother something that he was withholding from Francesca, some really incriminating piece of information.

As Francesca pondered the ins and outs of the case, she felt a headache coming on. There are so many possibilities here. How is Tony going to make sense of them? Now she glanced at her watch, realizing he would be at her front door in just a few hours. She also realized she would have to confess to him, once again, that she had butted into the investigation. She fed Tubs, took a shower, dried her hair, put on make-up, and straightened up the living room. Then she stood in front of her closet in her housecoat, wondering what to wear. She finally settled on white Capri pants, a black-and-white silky top, low-heeled white sandals, and large silver earrings. She rummaged through her lipstick collection, marveling as she always did, at the absurd names. Peachy passion, mango madness, violet vixen! She pictured a roomful of well-heeled advertising executives sipping expensive lattes as they debated the various possibilities. Sighing, she finally chose a bronze shade called chocolate kisses.

She had just finished twisting her hair into a chignon when the doorbell rang. She peeked through the opening and was surprised to see none other than Doris, carrying a grinning Mo-Mo who was clutching the lipstick-stained bear. Doris' eyes were puffy and red. I'll bet she didn't sleep at all last night, Francesca thought as she opened the door.

"Fran, I know this is short notice, but…"

"Sure. I'll watch her." Francesca could tell her sister needed a break. "When will you be back?"

The child trundled in the door and headed for Tubs, shouting, "Tat!"

"I'll be an hour," Doris said. "I just have some errands to run. You're a doll!"

Francesca mentally doubled the time, since Doris was always late.

Once her sister had left, Francesca found a pile of paper and some crayons and settled Mo-Mo at a table in her study. Tubs, she noticed, was hiding under the bed since small human beings perplexed and unnerved him. The next time the bell rang, there he was, her handsome Tony, looking as irresistible as ever. But when he walked in, she sensed something was wrong. He looked quite serious and businesslike as he took a seat on the couch.

"Do you want a beer before supper?" She asked with a smile.

He nodded, and she came back shortly with two chilled mugs of beer.

"Tat!" The shrill sound emanated from the study.

"Who the heck's that?" He put down the mug.

Mo-Mo zoomed into the room and stopped right in front of Tony.

"Tony, meet my niece, Mo-Mo."

"Pleased to meet you." Tony reached down and gently grasped the chubby little hand.

"This is Detective Viscardi," Francesca told the child.

"Cardie?" Mo-Mo flashed her dimples winningly at him.

Tony grinned. "Close enough."

Francesca caught a glimpse of Tubs scurrying down the hall, and then Mo-Mo was off again in pursuit of what she considered a moving stuffed animal.

"Here's to us." Francesca raised her mug playfully, but there was an odd expression in Tony's eyes. Was it distrust—or worry?

"Tony, is anything wrong?"

"No, everything's fine." He took a long drink of beer.

But in that moment, she suspected she knew what was bothering him: It had to be Frank. He probably thinks I'm dating him.

"Tony, look, if it's about Frank…"

But he cut her off. "Let's not talk about him tonight, Francesca. Let's not let anything interfere with our having a wonderful evening."

"Of course." What else could she say?

He took another long swig of beer. "You'll be happy to know I have some good news about Mauve."

"Really, what is it?" She could hardly wait to tell him her own news.

"We let her go. Her story just didn't hold water. We figure she was confessing to cover up for someone else."

"Someone else?" She suddenly remembered Brad's face when he had begged her to keep his secret.

"Francesca, this is all in complete confidence. I can't give out all the details, but we're taking someone else in for questioning."

"Is it her son?" The words were out before she could edit them.

He gave her an odd look. "Like I said, I can't say now."

"But you're looking for a woman, right, I mean, based on what Father William said about hearing laughter?"

"Not necessarily." He was studying the condensation on the mug. "That could be purely a coincidence."

She realized he was right. The woman Father William had heard laughing might have been Beatrice or someone else, but still there was no definite connection between that incident and the poisoning. Despite all the logic classes she'd taken, she was quickly realizing that Tony, a man who had never been to college, was much better at drawing the right conclusions than she'd ever be.

Now he put down the mug. "So what was it you wanted to tell me?"

"Well, awhile back, at a Choir Chicks' meeting, Mauve told the group about Augustine coming on to her one night. He was evidently pursuing her!" She delivered her information rather breathlessly.

But Tony didn't respond as she had expected. He just smiled in a somewhat mystifying way. "Well, things aren't always what they seem, you know."

"What does that mean?" She felt deflated now.

"Unfortunately, that's all I can say, without giving away inside information on the case."

She decided to take another tack. "Well, what about Beatrice? Has she been entirely dropped as a suspect at this point?"

"Well, I can probably tell you this much: It turns out Beatrice had an alibi after all. See, according to the report—the complete report, not the first draft I had earlier—it turns out she wasn't alone at home after all. She was with one of her boyfriends, and he vouched for her, plus a neighbor saw his car outside."

"Oh, but her grandmother said…"

"Yeah, Beatrice lied to the police, and to her grandmother, because she didn't want the old lady to know she was fooling around at home. But on further questioning she got nervous and admitted the truth."

"So is anything new with you?" He asked, and she sensed that he wanted to move on to a new topic.

At that moment she decided not to tell him about visiting Brad. He would just chide her for being nosy, and it would spoil the evening.

"Uh, not too much, really," she said evasively.

"Is Mo-Mo coming with us to dinner?" he asked.

"No, my sister should be back soon, and then we can go."

Mo-Mo wandered into the living room then, and climbed into Tony's lap. She was carrying a somewhat soggy storybook featuring a motley assortment of pigs and bears.

"Weed?" she inquired.

"I think she wants you to read," Francesca smiled. "And I think she likes you."

"Something about me—kids and animals just gravitate to me."

***

The food at Benedetti's was delicious as usual, but Tony thought the conversation felt stilted somehow. He knew Francesca had something to tell him, but she was holding back. And he was having trouble enjoying himself because he kept remembering that blasted call from Frank. His rational mind told him it was just a call, but his instinct said there was something going on between them. Of course, his instinct had been wrong before, he reminded himself.

His mind kept wandering as they ate. He found himself wondering if something had developed between Frank and Francesca, despite his warning her about the guy's past. After all, Tony thought, Francesca was a beautiful woman, and there was no reason she should wait for him. They weren't engaged.

"Tony, where are you?" She waded without warning into his uncomfortable stream of thoughts.

"I guess it's the case." He handed her the basket of rolls. "I wish I had been in charge from the start. That Baker guy... well, frankly, he's just not up to the job, and I'm starting to wonder if the real murderer might have already gotten away."

"Do you think the theft is connected in any way?" She selected a roll and placed it in her plate.

"That's another thing that's bugging me. Baker really dropped the ball on that one. Right from the start, he decided there was no connection." Tony added a dollop of butter to his roll. "You were at that masquerade thing, right? Did you notice anything suspicious?"

"Not really." She took a sip of wine. "I was trying too hard to keep Frank at arms' length."

"Oh yeah?" He felt a sting of jealousy, which he hoped didn't show on his face.

"Well, he had definitely had too much to drink—and then he just disappeared before the evening was even over." She dabbed at her lips with the linen napkin.

"Disappeared, huh? Do you think he was leaving with the cash?"

She had just taken a bite of manicotti, so she gestured toward her mouth, indicating it would be a few seconds before she could talk.

"I just don't know, Tony. All I know is he left early. Later he told me he had to help his mother with an emergency." She nodded as the waiter stopped by to see if they wanted refills on wine.

"So how did you get home?" Tony asked.

"Uh, well, there was someone there...who, uh, took me home," she replied evasively.

"Yeah, who was that?" Tony didn't dare look at her.

"Well, I feel like an idiot to admit it, but I don't know his name. He was dressed like a wizard." She took a sip of wine.

"A wizard, huh? Nice guy?" He could feel a giant chuckle developing, and he was willing himself to remain serious.

"Yes, he was a...well, a real gentleman."

Tony just nodded. Now I'm not only competing with Frank, he thought, but with the blasted wizard too.

***

Francesca didn't know what to think. Tony had just left her house after declining an after-dinner drink. He didn't seem himself, although he wouldn't tell her what was wrong. He claimed he'd gotten a call from the station, and had to work, and she hoped that was true. She hoped he wasn't having second thoughts about their relationship. After all, he could have met someone else in Miami. He was incredibly good looking. It would be just my luck if he decided to run off with some rich widow from Coconut Grove, she thought dismally.

She went into the kitchen and dug her hand into the cookie jar that she had ordered from a cloistered convent in Massachusetts where the sisters supported themselves by making pottery and chocolates. The porcelain jar was painted to depict a smiling, bespectacled nun wearing a traditional habit. Francesca removed the sister's head and fished around until she found a handful of hazelnut biscotti and stacked them on a plate. Usually she only made these cookies at Christmas, but she had baked a batch on a whim a few weeks ago. She knew she shouldn't be eating any right now because she'd had dessert in the restaurant, but she craved more comfort food.

She put on her robe and slippers, then sat on the couch and put Tubs on her lap. The old fellow was half asleep, but he opened one eye to stare at her before dissolving into purrs that quickly segued into snores. She munched on a cookie, noting with approval that it had just the right hint of anise flavoring. She decided to start re-reading one of her favorite books, "The Habit of Being," a collection of letters by Southern writer Flannery O'Connor. At nearly midnight, just as she was heading for bed, the doorbell rang. I'll bet that's Tony coming back for a drink, she thought excitedly. She was so sure it was him she didn't even look through the peephole before opening the door.

"Tony, I'm so glad…" But it was Brad's father, Andy.

"Can I come in? I know it's late, but I want to talk about getting help for my son."

The poor man looked so worried she couldn't refuse, despite the late hour.

"Sure, come in, but excuse me a moment while I put on some jeans." She opened the door and he came in, but some instinct prompted her to leave the door ajar after he entered. She gestured toward the plate on the coffee table. "Help yourself to some biscotti."

She went into her bedroom and changed into jeans and a T-shirt—a present from one of her nieces in Oklahoma—that proclaimed boldly across the chest: "Reduce your government footprint." When she returned to the living room, Andy was sitting on the couch eating a cookie, and Tubs was on the floor staring up at him. *Tubs is probably wondering why he isn't Tony*, she thought.

"What's wrong with Brad?" She sat in the rocking chair opposite Andy.

"Oh, he's OK." He bit into another cookie, spewing crumbs onto the couch.

"But I thought you said..."

"Look, here's the deal," he said gruffly. "My wife and I want a chance to start over. She's agreed to come back to me. We're going to be the mother and father Brad deserves."

After this proclamation, he suddenly seemed distracted. He picked up a copy of a woman's magazine from the coffee table and stared at the cover, which displayed a skeletal twenty-something woman in red jeans that revealed an almost total lack of hips. The fact that most women's magazines touted models with decidedly masculine physiques was something Francesca had long ago stopped trying to understand.

"It's funny how the covers always mention the latest diets and the most fattening desserts, isn't it?" Francesca figured she might as well engage him in light conversation.

But Andy didn't say a word. He just dropped the magazine onto the coffee table as if it had suddenly burst into flame. "We're getting out of town—tonight—to make a clean start. We have to get away before the police pull Brad in for questioning." His voice now had a sharp, almost angry edge to it.

"They told Mauve that was the game plan when they let her go," he continued, "and we don't have much time."

"If you run away, you know how that's going to look," she protested. "They'll think it's an admission of Brad's guilt."

"Yeah, we've thought that all out." He picked up the magazine and rolled it tightly in his hands, as if getting ready to swat a fly. "But we're going to get so far away, it won't matter one way or the other. We're going to start a new life."

He slapped the magazine against the table to emphasize his words, and the sharp sound sent Tubs running for cover beneath the couch. Francesca didn't say anything but was sure her curiosity was etched on her face. What does all this have to do with me? She wondered anxiously.

"You're wondering where *you* fit in, right?" His lips stretched into a fake smile that made her instantly uncomfortable.

"Exactly," she said. Oh, dear Lord, she prayed silently, why did I ever let him into the house?

"Mauve doesn't know I'm here. She'd never put up with what I'm going to do." He looked even more agitated now. "But I have to do this for the sake of my family."

"Do what?" She dreaded the answer.

Things happened quickly then, almost as if someone had hit the fast-forward button on her life. Andy reached into his jacket pocket and extracted a small gun, the very sight of which caused Francesca's heart to start pounding at an alarmingly fast rate. Am I going to have a heart attack or something? She worried. She willed herself to calm down so she could figure out what to do. She noticed that he looked frightened, as if he'd never pulled a gun on someone before.

"I don't want anyone to get hurt, but there's some stuff we need before we can leave town," he barked at her.

"What stuff?" Her voice was barely a whisper.

"Money, of course," he replied. "And that fancy ring of yours would help too."

He stood up now and gestured with the gun toward her diamond-and-ruby engagement ring, which Dean had bought for her. At the time she had protested that he had spent far too much on it, but he had insisted on doing something extravagant for her.

"My husband gave me this—my husband who died two years ago," she said emphatically. "There's no way in the world..."

"This isn't an invitation—it's an order! We need more cash to get out of town." He started moving toward her. "The decision is yours. You either give us what we need or..." He waved the gun.

She got the message quickly. She pulled off the ring and handed it to him, and he stuffed it into the pocket of his jeans.

"OK, now I need the key to the church," he said.

"The church?"

"Yeah, the church, what are you—deaf? Mauve told me you work over there. There has to be plenty of money there, what with the collection basket going around on Sundays."

"I don't have the key. I just ring the doorbell like everyone else." She hoped he couldn't tell she was lying.

Now Andy looked even angrier. "Well, I need some money, see, and I'm betting you have some squirreled away somewhere."

"I have some money in my dresser, but I have to dig through my clothing to get at it. I'll be right back." She turned to leave the room, hoping to surreptitiously call Tony, but Andy was right behind her.

"You're not going anywhere alone, see? I'm not that stupid." He motioned with the gun toward the hallway. "Let's both go and get the money, and move it!"

***

Frank decided to drive by Francesca's to see if her lights were on. If they were, he'd drop in for a few minutes. His decision to stop by her house a while back after two six-packs— and a few joints—had been really stupid. The truth was that she really wasn't his type. She was pretty, sure, but way too brainy. He'd seen all the books in her living room, and he figured she'd read them all. He liked girls who were a little more light-hearted. She was rather serious, and the kind of woman his buddies called "churchy."

He knew he should just leave her alone, but the whole Tony situation irked him. He was really going after Francesca to annoy Tony. He wanted to rattle Tony's cage. He still blamed Tony for everything that had happened to him, the jail sentence and all. When he got to her house, he saw another car parked in the driveway behind hers, but he didn't recognize it. He was relieved that it wasn't Tony's truck. He didn't particularly want to run into him. Maybe a friend of hers had dropped by. No harm in joining the party, he thought.

Frank had picked up a bottle of cheap red wine and some rather wilted carnations at the grocery store. He figured a peace offering couldn't hurt. He didn't want her badmouthing him over at the church. He needed the jobs over there. If she was busy, he'd come back some other time. He parked on the street and headed for the front door. Even from the yard, he could see the door was partially open. That's weird, he thought. I wonder what's going on.

***

Tony didn't feel right about the way the evening had turned out. His own suspicions were getting the best of him. This had happened before with other women. He started dating them and then found himself tied up in knots when he realized they were also seeing other guys. But he didn't step forth and say he wanted an exclusive relationship, so the girls got mixed messages.

They figured he didn't care that much about them and so he wouldn't mind if they saw other men. But he had a strong streak of jealousy. His mother had said it was his Sicilian blood and he shouldn't worry about it, but somehow that didn't comfort him. He didn't want to be a prisoner of his genetic make-up.

The truth was he'd never met a woman he really wanted to be exclusive with. Most of them had some flaw or another that would grate on his nerves, once he noticed it. But Francesca was different and she deserved better. He'd go over and lay the proverbial cards on the table. It was time to tell her how he really felt about her. As for the whole thing with the wizard, he could see now that he'd made too much of it. Sure, she'd admitted their relationship wasn't anything serious, but wasn't that the truth? And wasn't that partly his fault since he'd been out of town for so long?

He stopped at an all-night grocery store, where he picked up a bottle of champagne and a very large bar of her favorite chocolate, Hershey's with almonds. She had once confided that she didn't need pricey imported chocolates. That was what he loved about her. She didn't put on airs, and she was honest. As he thought about honesty, he realized he'd been falling down in that department. *I should come clean about my suspicions that she's seeing Frank, he thought, and tell her how I stretched the truth about him being a dangerous drug dealer and all.*

When he got to Francesca's house, he was relieved to see the lights were still on. *She must be reading with Tubs, he thought.* He parked a few doors down, because he wanted to surprise her and didn't want her to see his truck. Then he noticed there was a car he didn't recognize parked in her driveway. He got out of his truck and started toward her house. At that precise moment, he spotted a man walking toward her porch, carrying a brown paper bag and a bunch of flowers. In a flash, Tony recognized the man from the photo in his police file. It was that blasted Frank guy! As a bitter wave of jealousy overtook him, Tony gritted his teeth, got back in his truck, and drove angrily away. *OK, Francesca, I get the message, loud and clear, he thought.*

***

Frank peered through the screen door into Francesca's living room, but no one was there. He saw a plate of cookies on the coffee table and what looked like a rolled-up magazine nearby. *She probably went downstairs to get something, he thought—but where was her guest? And why had she left the front door open?* He decided to go on in and have a quick look around. But then he heard sounds coming from down the hallway, evidently from one of the bedrooms. He heard a man's voice. She must be entertaining someone, he thought. Well, I guess still waters run deep!

His first instinct was to turn around and leave, but then he became aware that the gruff male voice sounded angry, not amorous. As he listened, he realized something was wrong. He heard the words, "money" and "hurry." She's being robbed!

***

Francesca dug frantically through her lingerie drawer. She knew she had put some cash in there a while back, so where was it? She was so nervous she could hardly think straight. She suddenly remembered the time Mo-Mo had been wearing the socks on her head. A strong impulse to laugh seized her, and she was unable to squelch it. She began laughing hysterically and had to gasp for air. When she saw the look of utter amazement in Andy's eyes, it just made her laugh harder.

"What the hell is so funny?" He was clearly growing more impatient by the second.

"I...I...can't help it," she sputtered. "I just can't seem to stop."

"So where the hell is the money?" He prodded her in the back with the gun. "I haven't got time for this nonsense. Give me the money and I'm out of here."

She saw a mental image of her mother, who had always said the same thing to Francesca and her sisters when they were seized by a fit of giggles: "You're laughing now, but you'll cry later." Her mother had always been right.

"It's been a l-long time s-since I hid it." Tears of laughter were now streaming down her face.

"Hey, look, I'm not stupid, so quit playing the fool with me," he said savagely.

An image suddenly popped into her mind, and she acted quickly. She dug through the drawer and managed to unearth the massive Va-Va-Va Voom bra from beneath a pile of nightgowns. Then, uttering a silent prayer, she turned around quickly and swung the hefty bra toward Andy with as much force as she could muster. The helmet-like cups imbedded with rhinestones hit him squarely in the eyes, and he yelled out in pain. She repeated the gesture, and made another direct hit. Cursing, he brought his hands up to cover his eyes, and as he did, the gun fell from his hands and slid beneath the bed. Francesca continued swinging as he backed away, cursing at her and yelling about his eyes. Now that she had the upper hand, she chased him through the living room and toward the front door.

***

Frank had headed out to the front yard and ducked behind a tree. As he was dialing 911 on his cell phone, he saw Francesca's door swing open and a man came running out. The man, who was cursing up a blue streak, had a hunted look in his eyes and his face was bleeding. Frank almost dropped his phone when he noticed the man was being pursued by a wild-eyed Francesca who was wielding as a weapon—and here Frank could hardly believe his eyes—a hefty red-and-purple bra.

Still swinging the bra and yelling, Francesca chased the guy to his car, and he jumped in and took off at a fast clip. Then Frank rushed over to Francesca who was standing on the sidewalk, looking exhausted and dazed. The bra lay on the ground beside her, its rhinestones glittering in the moonlight.

"Are you OK? What happened?" Frank asked. He gave her a hand getting into the house. In the back of his mind, he was uneasy because he didn't want to be there when the cops came. He didn't relish a run-in with the police, even if he hadn't done anything illegal, well, not lately anyway. On the phone, he had described the man's car, and given some details about what he had seen. He figured they'd send an ambulance for Francesca, who looked like she was about to pass out.

He led her to the couch and helped her sit down. She was still shivering, but she managed a weak "thank you."

"Who was that guy?" he asked.

"Mauve's husband—he took my ring." She let out a shuddering sigh at the same moment that Frank heard sirens in the distance.

"Look, I gotta go. I...uh...I have another fire to put out." And then he was out the door.

CHAPTER 14

Father Bunt let himself into the rectory. He'd had a very late supper at the pub after stopping at the hospital to visit some parishioners. He'd spent most of the day visiting elderly shut-ins who said they needed the sacrament of Confession. He hated to admit it, even to himself, but the sins of people who rarely left their condos never failed to amaze him.

How could people get into so much mischief when they were in their eighties, using walkers, canes, and hearing aids, and suffering from a host of ailments? Still, every week he heard the old folks admit to sins that were usually on the roster of fit and hearty 20-year-olds: struggles with overspending, bitter disputes with family members, and the most unexpected one of all, lusting after others. Stranger still, sometimes the concupiscent desires were actually acted out. Either that, he thought, or these old folks have some really vivid imaginations.

It was late, but he felt wide awake. He put on his robe and slippers and decided he'd have another beer and read the paper. He would settle down in the sitting room and relax, and then head off to bed. He went into the kitchen and turned on the light, then leaned into the refrigerator and selected a beer. He liked basic American beer, which was a good thing since his paycheck wouldn't cover exotic imports.

On the kitchen table, he found an envelope addressed to him. Inside was a handwritten note: "Dear Father Bunt: I am sorry about what happened when the Archbishop came to lunch. You were right. I had been serving you and Father William vegetarian food, but that day the lunch really was pork. I hope you will forgive me. From now on, I will be cooking meat. Sincerely, Trudy Greenstone."

Well, that explains things, he thought. Just wish she had told me before I made an ass of myself with MacPherson. But at least now I know my suspicions were correct.

Just as he was leaving the kitchen, he heard a strange whirring sound and then a crashing noise. Who in the world could that be? He knew he was alone in the rectory, since William's car wasn't outside. The young priest tended to be a night owl, and sometimes went to a nearby fast food restaurant in the wee hours of the night to get a snack. That was his last thought before he tripped over something that was zipping across the floor. The beer bottle flew out of his hands and he felt a sharp pain in his knee.

He sat there on the floor a few seconds, making sure nothing was broken. It had just knocked the wind out of him, whatever it was. And then he saw the thing go zooming by again and realized it was the hamster in his plastic ball. William must have forgotten that Ignatius was roaming around. Father Bunt slowly stood up, brushed himself off, and then went into the kitchen and got paper towels to clean up the spilt beer. He reminded himself it could have been much worse. There were no broken bones. He would clean things up and then put Ignatius back in the cage.

***

Andy cursed under his breath as he was driving away from Francesca's house. Things had gone terribly wrong. All he'd gotten was the ring, and he couldn't pawn that until they were really far away from Decatur. He needed more cash, and he needed it tonight. He didn't want Mauve to know he'd lost the savings she had entrusted to him. There'd been a really big poker game at his friend's house the other night and Andy had enjoyed a winning streak.

He had doubled the five thousand bucks in two hours. But the temptation to make an even bigger killing had proved irresistible, and he had managed to lose every last dollar before the game folded at 3 a.m. There was no way Mauve would get back with him if she knew he still hadn't kicked his gambling habit. He decided to head to the church. It was a long shot, but if the lights were on, he'd give it a try. He knew churches always had plenty of money. He hadn't been to church in many years, even though Mauve was always nagging him to go. But he remembered from the early years of their marriage that whenever he did go, the collection baskets were crammed full of cash.

He was in luck. He spotted lights on in the rectory. He quickly parked his car and rummaged in his glove compartment for a gun. It had been fortunate that he'd thought ahead of time to pack two for the evening, since the other one was still at Francesca's. He stashed the weapon in his pants pocket and then rang the doorbell. He'd need a good story to get him in at this hour of the night. The porch light went on, and he stood there nervously on the stoop. As the door eased open just a crack, he heard a man's voice.

"Yes, who's there?"

"It's Andy Bundle. My wife's back home again, but she's sick and needs a priest." That should do it, he thought.

The door opened wide then, and he saw a man peering out. He figured it was a priest, although the man was wearing a robe and slippers.

"Certainly, come on in. It will take me a few moments to dress, and then we can head out."

As Andy walked in, Father Bunt looked startled. "What happened to your face? You've got some cuts there!"

Andy pulled out his gun and pointed it at Father Bunt. "Don't worry about me."

"What in the world?" Father Bunt gasped and drew back with a terrified look on his face.

"Look, just do what I say and no one gets hurt." Andy glanced around nervously. "Are you alone here tonight?"

"Yes, but…"

"Well, that works out fine. See, I'm in need of some money; I'm taking my family on a little vacation. So as soon as I get the cash, I'll be out of your way pronto."

"Cash?" Father Bunt repeated the word as if it were a foreign language.

"That's right, and I don't have much time, so no stalling!" Andy could feel the sweat pouring down his back.

"Well, I...I have about fifty dollars in my wallet." Father Bunt licked his lips nervously.

"I need more than that!" Andy exclaimed impatiently. "Where the hell is the collection basket money?"

"That's already been deposited at the bank. We don't keep cash here."

Andy could feel his heart banging around frantically in his chest. Time was running out. What if the police were already on to him? And here he was, stuck with this loser who only had fifty dollars!

"OK, give me your watch and your wallet." Andy figured he could at least use the credit cards for a while.

Father Bunt obediently removed his watch and handed it to him. "It's just a cheap one, I'm afraid. And as for my wallet, it's upstairs."

"Get moving then," Andy said harshly. "I don't have all night. Let's go get it."

As they started for the stairs, Andy saw something moving rapidly toward him out of the corner of his eye. He wheeled around to see what it was, and in his surprise his finger tightened on the trigger and the gun went off. The thing went careening out of the room.

***

The gunshot had nearly deafened Father Bunt, but he was grateful to be alive. The gunman was clearly discombobulated by what had happened. And the sound of the gunshot had another effect, quite unexpected, when, a split second later, a raucous string of curses and a woman's eerie laughter burst loose from another room. Andy stared, wild-eyed, at Father Bunt.

"Who the hell was that? I thought you said you were alone. Do you have a girlfriend or something?"

Father Bunt blinked nervously as his mind reached a quick and inevitable conclusion. Dear Lord, he thought, the laughter William heard that day wasn't coming from Beatrice—it was that blasted parrot! But he couldn't share this realization with the madman in front of him, so he said nothing.

Andy did some quick mental calculations. Whoever that was, I'll bet she's called the police, and they'll be here any moment. I'm getting the hell out of here. He then turned on his heel and rushed out the front door. Father Bunt glanced out the window and watched him get into the car and drive off. He fished nervously for his cell phone in the pocket of his robe and dialed 911. After giving a thorough report to the operator, he ran into the kitchen to check on the hamster.

Picking up the plastic ball, which was undamaged, he looked inside and saw a little furry face staring out at him. The ears were perked up and the whiskers were twitching, which he knew were good signs. He took the hamster upstairs to William's room and placed Ignatius safely back in his cage. He gave him a peanut as a treat.

***

"Hey, Viscardi, you're not going to believe this," Buddy Mills said, putting down the phone. "Some drunk just called and said a lady ran off a robber by hitting him in the face with—get this—a big padded bra!"

"That's a good one," Tony laughed. "Where did he say it happened?"

Buddy gave him the address, and Tony jumped from his chair. "Holy Toledo," he shouted, "that's Francesca's house. I'm going to go check it out. Who called it in?"

"Let's see," Buddy said, looking at his notes, "it was Frank Freeman."

As Tony was heading out the door, another call came through. The same robber, it seems, had gone to St. Rita's and held the pastor at gunpoint. Father Bunt had identified the man as Mauve's husband, Andy Bundle. He'd also mentioned the cuts on Bundle's face and described the car as a white Ford Focus. Bunt told the 911 operator that Bundle wanted to take his family out of town.

Tony now realized what had happened earlier, and he groaned inwardly. What an idiot he'd been! He had left the scene of the crime at Francesca's house! He had definitely drawn the wrong conclusion, something he hated to do as a detective. But he had seen Frank approaching the house, he reminded himself. Of course, that didn't mean Francesca had invited the man over, he realized. Because of his own jealousy, Tony had missed a chance to protect Francesca, who could have been badly injured—or killed—by Andy Bundle.

As much as he wanted to check on Francesca, he knew he'd have to get Bundle first. He asked Buddy to send a police car to her house, then jumped into an unmarked car and headed to Mauve's house. He had a strong suspicion about who had poisoned Hornsby. It could very well be the kid, Brad. Why else did Mauve confess to the crime? She could be covering for her son. And now the father was taking the family on a "vacation," which sounded mighty suspicious. So Tony might be able to kill the proverbial two birds tonight by arresting the father and talking to the kid.

Was the father stupid enough to return to Mauve's house, though? It was a long shot, but it could pan out. Tony knew from experience that many criminals did really dumb things, especially when they panicked. Tony parked a few doors down and walked toward Mauve's house. Bingo! There was the father's car, and there were lights on in the house. Tony figured the guy could have a whole arsenal of guns inside, so he approached cautiously. He called the station for back-up, and then pounded on the door, gun in hand.

"Police! Open up!" He hoped he wouldn't have to use his gun, since the woman and kid could be in there.

A terrified-looking Mauve opened the door a crack and peered out. "What's going on? What's happened?" Then her eyes widened as she recognized Tony. "Oh, it's you! Come in."

It was obvious from the disarray in the room and the suitcases open on the floor that the occupants of the house were in the process of packing.

"Going somewhere?" Tony looked around quickly to see if there were signs of the father or the son.

"Uh, yes, well, my husband, he's taking me and Brad away for a while," she replied nervously.

Tony raised an eyebrow. "Oh, yeah? Where to?"

But she didn't get a chance to reply, because just then a man came rushing into the room from somewhere in the back of the house. He had some bruises and cuts on his face, Tony noticed, so this had to be Andy, the husband. He was carrying a suitcase and had a frantic look on his face. When he saw Tony, he dropped the suitcase on the floor with a resounding thud.

Tony aimed his gun squarely at Andy's chest. "Get your hands up. You're under arrest for armed robbery."

"What the hell do you mean?" Andy put his arms ramrod straight into the air above his head.

"Don't play games with me. I got the report about Francesca. Someone called an ambulance for her." Tony had to control an impulse to punch the man in the face.

"What have you done?" Mauve shrieked at her husband. "Did you hurt Francesca?"

"Shut up! I told you I've got everything under control." Andy's face had reddened in fury. "I just went over there to borrow some money. While I was there, some other guy came in with a gun—and robbed her."

"Yeah, that's a real interesting story," Tony replied, "but we have an eyewitness who saw her chasing you out of her house." He couldn't resist adding: "And she was defending herself with a very interesting deadly weapon, namely a bra."

"Bra?" Mauve shrieked. "What did you do to her? Did you...?"

"Oh, shut up," Andy said rudely. "I didn't do a thing to her. She just had this...this killer bra and she came after me with it."

"Killer bra?" Mauve's face was contorted with what looked like a strange cross between disbelief and rage. "You mean to tell me that Francesca scared you off with a BRA?"

Two other officers now entered the room with their guns trained on Andy. Mauve stood ramrod still, her face ashen. When Tony nodded, the officers put handcuffs on Andy, read him his rights, and started escorting him from the room.

"Hold on a second," Tony said. "Where's your son?"

"What the hell do you want with him?" Andy sneered.

"We want to question him about the Hornsby murder."

"No, no!" Mauve screamed. "Brad had nothing to do with that. You wouldn't believe me when I confessed, and now you're trying to pin it on him! You can't do this!"

"We know *you* didn't do it," Tony said calmly. "Your story didn't check out, but there's always a big question mark when someone confesses to a crime they didn't do. Usually they're covering for someone—and I think it's your son."

"Where is he?" Tony again directed the question at Andy.

"At a friend's house," Andy muttered. "We were going to pick him up after we got the car loaded."

"Yeah, well, we need to know where the friend lives." Tony was starting to worry that the kid had already left town.

"You're not getting anything from me." The expression on Andy's face was venomous.

"Look, you can stonewall all you want, but you're just postponing the inevitable," Tony replied. "You're going to jail, and we'll station some plain clothes cops here for a few days— and your son will eventually return. We'll nab him then."

"Brad didn't do nothing," Andy growled.

"Yeah, well that will be for the jury to decide," Tony replied evenly.

"He doesn't need a jury." Andy looked over at Mauve before pronouncing the words that changed everything: "I'm the one who did it."

His statement magically caused Mauve to stop crying, as if the shock had dried up her tears. Tony didn't say a word. He usually got more information from suspects when he didn't try to fill the silence with words. He just hoped Andy was telling the truth. He didn't want another false confession in this case.

"Yeah, I knew what was going on," Andy said to Tony. "That young guy at church, he was trying to make the moves on my wife." Now he turned to face Mauve.

"You said he came over just to talk, but I knew you were lying to me." His voice was breaking now. "Brad said he heard you both laughing and talking. And once after the guy left, Brad said you were all upset. He also heard you talking on the phone to someone, some lady friend, and telling her how the guy was coming on to you. I knew there was funny business going on, and I had to stop it. I wanted us to be a family again. I didn't want anyone standing in my way."

"So you poisoned Augustine?" Tony asked quietly.

"It wasn't supposed to be like that!" Andy's face was beet red now and rivulets of sweat were pouring down his cheeks, looking like tears. "Something went all wrong. See, I just wanted him to get really sick. I'm no killer!"

Mauve covered her face with her hands, and she was sobbing. It took Andy a few seconds to compose himself before continuing.

"It was a joke that backfired. I just wanted to give the guy a stomach ache, a really bad one, and then I was going to send him an anonymous letter, you know, about how he should stay away from my wife, or he'd be sorry. I had Brad do it—put the stuff in the booze, but he didn't know it was poison."

He looked at his wife with a pleading expression. "I put the stuff in an unmarked bottle and told Brad it was a laxative. And I told him to wipe the bottle clean, so there wouldn't be any prints."

"You sent our son into the kitchen with poison?" Mauve was screaming at him now. "Why didn't you tell me you'd done that? I thought it was *his* idea!"

She suddenly grew quiet then, and the next words she spoke seemed like daggers aimed straight for her husband's heart.

"Brad never told me you had anything to do with it." The venom in her voice was unmistakable. "He was *protecting* you."

In that moment, Tony actually felt sorry for the poor devil. Andy seemed to be digesting the fact that he'd jeopardized a son who loved him enough to cover for him. But he wouldn't be cowed.

"Yeah, but if you hadn't been messing around with that guy," Andy said venomously to Mauve, "none of this would have happened."

"I didn't mess around with him." Her voice was shaky.

"Oh, yeah, well, what about the crying and the phone call and all that?" he shot back.

"I was crying because I made a fool of myself with him," she said. "I was the one pursuing him, and he made it real clear he wasn't interested."

"So why the hell did you brag to your friends about him?"

"It was a lie," she said quietly.

"Why the hell would you lie about something like that?"

Her voice was barely a whisper. "It made me feel, I don't know, young and attractive, to tell my friends this young guy wanted me."

Tony turned to Mauve. "So you confessed to protect Brad, right?" He wanted to get the facts out in the open.

"Yes, I'd do anything to protect him," she said, not meeting his eyes.

"And you're saying it was all a *joke,* the poisoning thing?" Tony asked Andy.

"Yeah, it was a lousy joke that back-fired." Andy was staring at the floor. "I just wanted to get him to leave her alone, but I didn't realize he would drink enough to…to die."

Now Andy glanced at Mauve. "It's your fault, really." His words had a hard, bitter edge. "Brad said you mentioned how the guy never drank more than one glass of that fancy booze. But you were wrong because one glass—with poison in it—wouldn't have killed him."

"My fault! God, Andy, why can't you ever take responsibility for anything?" Mauve cried out.

Her husband remained silent.

"How'd you figure one glass wouldn't kill him?" Tony asked.

"Oh, I did my homework on the Internet," Andy said smugly.

Tony mentally rolled his eyes. There was plenty of good, solid information on the Internet, and plenty of garbage too. Sadly, this fellow didn't seem to know the difference.

"Why didn't you just use a real laxative?" Tony had to ask the obvious question.

There was a pause and then: "I wanted him to really get sick. I figured a laxative wouldn't do it."

The response was woefully inadequate, making Tony wonder if murder had been Andy's plan along. But that would be for a jury to decide.

Tony had one final question: "Where did Francesca fit in all this?"

"At the last minute, I realized we needed more money to get out of town," Andy said. "I went over there for money and then noticed she had that fancy ring. I figured we could pawn it when we left town."

"You stole Francesca's ring?" Mauve screamed. "How could you? She's my friend!"

"I did it for you and Brad," he growled.

"Me and Brad? Don't you realize that now you'll be in jail forever—and Brad won't even *have* a dad?" Mauve collapsed into a chair and wrapped her arms tightly around her chest.

"Take him down to the station and book him," Tony said to the other officers. And then as they were escorting Andy out the door, Tony had another thought.

"Wait a second—where's Francesca's ring?"

"In my pocket," Andy replied.

One of the officers dug out the ring and handed it to Tony.

***

From his office window Father Bunt could see a large squirrel's nest perched in the nook of an oak tree. For the past half hour, one particular squirrel had been scurrying back and forth to the nest, with bunches of leaves crammed in his mouth. He seemed to be bolstering the nest for some oncoming catastrophe. Father Bunt glanced at the weather report on the computer. Sure enough, there was a good-sized storm on its way.

Two weeks had passed since Andy Bundle's arrest. That much at least was settled, thank God. There was no longer any question of a dangerous murderer being on the loose. Of course, there was still the matter of the stolen money, but Father Bunt had little hope of that ever being retrieved.

Father William was away in Valdosta visiting his parents, so Father Bunt was covering his responsibilities for a few days. He looked at his watch. He needed to be over at Eternal Sunrise nursing home in about 20 minutes. He heard a persistent whimpering sound outside his door and jumped up to open it. Dopey traipsed in and sat in front of his desk, tongue dangling wetly. The dog eyed his master longingly.

"Alright, just a minute, I'll get you something." Father Bunt quickly searched through his desk and found a handful of biscuits and watched them disappear almost instantaneously in the big hungry mouth. Then he grabbed his jacket and briefcase and hurried down the stairs. Mrs. Greenstone was there at the bottom, looking up at him.

"Will you be back for lunch or not?" she wanted to know.

He glanced at his watch again. "I should be, although I might be running a little late. Just a sandwich will be fine, nothing fancy what with William being away."

"Well, I thought you might like a BLT sandwich," she said meekly. "Would that be OK?"

It was one of his favorite lunches especially when the bacon was extra crispy, but he decided to make sure that he and the cook were, as the saying goes, reading from the same page. He was fairly sure that she had stopped sneaking in meat substitutes, but didn't want to take a chance.

"Uh, do you mean BLT as in bacon?"

"Yes, I mean *real* bacon, not fake." Her eyes darted nervously toward the floor. "Father, I guess you got my note of apology about the food situation."

"Yes, I did, and—there are no hard feelings."

"I came to realize that…" Her words fizzled out as if she couldn't bear to complete the sentence.

"Yes?" He glanced surreptitiously at his watch.

She sighed deeply. "Well, not everyone in the world is cut out for vegetarianism." She raised her eyes to meet his.

"Let's put it all behind us," he said, suppressing a grin. "And I'll be looking forward to that sandwich."

***

Grateful that the church was empty, Francesca dipped her hand into the holy water font and crossed herself. She wanted some time in silence before the 9:30 Mass. She took a pew on what parishioners fondly called St. Joseph's side of the church, where a life-sized statue of the saint held court. She would join the choir at the back of the church right before Mass started.

She closed her eyes and began her usual round of prayers for the repose of the souls of her parents and grandparents, and of course, Dean. As she was beginning to pray for the living, she sensed that someone had slipped in beside her. She opened her eyes and was very surprised to see that it was Beatrice.

"What are you doing here?" She immediately regretted her question, since it seemed to imply Beatrice was not welcome. "I mean, it's good to see you, but I didn't think you were, you know, a churchgoer."

Beatrice smiled somewhat enigmatically. "Things are changing." She looked around nervously. "Could we go outside for just a minute to talk?"

Francesca nodded, and quickly left the pew, following Beatrice into the narthex. The girl was wearing a tailored white skirt and a floral-print blouse.

In the narthex, Beatrice surprised Francesca by giving her a little hug. "Here's the thing," she said nervously. "I'm trying to make some changes—and I just wanted you to know."

She looked around now, as if confiding a huge secret. "I told you Augustine had given me some books to read, right?"

Francesca nodded.

"One of them is about this guy—Thomas Merton—you've probably heard of him. I gotta say, he was pretty rough when he was younger. It's *The Seven Storey Mountain*. It made me think I have a chance to turn things around." She hesitated for a moment.

"I'm starting to understand about Jesus and—you know—why he died on the cross and all. See, I went to Bible study when I was little, but I never thought the crucifixion was, well, a love thing, you know? And all this 'Jesus loves you' stuff—it didn't seem real."

She ran her tongue over her lips nervously. "My mom died of cancer a few years ago, and I went to live with Granny then. When my mom died, I really got mad at God."

Beatrice tugged nervously at a chain on her neck. "Then I found out your husband died in an accident—but that didn't stop you from going to church and all."

Francesca didn't trust herself to speak. She could see Dean so clearly in her memory right now.

"I just wanted you to know," Beatrice said, "that I understand now about Augustine. He did love me, really, but...well, not the way I wanted. He was trying to teach me about a different love. I was just too dumb to get it."

She pulled the chain up from her blouse. There was a tiny gold crucifix on it. "He included this in the package he gave me, with the books. I was hoping for something, you know, more romantic—but now I get it. Augustine's love wasn't romantic. It was—well I don't want to sound like some preacher or something—but it was higher, you know?"

Francesca nodded. "I do know. And I'm really happy for you."

Beatrice shrugged. "Well, don't get me wrong; it's not like I'm sprouting wings or something." She glanced at her watch. "I just wondered if I could sit with you at Mass, now and again."

"I'd love that, but be prepared," Francesca said. "We do a lot of standing up, sitting down, and kneeling."

Beatrice finally smiled. "Kind of like aerobics class, huh?"

"You got it!"

CHAPTER 15

Tony saw Francesca's car at the Dairy Queen and pulled in near it. He looked through the big glass windows and saw her standing inside with Mo-Mo in front of the counter. He came up behind them and whispered, "Make that a double!"

"Cardie," the child shrieked gleefully, throwing her arms around his legs.

"Hey, Mo-Mo, good to see you," he enthused, bending down to ruffle her curls.

Francesca's response was much more subdued, however. "Tony, it's, uh, nice to see you."

"Yeah, it's been a few weeks, way too long," he said. "I left you a couple of messages on your phone, but I wasn't sure you got them."

The girl behind the counter gave Francesca a chocolate-dipped ice cream cone, plus a small cup of ice cream for Mo-Mo. Francesca then busied herself getting napkins, avoiding Tony's gaze while he ordered an iced tea. The truth was, she had gotten his messages, but she was angry about something she'd learned through the grapevine. Someone had told her Tony had been at her house the night of the robbery—but he had driven away when he spotted Frank. She was miffed that Tony had jumped to conclusions about her and Frank—and quite angry that he had left her in the lurch that night.

"Oh, sometimes the phone machine just doesn't work," she murmured. "And I don't, uh, get all the messages."

Now he knew something was up for sure. He knew enough about her answering machine to know it worked just fine, since he himself had helped her purchase it a few months ago when the other one broke. There's something going on, he thought darkly, and I'll bet his initials are FF, as in Frank. I wonder if he's been putting the moves on her again.

They found a table and she settled Mo-Mo in first and then sat quietly, giving the child a spoonful of ice cream and then taking a nibble of her cone, all the while continuing to avoid his eyes.

"Well, how are things at church these days?" He took a long swig of the chilled tea. "A bit quieter now that the case has been solved?"

"Oh, yes, much better. You know, Father Bunt seems much more relaxed, even though there's still that problem about the stolen money."

"Yeah, that remains a mystery. I'm still looking into it, but it's been on the back burner what with the murder and all."

She dabbed at her lips with the napkin. "Tony, on a different note, there's something we need to discuss."

"Yeah, what's going on?"

She looked pained. "Well, Frank left me this long phone message. He told me about his past conviction for drugs, but he also said he hasn't had any problems with the law since then. Is that true?"

Tony shifted uncomfortably. "Yeah, that's right. We haven't pulled him in for anything."

Her eyes widened. "But you made him sound like he was really dangerous!"

"Well, I didn't like him going to your house in the middle of the night," he said.

"I-cweam!" Mo-Mo cried out, and Francesca gave the child another spoonful before continuing: "I just don't understand why you led me to believe he was a drug dealer, and maybe carrying a gun too."

Tony took another drink of tea to stall for time. "OK, you got me there. I really did stretch the truth about him, but he was bothering you in the middle of the night. And for all I knew, he could have had a gun. And there was that theft over at the church, and I didn't know if he was involved or not. To tell you the truth I still have my eye on him for that."

He crunched on a piece of ice before unknowingly adding fuel to the fire: "Besides, I was just trying to protect you."

"Well, you don't have to," she said huffily. "You know I can take care of myself."

He didn't reply because it would only make her angrier to hear how much he doubted that.

Now her mood suddenly changed. "Tony, why don't we call a truce?"

"Are we at war?"

"You know what I mean. We've wasted so much time talking about Frank. I'm not dating him, and I never was. I mean, he called me a few times, and we went to that party, but that's it. I could never trust him after he made up that stuff about being your cousin. Besides, he's just not my type."

"Is that right?" Tony hoped the enormous relief he was feeling wasn't too obvious on his face.

She nodded. "It seems that I like men who are...well, much more honest—even if they're somewhat overbearing at times." The ice in her voice seemed to be melting now.

"Bear!" Mo-Mo chimed in joyfully.

"Well, Francesca, I'll admit that I'm protective of women I, uh"—he knew he was blushing, a habit he detested but could not control—"really care about."

"So you do then?" She was smiling now.

"Do what?" He asked, feeling his face reddening more.

"Care about me?" She asked quietly.

"Of course I do!" he answered. "Why else would I give a damn about Frank?"

"Damn Fwank," Mo-Mo cried out.

"I always forget how kids repeat things," he said apologetically. His phone rang, and he dug it out of his pocket and glanced at the screen. "I have to get back to the station. Oh, look, before I go..." He reached into his jacket pocket and pulled out her ring. "I got this back from that Andy guy."

"My ring!" Francesca exclaimed.

"Wing?" Mo-Mo looked at the glittering object with interest.

"I guess she takes after you," Tony chuckled.

"What do you mean?"

"She's got a taste for fine jewelry, obviously."

Francesca laughed as he handed her the ring. "Oh, Tony, thank you so much. I've really missed it." She slipped it onto her finger, and then added quietly, "And you too."

"Same here," he said, standing up. "How about we have dinner one night this week?"

"I'd love that. Just give me a call." She fed another spoonful of ice cream to Mo-Mo, whose mouth was open like a little bird.

"And, um, by the way, there's nothing actually wrong with my answering machine."

"I figured that out already."

***

Tony was at the station filling out more paperwork. He was alone since his officemate, Buddy, was out on a case. The Hornsby death had been really tragic, he reflected, but what murder isn't? Andy Bundle was still insisting he hadn't really meant to kill Hornsby, but Tony had to wonder if the jury would buy it. The man didn't seem like a cold-blooded killer, but Tony had seen enough of jealousy to know it really was a monster, capable of goading even the mildest-mannered person into doing things he would later regret. I should know, he thought wryly, still embarrassed about the way he had lied to Francesca about Frank.

He looked at the snapshot of a smiling, hopeful-looking Hornsby in the folder. It was always sad when a young life was lost. This guy had his whole future ahead of him, and it had been taken away, just like that. Whatever justice the courts doled out for Bundle, nothing would make up for the loss to the family. Not to mention all the people Hornsby would have eventually ministered to.

It was really ironic that a man who was trying to walk the straight-and-narrow path had been so misunderstood and his actions misinterpreted, Tony thought. The way Tony saw it the seminarian hadn't died because he was a Romeo but because he was just the opposite—a guy trying to do the right thing. Going over to advise Mauve about her son had been a good deed, and look where it had led.

What a weird world it is, he thought. They say the good die young. I wonder if God takes them because He wants them in heaven with Him—or because if they lived longer, they'd do something bad. But that's too complicated for a cop to figure out. Maybe I'll ask Francesca if she ever studied anything like that in her philosophy courses.

He closed the folder and picked up a rubber band. He shot it across the room and hit a plastic cup perched on Buddy's desk. The cup hit the floor, emitting a river of pale brown liquid. He hadn't been aiming for the cup, but sometimes that was the way things went.

***

It was Saturday morning and Francesca was watching Mo-Mo for the whole weekend. As Doris had put it, she and Dan needed some time to themselves or they were going to go stark raving mad. Mo-Mo fortunately loved sleepovers at her aunt's, and Francesca enjoyed having the little warm body nestled next to her all night.

But today Francesca was exhausted. The child had tossed and turned for hours and had nudged Tubs off the bed a few times. His loud protesting meows had awakened them both, and by the time she got Mo-Mo and Tubs settled down again, Francesca had been wide awake. Now she was spending the morning trying to keep the two of them separated. The child apparently thought of the old cat as a living stuffed animal and loved to chase him around the house.

Although Francesca used to judge parents harshly for plopping little ones in front of the TV, she now understood their desperation. How else could she make a pot of coffee or scramble some eggs? Without the calming influence of the colorful dancing animals on the screen, Mo-Mo was a force to be reckoned with. But Francesca was determined not to make this a habit. She told the child she could watch a video for a half hour, and that was it.

Those golden minutes allowed her to get dressed and brew a pot of coffee. Then she switched off the TV and enlisted Mo-Mo to help her feed Tubs, something the child thought was much more fun than any video. It was 10:30 when the doorbell rang, and Francesca marveled silently that she'd actually managed to put on make-up and comb her hair, two accomplishments that had seemed unremarkable before she'd starting watching Mo-Mo.

Now she gasped as she looked through the peephole. It was the wizard!

***

Father Bunt settled in his recliner with the newspaper and sighed with contentment. Finally, things were back in order. The murderer had been captured, and Mrs. Greenstone was no longer sabotaging their meals. Not only that, but clerical transfers had just been announced in the archdiocesan newspaper, and he had noted with relief that his name was not on the list. Thus, despite any doubts the archbishop might have about his, Father Bunt's, ability to handle things at St. Rita's, it seemed he was in no imminent danger of ending up at some parish in the swamps. For this he was definitely grateful.

Things weren't perfect, of course, but he didn't expect them to be. He knew it was a fallen world, after all—and if he ever doubted it, a glance at Dopey would bring the truth of the dogma home to him. The dog still stuttered when he barked, but at least he was docile enough, and maybe in time could be trained to do a few tricks. Miracles really do happen, Father Bunt reminded himself. As for the missing money, Father Bunt had given up expecting that particular mystery to be solved. Someone at the dance—and he hoped it hadn't been a parishioner—had given in to temptation, and that was that.

He had learned a big lesson, namely to be far more cautious when holding social events at the parish. He knew it would be a long time before he gave the green light to anything along those lines again. But at least the negative publicity in the local papers had finally fizzled out. As he opened the newspaper, one of the phone volunteers—he thought she was named Andrea—buzzed him to tell him he had a call.

"Could you take a message?" he asked.

"Well, I tried, but she's kind of insistent, Father. It's Susannah Hornsby, Augustine's sister."

He took the call with a tremor of trepidation.

"Father Bunt, I'm calling with some news that might interest you," Susannah said cheerily.

"Yes?" A little spark of anxiety fired off in his brain. News, as he was well aware, wasn't always good.

"We've found a publisher for Augustine's book! Even though the manuscript isn't complete, the publisher thinks he can make a decent book out of it. Isn't that wonderful? I just know how happy that would make my brother."

Father Bunt winced. "Yes, that really is, uh, just wonderful."

"And the book will be called *The Secret Diary of a Seminarian,* just like Augustine wanted—but there's something I thought would especially interest you."

She took just a moment before dropping the bomb: "We discovered in his notes that he wanted the book dedicated to you, Father!"

He rubbed his forehead wearily. This, of course, would mean that anyone who wondered who the character of Father Dunce was would have their curiosity satisfied simply by opening the book to the dedication page.

"That's just terrific," he said.

"Yes, I knew you'd be pleased! And I'll keep you posted on the publication date. Take care, Father."

After the call, Father Bunt again picked up the newspaper and leaned back in his recliner.

"You idiot! Can't you do anything right?"

He jumped at the accusation, which seemed to eerily summarize how he often felt about his own ability to take charge of his life. He looked around the room nervously, expecting to see someone standing there—and then the phrase was repeated, this time even more forcefully.

It was then he realized it was that blasted parrot firing off a comment Father Bunt had never heard before. He wondered who had taught Leonora this phrase—and why she had chosen this moment to utter it. The bird seemed to have an uncanny ability to say the wrong thing at the worst times. Of course, Father Bunt reminded himself grudgingly, that surprise element had come in handy the night Andy had burst into the rectory.

Father Bunt fished around in his chair for his prayer book, which he knew he'd left there earlier that day. He gasped in disgust when his hand grasped a greasy, rather odoriferous pork chop bone, which he took as evidence of two things: One, Mrs. Greenstone had made good on her word about serving real meat at their meals, and two, Dopey truly was incorrigible.

***

"Please, come in," Francesca said, opening the door. "Pardon the mess, but I'm babysitting my niece for the weekend."

"No worries at all," the wizard replied with a little bow.

"Why don't you, uh, put your staff down and have a seat?" she smiled.

He put his staff in the corner of the room and removed his wizard's hat before sitting on the sofa.

"So how are things in the world of wizards?" she asked, taking a seat in the nearby rocker.

"I have no complaints," he grinned. "I've been pretty busy…you know, what with granting people their wishes and all."

She chuckled. "Well, there's one wish you could grant me, Mr. Wizard."

"What's that?"

"Well, you know my real identity, but I don't know who you really are."

He laughed, and there was something very familiar about it. "I think that's a pretty easy wish to grant." He slowly reached up and removed his mask and then began peeling off the beard and bushy eyebrows.

Francesca burst into delighted laughter. "Oh, I can't believe it! Tony, you really had me fooled!"

"Well, I guess this was a pretty good disguise if it fooled you so well that night."

Suddenly she remembered that night and what she had told him. Her stomach clenched as she recalled saying she really didn't have a boyfriend. Was that the reason Tony had seemed so standoffish for the past few weeks?

"Tony, listen, about that night," she said, sitting down next to him. "You might have gotten the wrong idea, I mean, when I said I didn't have a boyfriend and all..."

But he cut her off: "You don't have to say another word. You were right to say what you did. Really, we're not in a relationship with a capital 'r', are we?"

She didn't know what to say. They weren't, of course, but she would be overjoyed if they were. But she didn't want to make the first move.

"Look, Francesca, I was wrong to get all riled up just because you spoke the truth that night. I mean, I've been kind of...well, maybe gun shy is the word when it comes to women."

Now he moved toward her, and put his arms gently around her. "But when I was away, all I thought about was you. And how much I wanted to..."

He didn't finish the sentence, though, because he leaned down and gave her a long, delicious kiss right on the lips. She could feel herself relaxing in his arms. She realized how much she had missed him, and how much she really wanted him, in the truest sense of the word. She returned the kiss with deep fervor and let out a little sigh of contentment.

Suddenly all her defenses were down. She let him stroke her hair and give her another kiss. She felt like a starved person at a huge banquet. A warning went off in her head, but somehow the message didn't seem to be reaching her lips. He kissed her again, quite passionately, and she responded with deep fervor.

"Oh, Francesca, I…"

"Anny Fwan, kiss, kiss!"

Francesca drew back as if she'd felt an electric jolt. There was her niece, standing in the middle of the room, grinning with delight. The little girl was carrying—and here Francesca could hardly believe it—the famous Va-Va-Va Voom bra.

***

Father Bunt was grateful to find a parking spot near the front door of the nursing home. He hated to keep Mrs. Hartwell waiting. She had just called to say she needed to see him, although she had assured him it wasn't an emergency. Still, it was unlike her to call, and he hoped nothing was wrong. She was, as his mother would say, no spring chicken.

The lady at the receptionist's desk was not there, so he signed his name in the visitor's book and then went directly to Mrs. Hartwell's room. He was a bit apprehensive about visiting people in their nineties, ever since he had found one lady sitting in her recliner with a ladies' magazine in her lap, staring straight ahead—and quite dead. The image had been permanently branded in his memory, and he often puzzled over the fact that she had been reading an article entitled "Dance Your Way into His Heart." Was there some romance brewing in her life, he had wondered, or was she just reading the article to pass the time? He would never know.

He rapped on the door and heard a faint voice call out: "Come in."

Mrs. Hartwell was sitting by the window. When she saw him, she smiled, but she looked nervous.

"Oh, Father, thank you so much for coming."

He pulled up a chair and sat beside her. "I hope nothing is wrong. I was rather concerned when you called."

She twisted a handkerchief in her hands, and her eyes filled with tears. "There is something definitely wrong, Father. I just...well, I just have to come clean!"

"What do you mean? Do you need me to hear your confession?" Good God, he thought anxiously, what could be going on behind the closed doors of a nursing home to make this poor woman so desperate?

"Yes, please, Father," she replied eagerly.

He gave her a blessing and said the opening prayer for the sacrament of Confession and then waited for her to talk, all the while dreading what she might say.

"Bless me, Father, for I have sinned," she murmured. "It's been...let's see now...three months, I think, since my last Confession."

She went on: "Father, it's about the money that went missing at the masquerade ball."

"Yes?"

There was another pause and then she dropped the bomb. "I took it, Father."

***

"Mo-Mo, where in the world..." Francesca could hardly get the question out because she was laughing so hard.

"Nice to see you again, Mo-Mo." Tony was straightening out the front of his shirt. "What's that you have there?'

"Bwa!" the child proclaimed joyously.

Tony turned to Francesca. "Isn't that the weapon of mass destruction you used when fending off the Bundle guy?"

"It is." She turned to Mo-Mo. "Give Auntie Fran the bra, dear."

"My bwa!"

"Well, I guess it can't hurt if she plays with it a little," Francesca said. "You know, I'd be a terrible mom. I'm always giving in to her."

"Is she, uh, is she here for the rest of the day?" Tony asked.

"Yes, Doris begged me to watch her, and..."

"And you couldn't say no," he smiled. "Listen, why don't I take you girls out for pizza? Would you like that?"

"Pee-da!" the child screamed. "Want it now!"

Tony looked at his watch somewhat dubiously. "Well, I guess we could have an early lunch."

***

Talk about a chaperone, Tony thought, as he sat in the pizzeria with Francesca and Mo-Mo. The kid seemed to have some kind of radar when it came to anything even slightly physical between him and her aunt. Just moments ago he had reached over and taken Francesca's hand, and the child had broadcast to the entire restaurant: "Anny Fwan, kissy, kissy!"

Francesca blushed as she drew her hand back. "She certainly is observant, isn't she?"

"Yes, I wouldn't be surprised if one day she goes into detective work, just like her aunt."

"Well, bless her heart, isn't she cute?" A waitress was approaching the table carrying menus. "Oh, my, what's that she's carrying?"

"Bwa!" Mo-Mo shouted joyously, covering her head with one of the generously sized cups.

Francesca had tried to talk the child out of carrying the bra into the restaurant, to no avail. Mo-Mo seemed to think it was some kind of stuffed animal. Now Tony tried not to laugh as Francesca did her best to explain to the curious waitress why the little girl was carrying the oversized garment—and how she, Francesca, had come to possess it in the first place.

"It's a Va-Va-Va Voom, isn't it?" the waitress asked in a hushed tone, as if beholding one of the natural wonders of the world for the first time. She was fortyish with large, heavily made-up brown eyes and jet-black hair pulled back in a pony tail.

"Yes, that's right," Francesca admitted with a little smile.

"Wasn't there some lady in the news who chased a robber away using one of those?" the woman asked, once she'd taken their orders.

Tony glanced at Francesca who was struggling to keep a straight face. He couldn't wait to hear her response.

"Yes, I believe there was," Francesca said quietly, not meeting his eyes.

"That girl sure was a hero! I jes' loved the headline in the papers," the woman enthused. "Attack of the Killer Bra!"

"Yeah, it's funny how sometimes you don't even need a gun," Tony said drily.

"Kiwa bwa!" Mo-Mo yelled, and some people at the next table craned their necks to see what was going on.

The waitress returned a few moments later with big frosty glasses of iced tea, plus milk for Mo-Mo. And then, before anyone could stop her, the child gleefully swung the bra across the table, knocking over their drinks and creating a large flood of cold liquid, which made its way rapidly onto their laps.

The waitress frowned as she grabbed a cluster of paper napkins and began mopping up the spill. Tony watched with interest to see how Francesca would handle things. She managed to wrest the garment away from the child by offering her the bribe that always seemed to work, namely the emergency pacifier hidden in her purse.

"Well, she's something, isn't she? Bless her heart!" the waitress said. "How many more ya'll got at home?"

"Oh, we're not married!" Francesca said.

The woman's carefully penciled eyebrows went up. "Well, honey, I'm not gonna judge you. I always say what my grandma told me: If you ain't walked a mile in someone else's shoes, don't try to get the mote outta their eye. Or somethin' like that."

"Uh, what I meant was, she's my niece, you see."

The woman smiled fondly at Mo-Mo. "Well, she's jes darlin', and they all have their moments, don't they? You're sweet as sugar, aren't you?" she cooed.

The child pulled the pacifier out of her mouth, put it on the table, and delivered the line that Francesca had come to dread.

"DOPE!"

Francesca rolled her eyes. "I'm sorry; she's just ready for a nap."

The waitress smiled. "Sure, I know how they are. Heck, I raised three of my own." Here she paused. "But they never had one of them pacifiers, I'll tell you that."

She headed back into the kitchen.

"Well, there's never a dull moment with Mo-Mo, is there?" Tony commented. "It sure makes you realize how hard parents have to work to...you know, just get through the day."

Francesca nodded. "Yeah, I always wondered if I would have been up to it. You know, motherhood and all. It just seems really stressful."

"More stressful than detective work?" Tony couldn't resist asking.

She laughed. "Well, that might be a tie."

"What about you?" she asked. "Did you ever think about...uh...kids and all?"

Tony could feel himself turning a deep beet red. "Oh, sure, but, you know, with police work...I'd probably be gone most of the time. Probably not get the 'father of the year' award."

It was at this moment that Mo-Mo put a pudgy, sticky hand on his.

"Wuv oo, Cardie!" she chirped.

"Same here, kid," he replied. "And I gotta tell you, Mo-Mo, you make a pretty good case for parenthood."

***

"Father, please hear me out," Mrs. Hartwell said. "You see, I hated not having more money to give to the church. All I could give was the occasional ten dollars, and sometimes less." She looked at him with big, watery eyes.

"So I decided that night to take the money, Father. I just saw all that money sitting there, and I had this thought. You see, I didn't intend to spend any of it on myself—and I haven't, not a penny."

"What have you done with it?" he asked.

"Well, Father, I doubled it!" Her voice rang with pride.

"Did you invest it or something?"

"Oh, no, Father, I don't believe in investing," she explained. "It's way too risky, you see. No, I doubled it by playing poker. We get together here every Saturday night for a few hands of Texas hold-em."

She looked so pleased with herself that he didn't know what to say.

"And Father, here's the best part: I've given all my winnings back to St. Rita's, plus I still have two thousand dollars to give you today." Now her expression darkened. "But I just couldn't go on with the deception."

"But how did you steal it?"

"Well, Father, no one notices an old lady in the kitchen. So I just wandered in and started giving advice on the pimento-cheese-stuffed celery, and then I noticed the cash box. When no one was looking, I acted on impulse. I just grabbed all the cash and put it in my purse."

"Mrs. Hart—uh, Anastasia, you stole from the church—to give back to the church. He shook his head. "It just doesn't make sense."

"But I doubled it, you see," she explained.

"And you could have lost every penny, right?" he countered.

"Yes, that was the risk," she admitted. "Plus, I realize my intentions were...well, what's the word—murky? I mean, I did want to give more money to the church, but in a way it was because of pride. You see, Father, I was ashamed of having so little to give."

"I understand," he said quietly.

"And although it felt good to give more money, the guilt was just getting...intolerable, you see."

He nodded, trying to take it all in.

She looked at him with pleading eyes. "Father, will God forgive me for this? I know it's a big sin!"

"Do you have true contrition?" he asked.

"Oh, yes, Father, I'm very sorry," she said emphatically. "It's really been preying on my conscience."

He patted her hand and sighed. "Of course, God will forgive you."

He suggested that she say two Our Fathers for penance, and then, after she prayed the Act of Contrition, he gave her absolution, emphasizing mercy with the words "May God give you pardon and peace." Then, she bent down, picked up a red leather purse, rummaged around a bit, and finally extracted a large brown envelope, which she handed to him.

"This is all the rest of it. And Father, you can tell the police too. I can face the music, even if it means going to the slammer."

He suppressed a smile as he accepted the bulging envelope. "I'm not planning to press charges. I'll just tell the police that the money was returned, and that's that."

"You had good intentions, as far as helping the church is concerned," he added, "but you know theft is always wrong. Also, you caused people a lot of worry."

"Yes, I know, Father, and I'm truly sorry for that."

"Well, you made a good confession today." He patted her hand. "Let's put all this behind us."

They talked for a few moments and then he stood up to leave. As he was going out the door, she called out, "Oh, I almost forgot. Any time you have a Saturday evening available, come join us for cards. We start about seven and go on until someone falls asleep at the table."

"But you'll have to watch out for Aaron," she cautioned. "He's 98, but don't let that fool you. He has a real poker face." She smiled fondly. "It's almost like he's wearing a mask."

ABOUT THE AUTHOR

Lorraine V. Murray is the author of two other mysteries, *Death in the Choir* and *Death of a Liturgist*, both featuring Francesca Bibbo and Tony Viscardi.

Her other books include her conversion story, *Confessions of an Ex-Feminist*; a spiritual biography of Flannery O'Connor titled *The Abbess of Andalusia;* and *Why Me? Why Now? Finding Hope When You Have Breast Cancer.*

Lorraine writes regular columns on religion for *The Atlanta Journal-Constitution* and *The Georgia Bulletin*. She lives in the Chelsea Heights area of Decatur, Georgia, with her husband, Jef, and a hamster named Ignatius. When she is not writing, Lorraine enjoys taking care of her orchids and roses, watching hummingbirds at her window feeder, going for long walks, and baking bread. All her books are available on her website, www.lorrainevmurray.com.

CPSIA information can be obtained at www.ICGtesting.com
Printed in the USA
LVOW11s1327150614

390124LV00004B/282/P